YO-BZE-842

No Place Like Home

by

Rebecca Muddiman

Copyright © 2018 Rebecca Muddiman

The right of Rebecca Muddiman to be identified as the Author of the Work has been asserted by her in accordance Copyright, Designs and Patents Act 1988.

First published in 2018 by Bloodhound Books

Apart from any use permitted under UK copyright law, this publication may only be reproduced, stored, or transmitted, in any form, or by any means, with prior permission in writing of the publisher or, in the case of reprographic production, in accordance with the terms of licences issued by the Copyright Licensing Agency.

All characters in this publication are fictitious and any resemblance to real persons, living or dead, is purely coincidental.

www.bloodhoundbooks.com

Print ISBN 978-1-912604-63-0

Chapter 1

I can't wait to get home.

The rain pelts my face, and the wind just rubs the miserableness in. I'm desperate to get inside to shut the world out. To get into my pyjamas. To heat up some soup and devour the still-warm bread I bought on the way home. To watch something mindless on TV and forget about the chill in my bones, the stress of the day and the memories of worse days.

I decide to cut across the playing field behind the house. My eyes take in the almost empty space, and I think about the proposed housing development, about how the locals have been mounting a campaign to stop it, worried about the impact on house prices. It's never been something I've considered before, but I suppose now I'm one of them...

It's still light, just dull from the rain. I don't feel vulnerable, even though I probably should. I see a couple of people walking dogs in the distance but no one else. The play area in the centre of the field is desolate, and the remaining swings, the ones the vandals have yet to cut down, sway violently, creaking with each gust. I walk by quickly, desperate to get home.

I'm still in the honeymoon period with the house. It's been three weeks and I'm still excited by the thought of it. My own place. My own home. I never thought I'd have to wait this long, that I'd be renting until I was thirty-five. But that doesn't matter now. Now I have what I want.

I risk a blast of icy rain in the face and look up to the backs of the row of houses ahead. I count them, losing my place once as a plastic bag is blown into my face. Starting again, I count in my head. One, two, three, four, five. Five from the end. The fifth house. My house. And I can't help but smile.

I notice the extension on the house next to mine. Notice a window in the loft. I'll do that, when I've saved some money. The extra room will be nice, and it'll add value. I notice that next door's house has newer windows than mine too. Maybe that should be the first job. New windows. A period look. But double glazed, of course, to save energy, keep me snug.

I keep my eyes on the window. My bedroom window. And something catches my eye. Some movement. I feel a stab of fear and blink away the rain that has settled on my eyelashes. I look again. Nothing. I almost laugh.

I walk on, faster now, desperate to get home, to get dry, to get cosy. And then, I see it again. A shadow. Something moving within the gloom of the room.

I stop. It can't be. Maybe I miscounted. I'm looking into the bedroom of a neighbour. I stand still, buffeted by the wind, trying to concentrate. I count again. One, two, three, four. Five. The fifth house. My house. And someone is in there.

Someone is in my house.

I start to run. I don't know what I'm going to do. My legs are damp from the water splashed from puddles. I can hear my feet slam into the ground. I can hear my breath, making the burning in my lungs audible. The rain almost feels welcome now, cooling my cheeks, but the wind is my enemy, slowing me down, and I wish it would change direction and push me home.

I slow down as I get onto the road. A couple of cars pass and I see someone's face through the moving window, staring at me, seeing this woman in heels and skirt running through the rain. I wonder if they think something is wrong, or if they just think I'm one of those people afraid of getting wet.

My brain is going nuts, all the possibilities running through my mind at once like a zoetrope gone berserk. I'm wrong, there's no one there. I'm right, there is someone. It's nothing to worry about. It's everything to worry about. How did he get in? What should I do? What should I do?

What *should* I do? Call someone? The police?

I keep moving. The street is empty. No people. Not even any cars now. I realise I've got my keys in my hand. I don't remember getting them out of my bag. My mind is telling me to go inside, to stop this, to protect what's mine.

I look around the street. It's quiet, except for the rain and the occasional gust that rattles an awning or juggles some litter. I can't see life anywhere, not even inside the houses. There's not a single light on, no flickering TV. I could knock on a door, but what good would that do? I don't know anyone. I could knock. I could say I think someone's in my house. But so what? What would they do, these strangers? Who's going to come out in this squall to help some crazy lady who thinks there's an intruder in her house but won't call the police? Would *I* come out?

I stand there in front of the house, keys digging into my palm. It's freezing, but I feel the heat of something inside me.

I stand there, frozen, unsure what to do. And then I see him.

He's downstairs now. He's walking around my house like he owns the place.

He turns. He's put the light on now and I can see him clearly. I feel the heat inside me burn brighter. It's not fear. It's anger.

What's *he* doing in *my* house?

Chapter 2

Two Weeks Earlier

There were still things in bags, things I hadn't found a home for, even though I hadn't brought much with me. Or, at least, I didn't think I had. A clean start. That's what I was after. A new house, a new me.

But I was standing looking at stuff I didn't even know I had, never mind needed, and I wondered if I was turning into my mother. If they'd had those hoarder programmes back in the day, she would certainly have had a starring role. Even when we had to move into a smaller place, she had clung on to knickknacks and plain old rubbish as if her life depended on it. At least my stuff was functional. Maybe my mother thought that someday she'd get back what she'd lost and have room for it all again, but that was delusional to say the least. Dad was never coming back and with him went the good life. No matter how hard she worked it was never going to be the same.

I picked up a shoe box which rattled when I moved it. Not shoes then. I lifted the lid and found a few loose photographs and souvenirs from long forgotten holidays. I took the photos out and put them aside and threw the rest into the bin bag. New start.

The photo on top of the pile caught my eye and I picked it up. My mum smiled back at me; slightly mocking but in a loving way. The picture was faded, washed out with a yellow hue, and part of me felt it was a perfect image of her, if not then, now for sure. I could see her light dimming with each visit, and I knew one day I'd go and she'll have vanished completely.

I put the pictures down without looking at the rest of them. This was supposed to be a happy time, a new start. I turned to put some books on a shelf and stared at the wall. It was crying out to be demolished, to create one long room with more light, more space. I wondered if it was too late to start banging through walls, if there was anywhere open at this time to get a sledgehammer, or if it was even wise to start hammering myself. Surely there was someone I could get to do it for me. I stared at the wall, imagining what could be, trying not to think of what had been, that there had been someone, that maybe I'd been foolish to end things.

I shook myself out of it. The thought was ridiculous. It had ended for a reason. A very good reason. And there was no going back.

***

Later that night, I lay on the settee, staring at the ceiling, deliberating whether or not it needed a fresh coat of paint. I was tired, my arms and legs ached, mostly from moving things around but perhaps still an echo from that terrible week before. But I knew sleep would not come. Not for a while.

I stared at the ceiling a little longer, thinking about the best place to buy paint – decent stuff, not the cheap, nasty kind used in my last place – and noticed a cobweb waving gently. I sat up straight and searched for a duster, sweeping all traces of the past away. Standing, I looked around, realising that just because my things were here it didn't mean the past had been driven out completely. I needed to repaint it all. Tear up the carpets. God only knew what was lurking within those fibres.

I tried to work out just how much carpeting I'd have to buy. Or whether I could sand the floors, put down rugs. Then, there were the walls. So many walls I'd have to paint. How much money would it all cost? Too much. I knew I should just be happy that I had the house, a beautiful house, when I'd started to think I'd be living in crappy rented flats all my life; especially after the last attempt had fallen through. But I really wanted to make the place *me*. And there was so much temptation. It seemed like I couldn't leave the house without seeing a dozen things that would be just perfect, that screamed, *buy me, buy me, buy me*. I looked down at the pile of interiors magazines on the table, idly flicking through one. There was so much I could do with the place. But who has the money? No one. Not unless you're willing to make sacrifices.

I walked to the window, running my hand down the wall. It wasn't so bad. The decor was actually quite tasteful, considering. I could live with it. For now.

I looked out onto the street. It was dark, the streetlights were on. I pulled the curtain and noticed how heavy they felt. A hint of stale smoke wafted towards my face as they moved and my nose twitched. When I got the house, everything had been left inside – furniture, curtains, even personal belongings. The last proper owner had died, and no one wanted to clear the place. No one but me. So, the curtains would go, but for tonight, at least, they'd have to stay. I didn't want people looking in. Mum always said that as soon as the lights went on the curtains should be closed or else it invited people to stare. Burglars, perverts, nosy neighbours.

As I pulled the second drape, I saw him. He was standing across the road, facing my house. For a moment I thought he was looking right at me, but he was in the shadows so I couldn't tell. I pulled the curtain a little more and he moved, just slightly, closer.

My heart pounded. I froze. Had he seen me?

I ducked behind the curtain, too late for sure, and peeked round it. He was standing there, not doing anything. Just standing. I pulled the curtain closed. Mum was right. I needed to keep people like that out.

Turning to walk away, feeling secure inside my little castle, I decided to ignore him. *Don't let anything spoil this.* But before I got to the settee I changed my mind and turned back, opening the curtain a little, phone in my hand like a weapon.

He was still there and I felt butterflies crawl inside my stomach. Maybe he saw the phone in my hand, the silent threat of calling for help. Either way, he turned and walked away, quickly but somehow without purpose.

I let my hand drop, releasing my grip on the phone a little. I wondered how he must feel. Wondered, did he have anywhere to go? He looked dirty, cold. He could be homeless. I felt a tiny stab of guilt.

But I'd had my fair share of troubles, so I closed the curtain and lay back on the settee, the TV burbling quietly in the corner, and soon, I fell asleep and dreamt of my dream house.

Chapter 3

When I woke up I felt disoriented. I sat up too quickly, it made my head ache. I was in the living room, on the settee. I reached for my watch.

It wasn't quite dark outside, just dim, really, which could mean anything. Early morning, late afternoon. Perhaps I'd slept through a whole day, exhausted with everything that was going on. I picked up my watch and saw it was just gone eight a.m. and felt relief I hadn't wasted the day.

I stood up, feeling sweaty and disgusting in the clothes that I'd slept in, even though it was cold outside. As I turned around I could see the outline of my body imprinted onto the settee.

I walked through to the kitchen for a glass of water. I'd cleaned the place from top to bottom when I first arrived, but still, there lingered a stale smell, something ingrained so deeply into the linoleum floor, the plastic veneers of the worktops, even the fridge. At first I'd thought it was handy that things like that were already here, that I wouldn't have to splash out on new things right away, but after a while it began to feel dirty, haunted even. The old woman had died months ago, and yet, I could still feel her presence in the old-fashioned furniture and the smells in the cupboards. I needed to get new things. Surely I deserved it, after everything that'd happened?

For a brief moment, the night before came to mind. I saw him standing across the street, looking towards the house. I blinked the image away, telling myself it was nothing.

I ran the tap, letting the water tumble over my hand before I filled the glass. It tasted metallic but felt good running through my insides as I tried to get my head around what to do next.

Okay. Febreze the mattress, let it air, put the sheets on. They're new at least. Unpack the rest of the stuff. Find places for some pictures. Clean the fridge again and stock it with nice things. Find a throw for the settee, something to make it look new. Buy a new toilet seat and shower curtain. Clean the bathroom again. Buy some flowers, flowers make people happy. Take the curtains down. Buy some new curtains. Buy, buy, buy. Clean, clean, clean.

I walked up the stairs to the bedroom and stared at the bed. I desperately wanted to buy a new mattress but a good one cost a lot, so I'd have to make do with the memories coiled up in the springs of this one. I flipped it over and started spraying, the sickly-sweet scent cloying. After doing one side, I let it drop back onto the frame and opened the window. The air smelled of exhaust fumes and damp autumn leaves, but it was better than the flowery smell in the bedroom. I stood by the window and inhaled the outside for a while before returning to the mattress to finish the job.

When I was done, I stood back to look, as if the mattress would be transformed by a few squirts of air freshener. It wasn't. It still looked ugly, and I tried not to think of all the things that must have taken place on it over the years. Or whose bodies had lain there. I didn't want old memories. I wanted new ones.

I pushed the window wider to let some of the chemical odour out and went into the hallway and took off my clothes. I ran the shower, letting it heat up while I looked around, doubting that the place would ever be really clean.

Steam started to fill the small room, and I climbed into the bath, adjusting the shower head and the temperature. It switched from inferno to ice for no apparent reason, and I spent five minutes trying to get it right like some kind of aquatic Goldilocks.

As I stood under the flow of water, I felt a surge of something. Happiness? Pride? I'd worked so hard for this. When my last chance had fallen through, I thought it was over. I thought I'd missed my shot. But then, this came along. Was I just lucky? Or was it more than that? I wanted to show it off to the world, but it was too soon. I couldn't wait to invite the girls over. I knew they'd be envious and that Kimberley would be able to disguise it, but Sasha wouldn't. I knew that Kimberley's parents were willing to help her buy a place but had nowhere near enough for a deposit. Sasha's parents couldn't even do that after losing their own house when her dad's business got into trouble. I knew she was bitter about it, and I tried to sympathize, but I didn't get any help either. I did this alone.

I stood for a few seconds more, telling myself to forget other people, that I deserved this, until the water was too cold to bear. The cold or the mantra, something woke me up, and I knew I could do this. I might be on my own now, but I could do it. I got what I wanted.

I climbed out of the shower and stood in front of the sink, wiping the condensation away from the mirror with the palm of my hand. I looked myself in the eye and practised a smile until it didn't look like I was being smug. I got dressed and dried my hair, deciding to leave the mattress to dry out a little longer. I planned to go to the shops and buy something nice to eat. I still had one more day before I had to go back to work, so I thought I should make it count. I went to the window and pulled it shut. Although it was an upstairs window, I didn't dare leave it open while I was out. *Don't make it easy for the burglars*, Mum had always said. And Mum was always right.

Chapter 4

Ionly got to the end of the path before I went back and checked that I'd locked the door. I shook my head at myself, wondering when I'd got so paranoid. Slipping the new keys into my bag, I tried again and crossed the street to the bus stop. For a second my heart stuttered as a man walked past me too closely. I thought it was him. A dozen scenarios played in my head in the split second he looked up at me. But it wasn't him. This man hadn't been outside the night before. He was just some guy. He nodded an apology and walked on, head down, tucked into his jacket again and barely missed colliding with another woman.

I told myself to stop being stupid and got in the haphazard queue for the bus. When it finally arrived, I was soaked through from the sea fret style rain and wished, not for the first time, that I'd passed my driving test. I'd only taken it twice, not a lot in comparison to other people I knew – Sasha did hers *six* times – but having been failed by the same examiner twice, I decided I was going to be stuck with him forever and would just be throwing good money away; money I could be saving toward a place of my own. I thought I was being sensitive, but whenever I told anyone about the test, they all agreed the examiner was being overly critical, that he was on some kind of power trip. So, I stopped. Besides, there were always buses or people to give you lifts. And since I'd moved I could now get just the one bus to most places instead of two, instead of the daily panic of hoping the bus times will align, instead of running from one stop to another as a bus appeared in the distance. Another reason to love my new home. Excellent travel links, as the estate agents say.

I climbed on the bus and made my way to the back. There were plenty of seats at the front but were taken up with the bags and coats of the people who didn't want company, the kind who surreptitiously look from the corner of their eye to see if I'm someone who'll want to have a conversation. Or just keep their eyes firmly on the window while their headphones do the rest. It's usually the old folks who sit next to these people. Some, I'm sure, just get on the bus to have someone to talk to, and I wonder if my mum, if she wasn't where she was, would be one of those people, desperate for attention from strangers.

A few stops from the care home, an old lady got on, older than Mum, older than most people, and slowly made her way up the bus, nodding hello to people who refused to give up their seats. She lurched forward as the driver gave up waiting for her to sit down and had to reach out and steady herself on the shoulder of a middle-aged woman. The woman shrank away from the old lady's touch as if she was Death itself. We were at the next stop before the woman had made her way to the back and took the seat beside me. She smiled, shakily but sincerely.

'Nasty weather, isn't it?' she said, and I nodded. 'I wouldn't have come out if it wasn't for my Frank. He's in the hospital. Bad lungs. I go every day.'

'That's nice,' I said.

'Are you heading to the hospital?' she asked, her smile sitting unsteady on her lips, wavering with age. Or maybe it was just the motion of the bus. I looked closely at her face and saw a deep ingrained sadness. I wondered what had happened to her in her long, long life that had made her sad, that made her try to cover it up. I wondered if I'd get to the home and find my mum looking the same way.

'No,' I said, finally. 'I'm going to see my mum.'

I saw a new crease appear on her face. 'Oh.'

I could tell she wanted to know more. Where my mum was, why I was visiting.

'She's in the care home. You know, the one by the hospital?'

'Oh yes,' the old woman said, and I saw a flash of something. I hated to talk about it, hated the feelings it brought up whenever I mentioned that place. Hated the look on their faces – the look I was seeing now – when I told them she'd been shipped off somewhere, because I could tell they were thinking I was a terrible daughter, that *they* would never have done such a thing to their mother. But it wasn't my decision. It wasn't what I wanted. It was the last thing I'd wanted. But sometimes life just doesn't happen as we planned.

'She'd started forgetting things,' I said. 'Losing stuff. She was getting worse and worse. It's hard to see at first. But after a while, I'd go round and she'd tell me she was starving, and when I checked her cupboards, they'd be bare. Sometimes, I'd only restocked them a couple of days earlier. I'd find unopened tins and packets in the bin that she couldn't explain. Or piles of opened biscuits in the airing cupboard that she denied putting there.' I shook my head, and the old woman put her hand on mine. I smiled down at it, feeling like someone was listening to me, understanding.

'And then, she almost burnt the place down. She'd put sheets in the oven to warm up.'

The woman's hand left mine and went to her mouth.

'It was July,' I said, forcing a laugh as if this detail made it less awful. 'Fortunately, I came around just in time, before any real damage was done. She had some smoke inhalation so they took her to hospital and assessed her. It sounds terrible, but to me, she was in the right place already – the nuthouse as she called it. But the doctors knew best, apparently, thought she'd be fine at home, thought I could give her all the care she needed.'

'But she nearly burnt the house down,' the old woman said.

'Exactly. That's what I said, but they'd just look down at their shiny shoes and say there was nothing they could do.'

'Money,' the old woman said and shook her head. 'It's always about the money. We're just not important enough. My sister had cancer, and they wouldn't pay for her treatment because of her age.'

I shook my head in solidarity. She was right. It all came down to money. Everything.

'You wouldn't believe how hard it is to convince these people that someone is ill. Until, of course, they're lying on the floor, unable to move or speak. *Then* they believe you.' I stopped talking, hearing the anger in my voice. I'd thought after that they'd do something, that she'd be taken care of. I thought I'd even have some say in the matter. But after her stroke, they decided she wasn't capable of making decisions about what happened to her anymore. And apparently neither was I. Why doesn't anyone tell you about these things *before* something happens? Why don't they tell you that strangers can come in and decide how you'll be treated and where you'll live and how to spend your money?

I let out a breath and turned to the old woman who looked at me with sympathy. She put her hand on mine and squeezed, her bones fragile like a bird. 'The world can be a terrible place. But we have to make the best of things, don't we?'

I nodded, feeling better for getting things off my chest. And I knew she was right about making the best of things. It was what I'd always tried to do. When life gives you lemons and all that.

'You'll be fine. You and your mum,' the old woman said. 'I can tell.'

'Thanks,' I said, and the woman reached over and pressed the bell, trying to get to her feet while the bus was still moving. 'I hope your husband's okay.'

The woman nodded, and I watched her make her way off the bus. She smiled and waved through the window, and I waved back.

The bus drove on, leaving the old woman behind as we passed the second stop for the main hospital. The next stop, that was for the new unit. The one that replaced the old unit, the one people said was haunted, the one I remembered visiting with my mum a long time ago. If you got off at that stop, they all knew. It was something with the mind, either you or someone you love.

Something had gone wrong *up there*. I almost stood up to go, before remembering Mum wasn't there anymore.

A few stops down the road, I got off, immediately feeling the rain soak right through to my bones once again. I took a shortcut through the bare trees, feeling the mud squelch beneath my boots, wondering if the staff would object to me dragging muck inside. The care home prided itself on being spotless, a reason they probably charged so much, as if cleanliness wasn't a basic human right.

I found myself getting wound up with each step, thinking of something else that bothered me about the place, about the situation. It was the same every time. I'd get there and couldn't help but feel angry about everything that'd happened. How strangers had taken over Mum's life, how they'd taken everything from her, from me, because she'd had the misfortune to be ill.

I tried to shake myself out of it. It was hard enough as it was, seeing her like that. I thought about the old building that once stood further up the road, and I recalled walking across the grass, hand in hand with my mum, as we went to visit Granddad. I could almost smell her perfume on the wind, the same one she wore every day...until one day, she didn't. I remembered her chatter, telling me things I didn't really care about, and she probably didn't either, but it was better than thinking about the reality of what we were about to walk into. I remembered her letting go of my hand as we got to the locked door, and she'd press the buzzer and wait to be let in, squeezing her hands into fists as she did. I remembered the look of pity the nurses would give her and the fake smile they'd aim my way as if I didn't understand what was going on. Someone would point to the end of the high-ceilinged room, and we'd walk through, listening to strangers tell us their secrets, showing us their flesh. No one stopped them, and I'd wondered, even then, why no one cared enough to protect their dignity. But maybe it was too late. There is no dignity in the end.

I remembered sitting beside my granddad, Mum on the other side, and trying not to slide off the wipe clean seats, trying to breathe through my mouth, the chemical smells burning my nose and throat. I remembered Mum talking to her dad about day-to-day things and him not caring anymore. And then she'd glance at me, as if to say, *Say something!* I never knew what to say, so Mum would just carry on, and then, when it was time to go and she'd kiss him on the cheek, we'd be buzzed out, and walking back across the grass she no longer reached for my hand. I sometimes wondered why she took me there when Granddad had no idea who I was. I wondered if it was for him or for her.

I was suddenly standing outside the home, an ugly new building with posters in the windows of smiling carers and even happier residents. It was all a lie, of course. No matter how new, how shiny, how high tech they made the place, inside, the people were the same. Sad, desperate, clinging to life.

I faltered. There'd be another bus soon, one to take me home. I wondered again why I was here – for me or her. To assuage guilt or to help her? It wasn't my fault she was here, but still…

The door to the home opened, and the man leaving held it open for me, so I forced myself to move inside. Maybe things wouldn't be so bad. Things were looking up elsewhere. I had the new house, after all. Maybe these things were like buses. They always turn up at the same time.

Chapter 5

When I walked in to Mum's room, Cathy, her nurse, was standing in front of the chest of drawers opposite the bed. She closed one drawer, quietly, and opened the next, rummaging through Mum's nighties.

I was about to speak when someone dropped something in the hallway, and it thundered along before clattering to a stop. Cathy turned and saw me standing there, her hand going up to her ample chest.

'Polly,' she said, breathless. 'I didn't realise you were there.' She closed the drawer and turned to Mum who was propped up in bed, staring out of the window, a blank expression on her face. She didn't seem to notice me, and I watched her for a while. Beneath the facade of an old woman, I could see the person she used to be, the same face that I wear these days. I thought about how hard it'd been for her, that when she was my age, she was suddenly alone after so many years; she had been thrown out of the house that she loved and into a crappy flat, struggling to manage on the wages she brought home from a job she despised. It took a long time and a lot of hard work for her to get out of there and back into a house she could think of as home. I wondered if the weight of all that was recorded in the lines on her face. She looked old before her time. I wondered if I'd been heading the same way.

'Polly's here, Margaret,' Cathy said, her voice too loud, and Mum turned around and almost looked through me. 'I'll leave you to it, then, shall I?' Cathy said, patting Mum's knee as she walked out.

Mum smiled at her, and I felt a stab of sadness. She hadn't smiled at me when I came in, for all I knew she *couldn't* smile anymore.

I walked to the bed, leaned over and kissed her cheek, which was smooth and dry and smelled of institutional soap. I took a seat on the edge of her bed. 'How are you, Mum?' I said, and she blinked slowly.

'Not bad,' she said. Or at least I thought that's what she said. Her words were still slurred, though getting better all the time. I smiled and tried to think of something to say. I could feel the weight of her stare and picked up a get well soon card from one of Mum's oldest friends, Joan.

Joan had been in our lives for as long as I could remember, and although Mum thought of her as one of her closest friends, as I'd got older, I started to notice how Joan looked down on Mum, how she patronised her once Dad had gone, how she used to say, 'Well done you,' whenever Mum told her she'd applied for a new job or had managed to fix the sink herself.

After Mum's stroke, she'd shown up at the hospital, discussing Mum's outlook with the doctors, even though she'd been a medical secretary rather than a doctor herself. And then, she started talking about Mum's affairs, that she and Mum had often talked about being there for each other, that Mum had wanted her to take care of things should anything happen. Mum had never mentioned any of that to me, and so, we'd argued – me believing it was only right that as her daughter, I should be the one to speak for her, Joan believing because she was older and wiser that she was the best person for the job – and all the while, Mum lay there unable to do anything about her own life. Nothing had been signed, and now, it was too late.

But Joan hung around for a while, organising this and that, giving her opinions on what Mum would've wanted, as if Mum was no longer there at all, and we both tried to stay out of each other's way until one day Joan just stopped coming and the occasional card was all Mum was worth.

I put the card back and saw Mum's eyes move back to the window. I knew she was angry with me, knew she blamed me for what'd happened, for her ending up in this place. And though it wasn't my fault, I knew I hadn't dealt with things very well, not then and not now. I still got frustrated at my inability to understand her. Patience was never my strong point. But it still hurt that she could smile for a stranger and not for me.

'I've got a new house,' I said, and she finally turned back to me.

'A house?' she mumbled.

I nodded. 'Yep. My own house.' I smiled and waited for her to do the same.

'How?' she said, although I wasn't sure if that was what she meant, her words would get jumbled sometimes.

'Do you mean *where*?' I said.

She shook her head, and her breath quickened, frustration rising. 'How?' she said again. Another sound came from her lips, and I struggled to make it out.

'I've been saving, Mum.'

'How d…d…' she stuttered before stopping, frustrated with herself. I leaned in, about to put my hand on hers to let her know it was okay, that she didn't have to keep going if it was too much. She closed her eyes and fell silent, remaining that way for several minutes, until I thought she'd fallen asleep. I was about to stand up and tiptoe to the door when she opened her eyes again.

'Fire,' she said, and I froze. A chill went through me, and I pulled back.

'Why are you talking about that?' I asked.

'Fire,' she said again, lifting her good hand which trembled.

'Mum, you're upsetting yourself. Maybe I should speak to your nurse.'

'What for?' she said slowly, her voice sounding like she was under water.

I went to stand, but she gripped my hand, her nails digging in to my skin, her mouth twisted as she stuttered and stumbled over her words.

'Stop it, Mum,' I said, pulling my hand away. I walked to the door. 'I'll see you tomorrow.'

'Polly.'

I could hear her calling me all the way down the corridor. I could see the care assistants staring at me for abandoning my poor ill mother. But I couldn't stand it anymore. I couldn't take it when she became agitated.

'Miss Cooke?'

I turned, and Cathy was coming out from behind the desk, hurrying after me. Suddenly, I couldn't be bothered to speak to her, knowing she'd just say the same old thing about mum – "Give it time".

'Can I have a quick word?' she asked. 'I've been trying to contact you. Your flatmate said you'd moved out.'

'That's right,' I said, and wondered who Cathy had spoken to. When I'd told Kimberley and Sasha about my mum's nurse, they'd agreed she sounded patronising. Condescending Cathy was what Sasha called her, and we'd all laughed and then, one day, I'd called the home and it almost slipped out.

'Well, it makes things difficult for us if we have no contact information for you. In case of emergencies and so forth.'

'I'm here almost every day,' I said.

She looked down her nose at me. 'You haven't been here for a week.' She looked me up and down, and I wondered if she was noticing the last remaining bruises or if she was just being judgemental again.

'I've moved house. You must know how stressful that is,' I said.

'Yes, and I know things have…difficult for you recently. But you should've let us know if you changed your number, at the very least.' She waved a sheet of paper in my direction with little boxes for my details. She handed me a pen, and I pressed the paper against the wall, trying to keep my writing inside the boxes.

I had to get my new phone out to find the number, and Cathy sighed and pursed her lips. I wrote the numbers down carefully and handed over the pen and paper.

'Anyway,' she said, clicking her pen off and sliding it into her pocket. 'You might've noticed your mother was a little quiet today.'

'Yes,' I said.

'She's been doing so well lately,' Cathy said, 'but these past few days, she's been very down, agitated, you know.'

'About what?' I asked, wondering if something had happened to make her bring up the fire again.

Cathy shook her head. 'I don't know, that's what I was wanting to ask you.' She leaned in closer, and I could smell coffee on her breath. 'I know you were…the last time you came, I know something had happened. I thought maybe it was that?'

'Mum was out of it last time I was here,' I said. 'She didn't even know I was here.'

'Right,' she said, nodding slowly. 'She did keep calling for you, though. So, you can see how important it is for us to be able to get in touch?'

'She seems okay,' I said, eventually.

Cathy looked past me to Mum's door and gave a half smile. 'Well, perhaps she just wanted to see you.' Cathy turned to walk away.

'Could she be having delusions again?' I asked, and Cathy turned, a look of surprise on her face.

'Has she said something to make you think that?' she asked.

I sighed. 'I don't know. She's started talking about the fire again. I thought she was past that,' I said and glanced back at Mum's door.

'But there *was* an incident at the house, wasn't there? She's not imagining that,' Cathy said.

'No, it's just…it was the *way* she said it, as if…' I shook my head, wondering if it was worth worrying about. 'She was having weird thoughts and ideas when she was in the hospital. She was saying all kinds of things then. I just don't want her to go back to that.'

'I don't recall seeing that in her records. She wasn't treated for it, was she? Wasn't on medication?'

'No,' I said. 'They thought it wasn't serious enough.'

Cathy frowned. 'Delusions after a stroke aren't very common,' she said. 'And if a patient does experience them, they usually disappear quickly.'

'But she could have them again, couldn't she?'

'Well, it's not likely. And I've not witnessed any behaviour that's concerned me.' She put a flabby hand on my shoulder. 'What is it that's making you think she's delusional?'

'I don't know,' I said, shaking my head. 'I just thought you should be aware. You know her history, don't you? You know she was having problems before the stroke.'

'But she was never diagnosed, was she? With dementia?'

'No. But only because they wouldn't listen to me. She almost set the house on fire!'

Cathy squeezed my shoulder. 'Dementia is difficult to diagnose. But I'm sure if the doctors thought something was really wrong, they'd have done something.' Cathy smiled. 'I wouldn't worry, Polly. She's making good progress. Her speech is improving day by day. She even wrote a little earlier in the week. She'll be back to her old self in no time.'

Someone shouted for Cathy from behind the desk, and she toddled off to answer a call. She held her finger up to me as she went, presumably wanting me to stay, to continue the conversation, but I needed to leave. I needed fresh air.

Part of me wanted to go back, find out exactly what Mum had wanted to say. But I tried to tell myself it didn't matter. That it was all in the past.

Chapter 6

The bus took forever to get me home, and when it finally pulled up on my street, I hurried off, knocking into some bloke's bags of shopping as I did. I made my way to the house quickly, not looking back, not looking up, not wanting to see if anyone was around. So far, no one had spoken to me on the street, no neighbours had come round with a friendly hello, and I wondered if I should make more of an effort. I made sure I had my keys in my hand before I got to the door, not wanting to linger on the doorstep in full view for longer than necessary. The memory of the night before pulled into view, and I felt a shiver go through me. I could see him standing there, watching. Watching me.

I got the key into the lock and breathed a sigh of relief. After visiting Mum, I'd had this terrible feeling that she was right in asking me *How?* That in reality I'd never get a place like this. That I'd come back and find the key wouldn't work, that it'd all been some fantasy. But it slid in easily, and I opened the door. As I walked inside, I chanced a look back, up and down the street, across the road. There were plenty of people about, but no one watching me, no one paying attention at all. I closed the door, shut out the world, and realised I was being ridiculous.

I dropped my bag onto the floor in the hallway and closed my eyes. No one was taking the house from me, no one was going to ruin it this time.

I walked through to the living room, and as I passed the bottom of the stairs, I could smell the lingering odour of the air freshener I'd used that morning. It stuck in my throat, and I ran up the stairs to open the window again. The room was stuffy with the scent, and I pushed the window as far as it would go, even though it was chilly. I found the clean sheets and put them to one side, on top of the dressing table, ready to go once the smell had disappeared.

Needing a cup of tea, I walked to the stairs, but suddenly stopped. Something caught my attention. A noise somewhere behind me. I went still. It was a tapping sound, insistent and loud. I could see the open bedroom window and let out a breath. Something was being blown against the pane. I went back in and looked around but found nothing.

Coming back onto the landing, I could hear it again. *Tap, tap, tap*. What was it?

I turned to the other bedroom, wondering if it was coming from there, trying to work out what it could possibly be. As I turned, something caught my eye in the other direction. A shadow. Something moving.

My heart stopped. Was there someone in the house?

I couldn't move, my feet felt stuck to the deep pile carpet. But now I was facing the bathroom, I could hear it more clearly, I knew it was coming from in there.

It stopped. I was imagining things. Scaring myself with stupid thoughts, just like I did when I was a kid. Telling myself vampires lurked outside the front door at night, and if I lingered too long, they'd get me.

And then, I heard it again. This time, I moved forward. I looked around for something to grab, something I could use as a weapon, something to defend myself. There wasn't much choice, and in the end, I picked up the can of air freshener.

I edged forward, still listening to the noise, and pushed the bathroom door, gently at first, but when it didn't budge, I shoved it hard, hoping to scare whoever was in there. With the aerosol held up in front of me, I charged in.

The room was empty. The door slammed into the wall behind it, making it clear no one was lurking behind there. My hand dropped to my side, and I finally noticed the window was open.

It wasn't on the latch, instead opening and closing with the wind, tapping in time. I felt ridiculous. Leaving the can on top of the cistern, I pulled the window shut.

As I started to walk out, I caught sight of myself in the mirror. I didn't look my best – tired and pale. *It's the stress of the move.* And maybe I wasn't eating enough. As soon as I thought about food, my stomach started to rumble, and I knew it was time for something to eat.

I'd forgotten to go to the shops, forgotten to stock up the fridge, so I decided to head back out. I got halfway down the stairs when it occurred to me that I hadn't opened the bathroom window. I was sure I hadn't. And even if I had, I never would've left it open when I went out. I never left the windows open.

After turning back up the stairs, I looked around for things out of place. There was nothing obvious, nothing broken, nothing gone from what I could tell. But I felt a chill go through me.

Standing on top of the toilet seat, I checked the window frame. Nothing looked broken there, either, it didn't seem to have been forced. I jostled the latch, wondering if it was loose, if it could've come free by itself, if the wind could've caught it. But it didn't seem likely.

I stepped down and looked around once again, unable to shake the feeling that someone had been there. That someone had been inside my house while I was gone.

Chapter 7

I walk up to the door, feeling the anger rattling around me, battling with the fear. I try to push it open but find it's locked. Of course it is. He couldn't have got in like that, he'd have to find another way.

The keys jingle in my hand as I try to unlock the door and I drop them. After a fluster, I finally make my way through it. Once I'm in, I slam the door back hard, hoping it frightens him away.

I stomp through to the living room, expecting to find him there, but the room is empty. I wonder if he's gone, slipped out when he saw me coming. Maybe he was trying to scare me, trying to get in my head by moving things about when I'm not here. But I've caught him in the act.

I pick up the cricket bat that stands in the corner of the room. It'd been in the house when I arrived, but I kept it because it reminded me of my father. I grip it tightly by my side. I walk quickly to the kitchen and find him there. He doesn't seem shocked to see me, he obviously heard me come in. But he looks afraid, as if he only thought part of the way through his plan. As if he hadn't thought of the consequences. He doesn't know what to do.

'What're you doing?' I say, and he stands there, hands in pockets, eyes going somewhere beyond me. He looks rough. I can smell his clothes from where I stand, as if he hasn't washed or changed in weeks. His nails are long and filthy, his hair is greasy and needs cutting. 'What're you doing?' I say again, slower, and take a step closer to him. He pulls his hands from his pockets, and I stop.

'Polly,' he says, and his eyes dart about, never staying on me for more than a fraction of a second. I don't like him using my name. It makes me sick. He sees the cricket bat and frowns. He reaches out for it, and I tighten my grip, raising it slightly as a warning.

'How did you get in here?' I ask, and he opens his mouth but says nothing, instead his eyes swivel to the window behind him. I notice for the first time it's broken, fragments of glass are scattered all over the floor.

I raise the cricket bat, and he ducks. 'Please, don't,' he says.

'You're an idiot, Jacob,' I say, pitying him. 'Just get out now, and I won't call the police.'

'I just...' Jacob says, mumbling, looking anywhere but at me.

'Just what?' I say, dropping the cricket bat onto the floor, knowing I don't need it anymore.

'I just want...'

'Go away, Jacob,' I say and grab his sleeve. He pulls away from me, but I hang on this time, grabbing his arm too. 'Go now, and I won't call the police. I promise.'

He pulls away again, more violently this time, and I suddenly remember how he used to be. How he'd have his little outbursts, a few seconds usually, occasionally more, where someone would get hurt, and then, it'd be back to good old Jacob. Such a nice boy.

'What's going on?'

I spin around before looking at him again. He seems more nervous now, and his eyes are on the floor. I look back to the hallway and see a shadow move, someone coming down the stairs.

There's someone else here. Jacob brought someone else into my house.

The anger is taken over by fear. The certainty replaced by doubt. I thought I could beat him, thought I could handle this by myself. But he's not alone.

Jacob is not alone. I am.

Chapter 8

I missed the good bus again, the one that drops me almost right outside my house. I'd have to wait another hour for the next one, so instead, I got the other bus – the one that drops me behind the house. It wasn't so bad, it just meant walking around the block to get home or else cutting across the playing fields. For the first time in days, it wasn't raining, so I decided to go the longer route around the block and stop at the shop on the way home.

My feet were sore from the new shoes I'd bought myself as a moving in present, and I added plasters to the shopping list in my head. Plasters, tea bags, onions. I repeated it over and over, trying to keep it in my head. Plasters, tea bags, onions. I should've gone to see Mum, too, but I was tired and planning to cook from scratch, wanting to try out my new food mixer. There wasn't time to do it all.

I turned the corner and walked up the little street adjoining the two main roads, where the bus stopped and where *I lived*. I liked this street, it was mostly bungalows, mostly older people, but they were all pretty places with immaculate gardens with scatterings of gnomes. The kind of houses retired baby boomers moved to in order to spend some of their hefty pensions. The prices alone made sure there was no one under fifty living there, not unless they'd had the good fortune to be left the house in someone's will. If things had been different, maybe Mum and Dad could've lived on this street, in one of these houses. But things weren't different, so she was where she was, and I was in my own place. Of course, my place wasn't as fancy as these bungalows, but it was more than I'd ever expected to get with my budget, more than any of my friends could get. Kimberley and Sasha had once talked about getting a mortgage together, but it seemed like madness to me. Sooner or later, somebody's circumstances would change, and everyone's dream would come crashing down. I guess I'd lucked out with my place.

I quickened my pace at the soothing thought of getting home, getting out of my uncomfortable shoes and sitting down in *my* house. I smiled at the thought of it, the idea still exciting to me. After everything that'd happened, I almost couldn't believe it was true.

An image of him came to mind, those sad little eyes staring at me, unable to comprehend it was over. No. I shook my head. I wasn't going to think about him. Not anymore. He was in the past. I had to think of myself now. Like Mum always said, you have to look out for yourself.

I walked on, almost at the little shop that seemingly sold everything, forcing my brain to think *plasters, tea bags, onions*, instead of thoughts of him. I could see my house, almost. I could see the promise of my house anyway. And then, my eyes shifted across the street as a car honked its horn at someone taking too long to cross the road. And I saw him.

Sitting on the wall across the street from my house, there he was again. Jacob.

My breath caught in my throat, and I stopped. I tucked myself close to the wall, wondering if he could see me. But his eyes were firmly on the house. Maybe he thought I was in there. Maybe he thought I wouldn't dare leave. That his little games would freak me out.

After that night I'd seen him hanging around, I didn't see him for a couple days, but I'd felt his presence in every little noise, every shadow. The incident with the bathroom window had worried me, and for a little while, he almost won. I didn't go back out that day, instead of getting something nice for my tea, I'd had to make do with beans on toast and whatever scraps I could find in the cupboards. But it didn't last. I told myself not to let him scare me, not to let him dictate what I did. So, the next day, I went out – and the day after that. When I returned, sometimes the window was open again, but in the end, I told myself it was the wind and bought some nails, found a hammer, closed it for good.

But yesterday, I saw him again. In the morning when I woke up and pulled back the curtains, there he was, lurking across the street, watching, waiting. I hid. And when I looked back, he was gone. I told myself it was nothing. He was just messing with my head. I had to give it to Jacob, I never thought he had it in him. Never thought he was clever enough for mind games. So, I readied myself for trouble, but he vanished again before I could take action.

But now, he was back. And I was no longer behind the safety of my four walls. I looked around, wondering what to do.

I hid.

Chapter 9

I'd hung around in the little shop so long, I think they started suspecting me of shoplifting. There's only so long you can look at tins of beans and weigh up the best value toilet rolls without looking odd. But I couldn't go back out there if he was still waiting. I didn't want the hassle of a confrontation, didn't want my new neighbours to witness what would inevitably be a scene.

I wondered what he wanted, or rather, what he thought he would get out of hanging around all the time, from seeing me. I just wished he'd leave me alone. It was over.

'Can I help you?' the man behind the counter asked, trying to smile.

'No,' I said, and took my basket, which still only had two items in it – tea bags and onions – to the till. 'Actually,' I said, and tried to work out how friendly the man was and how ridiculous I'd sound. 'There's a man out there. Across the street, sitting on a wall. He's waiting for me, but I don't want to see him.'

The man behind the counter nodded, and his look of slight worry changed into slight impatience. I might've been paranoid, but at least I wasn't going to rob him. He put my shopping through the till and dropped them into a plastic bag. 'Four eighty-five, please,' he said and held out his hand. I had to rummage in my bag for my purse and then counted out the money in change. I heard him sigh, but he never let his hand drop.

'Five pence change,' he said, and dropped the little coin into my hand, holding up the bag for me to take.

I reached for the bag, my hand brushing his. He started to turn away to the little TV tucked beneath the counter, but I smiled, and his eyes drifted back to me.

'You couldn't…' I started, and the man narrowed his eyes. 'I hate to ask but… You couldn't take a look, could you?'

'A look?' he said.

'Outside. See if he's still there.' He glanced at the door. 'I'd really appreciate it. It's just, this man has been harassing me.'

The man squinted again, but I thought I could feel him softening. He looked back to the door, ducked his head as if he thought he was doing me the favour from there. 'How will I know who to look for?'

'He's just across the street, a little bit further that way,' I said, pointing to the right of the shop. 'He's dressed scruffily. Possibly smoking.'

He opened the door and stepped outside. I could see him looking down the street, moving his head to see past passers-by. He turned back to me and shrugged his shoulders before coming back inside.

'I can't see anybody. Not across the street, like you say,' he said.

I let out a breath and thanked the man before grabbing my bag and heading outside. I glanced across the street and saw an empty wall where Jacob had previously been. I looked back into the shop before walking home and mouthed 'thanks' to the man. He just nodded and went back to his TV.

I was halfway home when I realised that the man had said he couldn't see anyone across the street. Did that mean Jacob had gone? Or was he now waiting at my door?

I stopped abruptly, and a few people walked around me, just another obstacle on their way home. I craned my neck to see the house, wondering if he'd be there, ringing the bell, sitting on the step. I started moving again, bracing myself for a run-in, but when I got to my door, he wasn't there. I let myself in and closed the door behind me, making sure it was locked. I went straight into the living room and pulled the musty curtains closed.

Relieved, I pulled off my shoes and remembered, too late, that I'd forgotten the plasters. 'Shit,' I muttered to myself. All that bloody time in the shop and I still forgot them. I threw the shoes across the room and took the carrier bag with the tea bags and onions to the kitchen.

I found the recipe I'd planned on making but suddenly felt tired. *Maybe tomorrow*, I told myself and tossed the onions onto the vegetable rack. I stood in the kitchen for a while, leaning against the worktop, thinking about Jacob and what I would say if he finally got hold of me. I'd been paranoid that he might show up at work if I kept ignoring him, and wondered which would be worse, a fight here or at work. He'd never been there before, but he knew where it was, it wouldn't be hard to track me down. But no one at work knew him, so I could easily pretend not to know him, say that he was just some nutter and get him thrown out. But I wondered if the same would work at home. If he showed up and caused a scene, would the neighbours call the police? Would he start saying things that made trouble for me? I'd thought about it a lot when I was ending things with Jacob. I was a normal, responsible person with a job, a real life. What did he have? Besides, the police were already looking for him, and Jacob knew that. I'd thought that would stop him from coming, but it hadn't. Maybe Jacob wanted to get to me more than he cared what happened to him. Or maybe he was just thicker than I thought.

I tried to tell myself that everything would work out. That if it came to it, and the police were called, it'd be for the best. But what if they dug deeper into what'd happened? Maybe they'd find things out about me that no one could ever know.

Chapter 10

I spent the rest of the evening feeling on edge, wondering if he was out there somewhere, watching me. Every few minutes, or so it seemed, I'd get up and walk to the window, peeking out from behind the curtain, sure I'd see him standing there. But he wasn't. Not once.

After a while, I started to think maybe he'd never been there. That he was a figment of my imagination, my subconscious conjuring him up. Maybe everything that'd happened between us was haunting me, making me see things that weren't there.

I tried to concentrate on the TV – some programme about polar bears – but my mind and eyes drifted to the window constantly. In the end, I decided to do something to take my mind off it and started tearing at the wallpaper again, feeling pleased with myself when I pulled off big strips. By the time I was done, the whole room was stripped with the exception of little bits here and there. I stood back and admired my efforts and made a note to go to B&Q one night after work and find some tools to finish the job along with some new paper or paint to replace it.

It was late when I finally headed to bed. I was feeling better but figured a good night's sleep would help get rid of this spectre hanging over me. When I'm unconscious, I don't think about him.

I'd brushed my teeth and was changing into my pyjamas when I first heard it. To start with, I didn't know what it was, a sound without a source. I stood at the top of the stairs and listened. It sounded like scratching but I couldn't tell where it was coming from, and after a few seconds, it stopped. I stood still, foot on the top step, for a minute longer, waiting for it to start again, but there was nothing. Finally, I went into the bedroom and climbed into bed. The sheets were fresh and crisp and felt good against my skin. The awful flowery smell was gone.

Lying in the almost-dark, I thought about Jacob. I didn't want to, but my brain couldn't help itself, and I wondered if I'd ever be rid of him, in person or in memory. It seemed unlikely I'd forget him now, not after everything that'd happened. In a lot of ways, I'd never forgotten him, even when he'd disappeared from my, and everyone else's, life for so many years. It wasn't like I thought of him all the time. Why would I? But there was always a hint of him somewhere in the back of my mind, a lingering presence that a certain smell or sound would bring to the forefront. He was one of those people; not important, not special, but unforgettable.

I rolled over onto my side and could see the light from the moon sneaking in through the gap in the curtain. I tried to stop thinking about Jacob, but the more I tried, the harder it became. I wondered where he was, if he wasn't lurking outside my house. Whose bed he was in, if he'd found someone else to take care of him. If he'd told them about me.

I turned again, onto my other side, the light keeping me from sleep. But I still couldn't drift off, Jacob's face appearing before me every time I closed my eyes. *Go away.* I turned the pillow and punched it down, trying to get comfortable. And then, I heard it again. The scratching, louder this time.

Sitting up straight, I turned my head towards the sound. It was downstairs, I was sure of it. I pulled back the covers and walked out to the landing, listening intently. It'd stopped again, but I knew I wouldn't be able to sleep until I'd found out what it was.

The bang made me jump, and I ducked back behind the banister. There was someone outside, at the door. I started to move, to go downstairs, but stopped and went back to the spare bedroom. I looked around and found a cricket bat, the twine at the top dirty and frayed. I picked it up and carried it downstairs.

As I looked out of the peep hole, I saw a shadow as someone ran away. I could hear my own breath and saw the condensation on the door. I knew it was him. It had to be. But he'd gone now, scared away when he'd heard movement.

I wondered what he was playing at. If he wanted to see me, why had he run away? Was he just trying to scare me? Trying to hurt me? The door was open before I realised what I was doing. I ran down the path and looked around, no longer caring what the neighbours thought. But the street was empty, not a soul about.

I turned to go back inside and saw it. On the doorstep was an envelope with POLLY scrawled across the front in child-like handwriting. Jacob's handwriting. I was going to ignore it, but curiosity got the better of me, and I bent down to pick it up.

Wide awake now, I took the envelope into the kitchen and turned on the light. I put the kettle on and sat at the little round table while I waited for the water to boil. I stared at the envelope, trying to decide if I really wanted to open it, if I really wanted to find out what he'd left for me.

The kettle clicked off, but I didn't move, I had hold of the packet, turning it over and over in my hands. Finally, I tore it open, half expecting something nasty to spill out. Instead, I found nothing more than a sheet of paper. I turned it around, and as it dawned on me what I was looking at, I dropped it, watching it float down to the floor.

It landed face up, and I looked down at the drawing he'd left. A picture of me, half undressed, sitting on a bed. His bed. I felt bile come up my throat, stinging the back of my tongue. I couldn't decide if he was trying to creep me out, or if he thought, in his twisted little mind, that it was a nice gesture. Either way, I didn't want to look at it, didn't want it in my house. I picked it up and tore it into little pieces. I opened the bin and then changed my mind, wanting it out completely. I opened the back door and threw it outside, letting the wind carry it away.

'Polly?'

He came out from the shadows and walked towards me. I slammed the back door, locking it and sliding the latch. How long had he been there? Had he been watching through the window? Did he see me open the envelope, did he get pleasure from it?

'Polly, it's me,' he said, and I could tell he was right at the door. 'Let me in.' The handle jiggled up and down, and I ran from the kitchen. He started banging on the door, asking for me to open it, over and over.

'Go away,' I screamed and crouched down in the hallway, out of sight.

'I just want to talk to you,' he said.

'Leave me alone!'

He kept knocking, kept calling out to me, and I couldn't take it anymore. I got up and ran to the door but stopped myself from opening it, unsure what he'd do if I gave him the chance.

'I'll call the police,' I said, but he kept knocking. My mobile was upstairs, but he didn't know that. 'Hello, police? There's someone outside my house, he's trying to get in. I'm frightened.'

I stopped talking and realised the knocking had stopped. Had he believed it? Did he think the police were coming? I moved to the window, trying to see if he was still there, but I couldn't make him out from my position. I went back and pressed my ear to the door. I couldn't hear anything, but it didn't mean he'd gone.

After a few minutes, having heard no more noise, I walked away from the door and turned off the light, going back upstairs. I went into each room, looking out of each window to see if he was still hanging around. Guessing he'd given up, I climbed back into bed and was just beginning to calm down when I heard it again.

'Polly. Let me in,' he shouted, his words slurred. I closed my eyes and wondered how much he'd had to drink. The neighbours were bound to be awake by now. Even if I didn't call the police, someone would. I sat with my arms wrapped around my knees, rocking back and forth, listening to the pathetic cries from beneath the window.

'Leave me alone,' I mumbled to myself, too tired to go back downstairs.

I watched the clock tick its way around to three a.m., and still, he continued. At one point, I thought I heard someone else shout, an angry voice telling him to shut up. But he didn't stop. I lay down and shoved the pillow over my head, trying to drown out the sound. And not for the first time, I wondered if I'd done the right thing getting involved with him again. I could still hear his voice through the pillow, and I knew that it had all been a terrible mistake. One I was going to pay for.

Chapter 11

I woke late the next day, the alarm turned off subconsciously, if I'd even remembered to set it at all. I scrambled out of bed, the panic of being late for work forcing me up, even if what I really wanted to do was stay in bed where it was safe and where no one could see me.

I picked up my phone to call work, to let them know I was running late, my mind furiously trying to think of an appropriate excuse. I'd missed so much work already because of Jacob. I knew I was risking everything, but I just couldn't face it. I was surprised no one had said anything to me yet about my absences. And there'd been days when I barely focused at all, my mind drifting, my hand scribbling Jacob's name over and over again like a schoolgirl hoping to marry her crush.

I noticed several missed calls, and for a second, I thought it was him, that he'd given up on calling out my name from outside and had started calling my phone instead. But I remembered changing my number afterwards, making sure, or at least I thought, that he wouldn't be able to get hold of me. Of course, that was naive. He knew where I was, and that was much more dangerous than him being able to call. I could ignore calls, block them even, but there was nothing I could do to stop him showing up here. Maybe I'd been foolish to think he'd just walk away. I guess deep down I knew this would happen, but I'd fought the thoughts away, not wanting them to be true.

I looked at the phone in my hand, and the realisation hit me. The calls were from the care home. Something had happened to Mum.

'Hello?' The voice on the end of the line sounded impatient, and I realised I'd zoned out again.

'Hi, this is Polly Cooke. You called me,' I said.

'Oh yes,' the woman said. I tried to decide if there was a hint of pity or fear or something in her voice. 'I'll just find Cathy for you, she's dealing with your mum.'

'But–' I wanted whoever this woman was to just tell me what was going on, but she'd put the phone down. I could hear the background noise of the place, the chitter-chatter of the nurses and care assistants. I could hear someone shouting nonsense, presumably a resident. I could hear the clatter and tinkling of the drinks trolley being rolled along the lumpy linoleum floor.

I was getting impatient and paced up and down the bedroom, my mind flitting about from Mum to work to Jacob to the situation I found myself in. I couldn't help thinking that at least now I *did* have an excuse for being late for work and then felt bad.

'Ms Cooke?'

Cathy's voice brought me back. 'Yes,' I said. 'Has something happened? Is she all right?'

'She's fine, Polly,' Cathy said, her voice calm. 'She had a fall last night. She's a little bruised, but nothing's broken, and she's had some breakfast this morning. The doctor will be along shortly to check on her, but I think she's fine.'

I heard myself let out a deep breath, and I wondered if Cathy would think it was a sigh of relief or a sigh of annoyance that she'd left so many messages about nothing.

'She might like to see you, though. Will you be visiting today?' Cathy asked.

I thought for a moment. 'I'll be there shortly.'

***

I dressed quickly and crammed a couple of biscuits into my mouth in lieu of breakfast. As I stood over the sink to catch the crumbs, I looked out of the small kitchen window and thought about the night before. I'd been genuinely scared, and the memory ran through me like ice.

I'd never really been as afraid of Jacob as perhaps I should've been. I thought I had him worked out, but how well do we ever really know someone? Maybe everything I'd assumed about him was wrong, and I realised that my assumptions could've put me in danger.

I washed down the biscuits with some water and rinsed the glass before leaving it on the drainer. I was about to leave but stopped and turned to the back door, wondering if Jacob had left any more gifts. In the light of day, it didn't feel as frightening to open the door, even if it meant, as I thought as I unlocked it, that he could still be out there. He could've worn himself out shouting like that and fallen asleep in the yard.

Pulling open the door, I steeled myself, but there was nothing there. No Jacob, no gift. Just a couple of cigarette butts. I sighed and picked them up, throwing them into the wheelie bin. As I washed my hands, I decided I was being ridiculous. Having someone banging at your door and screaming your name in the middle of the night would freak anyone out. There was nothing to worry about. Jacob wasn't dangerous. I knew that. I'd known him most of my life.

I picked up my bag and headed out thinking everything seemed worse in the dark. Every problem seems bigger, unsolvable. But I had nothing to worry about. If anything was going to happen, it would've happened already. I was safe. I'd done what I thought was right, what was best for me. And that's all any of us can do.

Chapter 12

I called work while I was walking to the bus stop. The exertion of walking quickly made me sound out of breath, desperate even. 'I'm really sorry,' I said to Janet, my boss. And I was sorry, knowing they'd be struggling without me there.

'Don't worry about it, Polly,' Janet said, her voice oozing patience. 'Just go and check on your Mum. Don't worry about us, we'll cope. And take care of yourself too.'

'I will. Thanks.'

'Just call me later, let me know how she is and if you'll be back tomorrow.'

'I will,' I said again. 'Bye.'

As I took a seat on the bus, I thought about what Janet had said and realised I could take the whole day off, maybe even the next day, too, if I wanted to. If I had a couple of days to myself, I could really make inroads with the house. Maybe it was wrong, especially using Mum as an excuse, but I decided work would have to learn to cope without me sooner or later. I'd already applied for a couple of better positions, and besides, I was always doing them favours, working extra shifts, staying late to mop up other people's mistakes. I guessed they owed me one.

As the bus passed through the town, past the shops – those that were still in business, anyway – I tried to decide what to do with the rest of my day. I started making a list in my head. I'd get a blind for the kitchen window. I didn't want anyone, least of all Jacob, looking in at me, especially at night. Plus, I had my eye on a fabric that would perfectly match the paint I'd picked out in my head. I'd finally do some proper shopping for some proper food and maybe even make that casserole I'd planned the night before. But mostly, I'd have some time alone, just relaxing. It'd been a stressful few weeks with the move and everything. And it wasn't as if the months before had been easy. All the stuff with Mum and then Jacob – I was surprised I hadn't gone mad too.

The bus stopped by the home, and I hopped off, feeling lighter than I had in days, despite my disturbed sleep. I didn't even feel like turning back as I got to the doors. As I walked through, waiting to be buzzed in, I could see Cathy lurking by the nurses' station. I wondered if I could get by without her seeing me. I always got the feeling she didn't like me no matter what I did. I'd brought boxes of cakes and chocolates for the staff when Mum was first brought in, but it did nothing to endear me to Cathy. It always seemed as though she thought of us, the relatives, as the enemy. That we were somehow lacking by letting our parents be dumped in such a place. It didn't seem to occur to her that if we hadn't brought our loved ones there, she wouldn't have a job. I guess it's impossible to understand some people.

'Ms Cooke,' Cathy said as I walked along the corridor. 'I informed the doctor you were coming, but she had an appointment elsewhere so couldn't stay. But she said your mum is fine, and if you want to speak to her, you can call her secretary to arrange a time.'

'That won't be necessary. Thank you.'

'Oh,' Cathy said, looking put out. 'Well, I'm sure your mum will be pleased to see you, anyway. You left in such a hurry the other day.'

'What happened? How did she fall?' I asked.

Cathy looked down at her sensible shoes, and I wondered if she was responsible for what'd happened, if she'd been negligent. 'She was trying to get to the phone,' she said.

'What for?'

'She wanted to call the police.'

'The police? Why?' I said, an unsettled feeling coming over me. 'I told you something was wrong,' I said, angry they'd allowed this. 'She's done it before, you know. Called the police because she's gotten something in her head.'

'I think it might've been the man who came to visit her.'

'What man?' I said, but I could hear the blood rushing in my ears. I tried to tell myself it couldn't have been him. He wouldn't come here. He wouldn't do that. 'Who was it?' I asked.

'I didn't let him in,' she said, quickly. 'But I put my head round the door and saw him talking to your mum. She seemed worked up about something, so I asked if everything was okay, and he took off. I couldn't catch him. I tried to ask your mum who he was, but she was in a right state. I couldn't work out what she was saying at all. She was so upset, I thought she was going to have another turn. I couldn't calm her down, so I came out to call for the doctor. Next thing, she's dragged herself out of bed, crawling across the floor. Comes out here, trying to get to the phone. Shouting for the police. Took three of us to get her back into bed.' She shook her head. 'She was upset all night. Something really got to her. She kept saying a name. Jake. Jacob, maybe. Does that ring a bell?'

I thought I was going to be sick. Of course it was him. Who else would it be? No one. There was no one else.

'Polly?' Cathy said, coming towards me and putting her hand on my arm. 'She kept saying your name too. Is he someone you know? I know something happened to you last week. I saw the bruises. Should we have called the police?'

I could tell she was trying to work out if she was in trouble. If I was going to sue or something. But I had more on my mind. I wanted to scream at her, to tell her not to let him in again, but I was frozen. I couldn't speak, couldn't move. Why would he come here? What was he trying to do? Was he threatening me? Or Mum?

I could feel anger surging through me now. How dare he come here? How dare he try and get to me through my mum? I thought about telling Cathy to call the police on him, but I knew I had to deal with it myself.

'He's my ex. There's no need to call anyone, he's not dangerous. But Mum doesn't like him, so just don't let him in again.' Cathy stood there, wringing her hands. 'There was nothing you could've done,' I muttered and left Cathy standing in the hall, mouth gaping like a fish let off the hook.

I found Mum in bed, her eyes on the TV in the corner. Some cooking show was on, and even though Mum had never been into cooking, had never once made anything other than ready-made meals, she was engrossed, barely glancing at me as I went in.

'Mum? Cathy said you had a fall. Are you okay?'

'Fine,' Mum mumbled, keeping her eyes on the TV. I could see bruises snaking down her arm to her wrist.

'Have they given you anything? Painkillers or something?' A tiny shake of the head. 'Do you want me to go and ask someone?' No response.

We sat there in silence for a little while, watching the chef on the TV create something that looked pretentious and inedible. There was a time when Mum and I would've laughed at it together, she'd have made some comment such as 'what's wrong with egg and chips?', and I would've reminded her about the time she was offered oysters at a dinner party, and she'd vomited onto the host's lap. But now, we just sat in silence, keeping our thoughts to ourselves.

'I'm sorry I ran out the other day,' I said and bit my lip. 'I was just upset. You know I don't like you talking about the fire.'

Mum's eyes met mine, and I turned the TV off. The room was too quiet without the TV, or maybe it was that it was no longer drowning out the noises from other rooms. I could hear voices shouting out, eighty-year-olds calling for their mothers.

'What happened, Mum? What happened with Jacob?'

Her eyes widened, her mouth opened slightly.

'He came to see you, didn't he?' I looked behind me, towards the door. 'Cathy told me. Said he upset you.'

I could hear her breath, heavy and ragged.

'I know you never liked him,' I said. 'And I should've listened to you. He's not a nice person.'

She still didn't even attempt to speak, and I could feel myself getting angry. If she was so upset about it, why wasn't she saying anything? Cathy said she was getting better. Was she just punishing me for Jacob coming to see her?

'I'm sorry he came here,' I said. 'I'm sorry if he upset you. But I've told them not to let him in. You won't see him again.'

I could see tears in her eyes, and she tried to lift her hand. She closed her eyes, out of tiredness or frustration. Maybe both.

'Cathy said you tried to call the police. That's when you fell. Why were you calling the police? Because of Jacob?'

Mum wouldn't look at me, her hands twisted at the blanket on her lap. I put my hand on hers, and she jerked away. 'Why were you calling the police?' I asked, shaking her now. 'Mum?'

'Everything all right?' Cathy said, poking her head around the door. I stood up, and Cathy smiled at Mum. 'Polly was telling me that man was her ex-boyfriend. That you don't like him so much. Is that why you were upset, Margaret? Well, don't worry, pet, we won't let him in again if you don't want to see him.'

I waited for Mum to look at me again or to say something, but she just stared at the wall, not even acknowledging Cathy. Cathy looked at me, raising her eyebrows.

'He won't come again, Mum. I promise,' I said, although I knew I couldn't stop him trying. I should've realised he'd try dirty tricks to get to me.

'Margaret?' I looked from Cathy to Mum and saw that she was crying. She shook her head as Cathy offered her a tissue. 'I think your Mum's tired,' Cathy said, and I nodded and stood, gathering my things. I leaned down and kissed the top of her head before walking to the door, Cathy right behind me.

'Cathy,' Mum said quietly, and I stopped, wondering why she wanted this stranger and not me.

Cathy went back to her, leaning down and listening as Mum said something. Cathy looked up at me, worry creasing her face. She patted Mum's hand and came back to the door.

'See you soon, Polly,' Cathy said and closed the door on me, leaving me alone on the outside.

I stood there a while, trying to hear what was going on inside, but all I could hear was the sound of the TV again, so finally I walked away, fighting back the tears. I could feel tension building up inside me, like elastic bands were tied tight around my guts. I walked quickly, almost running, out of the building. I could see the other nurses following me with their eyes, but I didn't look back. I needed to get out, and I didn't want to come back.

Chapter 13

I made my way off the bus and ran across the street, barely pausing to see if he was there, part of me thinking, *If I can't see you, then you can't see me*. I was still wound up and wishing I'd never gone to see Mum. Wishing I'd never done a lot of things.

As I unlocked the door, I noticed an old woman at the house next door. I couldn't decide if she was coming out or going in, whether she lived there or was just visiting. Either way, she glared at me as I struggled to get the key in the lock. I could tell she wanted to say something. Once I'd opened the door, I chanced a look, and the woman opened her mouth, just as I closed the front door. She probably wanted to complain about the racket the night before.

I stood with my back against the door and closed my eyes. This was so much harder than I thought it would be. All of this. There was a part of me that wished I'd never left the flat, that I hadn't taken a chance on making things better.

The knock startled me, and I jumped away from the door. Was it him? Had he been waiting for me to come home? I leaned in and checked the peep hole. The old woman from next door. I stood back from the door and waited for her to leave. I didn't want to have to explain Jacob and what had happened.

I waited a minute longer and looked out again. She was still there, standing back, looking up at the windows. She came back to the door and knocked a second time. *Let her think what she wants. Who cares?*

I walked away from the door, into the kitchen and threw down the blind I'd bought for the window. I thought about calling Janet at work and telling her I'd be in the next day, maybe even that afternoon. At least then I'd be out of the house. I slumped down on one of the wobbly chairs and rested my head on the table. How had it come to this? I loved this house. I'd been so excited to get it. I'd put myself through so much to get it. But now...

I could feel tears burning the backs of my eyes, but I refused to let them fall. I wasn't going to let them win. This was my house now. This was my life now. I wasn't going to let anyone ruin it. Not Jacob. Not Mum. Not anyone.

Pushing myself up from the chair, I decided to put up the blind, taking out my frustrations with a hammer, before tearing up a threadbare carpet, sweating with the effort. I stood back and looked at the room. It suddenly looked unlived-in without the carpet, but it didn't matter. It hadn't been my life that'd lived on it.

Tired and achy, I decided to take a bath, to try and relax a bit before deciding what to do next. As I walked down the hall, towards the stairs, I noticed there was some post on the mat. I was going to leave it, doubting it was for me. I was still getting the previous occupier's mail, and I was yet to organise re-directing mine. Another thing on my to-do list. But something about the envelope on top of the pile stopped me.

My stomach tightened as I realised it had no full address, just my name. It was from him. I stood there for a moment, trying to decide whether I should read it or put it straight in the bin. Before I knew it, I was striding forward and scooping up the pile of letters. I walked back to the kitchen and threw the pile, save the one on the top, into the bin. I was sick of getting their stuff, and it was all junk anyway.

I took Jacob's letter to the table and sat down. The writing looked even worse than it had the day before. Tearing into the envelope, a small piece of paper ripped at the edges came out, and I thought I'd done it with my carelessness. But as I tipped it up, several pieces of paper fell out of the envelope, and I realised what they were.

On the table in front of me, I started to put it together like the world's worst jigsaw. The drawing of me started to reappear in front of my eyes, a few pieces missing here and there. The rest must have blown away, but Jacob had somehow managed to collect most of it. I pushed it aside and took the other bit of paper from the envelope. This one was complete.

I THOUGHT YOU LOVED ME. BITCH.

He hadn't signed it, but he didn't need to. I dropped the note on the table and sat back. I could go to the police, he was harassing me, after all, and it wouldn't look good for him after everything else that'd happened. But I didn't really want to do that. Not until it was absolutely necessary. I almost laughed. When, I wondered, would it be absolutely necessary to call the police? How far would it have to go before I thought that was a good idea?

Pushing the scraps of paper back into the envelope, I screwed the whole thing up and shoved it into the bin with the other junk mail. He'd have to do more than that to scare me.

Chapter 14

I came out of the bath feeling relaxed. There'd been no more people at the door, no more malicious notes, just me and some candles and bubbles. I hadn't called Janet back, deciding to wait until morning. I was sure she'd forgive me not calling back. I just couldn't think about that now. Not about Mum or work or Jacob or anything. I just wanted to be alone.

I was in my pyjamas, even though it was just gone four p.m., and it was still light, just. There was maybe a couple of hours daylight left. But I wasn't planning going anywhere else, so why couldn't I dress however I liked in my own house? My house, my rules.

I wished I had some wine in the fridge so I could start drinking early, too, really show them I didn't care, but the best I could rustle up was a half empty bottle of port in the back of the cupboard that'd been left when I moved in. I decided things hadn't got that bad yet, and I didn't want to make my point *that* much. So, I opted for a cup of tea instead and took it through to the living room and stretched out in front of the TV for the night.

It was after nine when I woke, knocking the cushion onto the floor, which spilled the cold cup of tea I'd left there. I had no idea how long I'd been asleep, but I felt woozy, disoriented.

I sat up slowly and tried to get my head around what day it was, what I should be doing. The TV was talking to itself in the corner, and the curtains were wide open. I stood up quickly and went to the window, panicking in case he'd been looking in. I felt vulnerable all of a sudden.

As I crossed to the window, I let out a cry. He was staring right at me. He wasn't across the street this time, he was right in front of the house. He'd probably been watching me sleep, and the thought made me feel sick. He caught my eye and something passed over his face, something I couldn't quite make out. It looked as though he was speaking, but I wasn't sure.

We stared at each other, and it felt intimate, somehow, the memories of things we'd done flashed through my mind. I felt the shudder of nausea rise in me again. I guessed this was what he was counting on. Either to make me sick or to try and win me back. But it wasn't going to work.

I felt the anger rush through me, about how he was trying to get to me, about how he'd used my mum to do so, and I ran to the door, the faster I moved, the more the anger grew. I struggled with the lock, but once I was outside, it all came rushing out.

'Leave me alone!' I screamed at him, running up to him, my face just inches from his. He looked perplexed, as if he never expected me to come out.

'Polly,' he said, stuttering over my name and reaching for my hand. I pulled back, his touch felt like creepy crawlies on my skin.

'Don't touch me,' I said, stepping back so it wouldn't happen again. 'How dare you go and see my mum? You've no right. And if you go there again, I'll call the police. If you come *here* again, I'll call the police.'

Jacob looked unsure now, as if he hadn't thought it through. I watched as he looked around the street, nervous in case the police were already on their way. We were both gambling on what we thought we knew about each other. Jacob thought he had a right to do this to me and hoped I wouldn't call the police, hoped that I wouldn't be brave enough to do it. And maybe he was right. I didn't really *want* to. I didn't want to see him carted off, didn't want him locked up and ground down by some copper. But he couldn't know that, it was all I had to cling to. Besides, if it really came to it, I *would* do it. It wouldn't be the first time.

'You can't keep coming to my house. I'll have to call the police if you don't stop. You know that, don't you?' I said, my voice gentler now.

'But…' he said and stepped closer to me again. I was being too nice. I was encouraging him. Showing sympathy, letting guilt get to me. It was dangerous. It would lead me somewhere I didn't want to go again.

'You sent that nasty letter. I can take it to the police. I *will* take it to the police if you come here anymore.'

'Polly,' he said again and it was like fingernails on a chalkboard. I hated him saying my name. 'You said you loved me. You lied.'

'You're right. I did,' I said. 'So just leave me alone. And leave my mum alone. Don't ever talk to her again. Understand? You don't belong here.' I could see tears in his eyes now, and I knew I was breaking him. It was the only way to make it stop. 'Go away, Jacob. Or I'm calling the police, and you'll go back to prison. Is that what you want?'

I guess I'd gone too far. He ran at me, and I stumbled back, tripping on a loose paving stone, falling back, landing on my hands. The pain shot up my arms. Jacob was standing over me now, his face red, spit at the corner of his mouth.

'You lied to me!'

He grabbed hold of my pyjama top, screwing it tight in his hand and pulled me towards him. I tried to prise his hand away, but he was too strong. I always forgot that about him, how strong he was.

'Jacob, please,' I said, but he just pulled me up further, closer to his face.

'I loved you,' he said.

'I'm sorry,' I said and put my hand over his. 'I do love you, really.'

'Liar!' He let go of me, pushing me to the floor, and I felt my wrist crack as I landed.

I was too busy rubbing at my wrist to notice what Jacob was doing, but when I finally looked up, I saw him staring in to my house, his eyes flickering back and forth. I knew what he was thinking. He wanted in.

I stood up and raced to the door, Jacob on my heels. He tried to grab hold of me, but I pushed him away, and he stumbled over the same paving stone I'd tripped on. I ran into the house and pushed the door, but Jacob was already up and pushing back. His hand was inside, trying to grab at me. I could hear him screaming something but couldn't make out the words over my own voice, screaming at him to go away, to leave me alone.

I thought the old woman would be out soon, the whole street maybe. Perhaps the police would come.

I bent over and bit his hand. He screamed out and withdrew his hand, and I used the advantage to throw my weight against the door. It slammed shut, and I locked it before sliding down to the floor, exhausted.

But Jacob didn't give in. He threw himself at the door, and the wood rattled as he did, vibrating against my back. I closed my eyes and wished it would stop. That *he* would stop. But I knew now that he wouldn't. I'd underestimated him, what he was capable of.

I realised I was crying. Big, heaving sobs that made my chest hurt. Everything that'd happened, everything I'd tried to control and tell myself I could deal with, it was all coming out. 'Leave me alone,' I said between sobs, banging my head against the door. 'Please, leave me alone.'

The banging suddenly stopped, and I let out a long, shuddering breath. Maybe he'd exhausted himself too.

I heard the letterbox open, and before I could move his hand was in my hair, pulling it hard.

'Why did you do this, Polly?' he said, and I tried to get away. I scratched at his hand, but he held on tight. I twisted, feeling the hairs pulling my scalp, and tried to push the letterbox onto his fingers, punching it hard trying to make him stop. Finally, he gave in, and it slammed shut, taking a chunk of hair with it.

I backed away from the door, still cowering on the floor, tears streaming. I couldn't do this anymore. I couldn't live like this, couldn't take it any longer. I was going to have to leave. Leave it all behind. The house, Jacob, Mum. I couldn't take it anymore. In the morning, I was going to walk away and start again. Somewhere new.

Jacob had won.

Chapter 15

I'd fallen asleep on the floor in the hallway, curled up like a baby. When I woke the next morning, I ached from top to bottom and wondered how much was from sleeping on the hard floor and how much was down to Jacob.

My face felt puffy from crying, and my throat was sore. I had no idea what time it was or how long I'd been asleep. For all I knew, Jacob was still there. I couldn't hear anything, but that didn't mean much. He could be sleeping on the other side of the door, as exhausted from our fight as I was.

I peeled myself up off the floor, stretching my arms and legs, pushing my shoulder blades back and rolling my neck. I heard a few clicks and crunches but felt no better. My wrist throbbed, was swollen too.

I went into the kitchen and ran the tap as cold as it would go and filled a glass to the top. It felt good sliding down my throat, soothing it momentarily. I was about to put some bread in the toaster but stopped myself. I didn't think I could eat anything.

In the living room, the TV was still playing from the night before, the blanket I'd been beneath on the settee was on the floor by the window where I'd dropped it as I ran out to confront Jacob. Why had I gone out there? What did I think I'd achieve?

I turned off the TV and sat down on the settee, head resting in my hands until I realised it made my head and my wrist hurt even more. I leaned back and closed my eyes, thinking about what'd happened.

Why had I never been afraid of Jacob before? I knew about his past. I'd seen what he could do, seen his temper aimed at other people, but somehow, I'd always managed to avoid it, and that had led me to believe I was safe, immune maybe. But that was then. Last night, I knew I'd made a huge mistake getting involved with him. How I ever thought it would be all right, I just don't know.

I thought about my decision to leave. Perhaps it'd been a little melodramatic thinking I'd leave *everything* behind. But something had to give. Jacob wasn't going to give up. And living in this house, knowing he could show up at any time…maybe that was the biggest problem.

But I loved this place. I opened my eyes and looked around. This was my home now. I didn't want to leave, certainly didn't want to be pushed out by him, it just wasn't fair. I sighed and looked at the clock. It was gone eight-thirty. I needed to call work.

'Hi, Janet,' I said as she picked up. 'It's Polly. Sorry I didn't call you back yesterday.'

'Oh, honey, you sound terrible,' Janet said. I could hear my voice, it sounded shaky, raw. 'Is it bad?'

'Yes,' I said and started to cry.

'Oh, sweetheart. Look, don't you worry about this place. You just take your time and call me if you need anything. Okay?'

'Okay,' I sniffled and hung up, already thinking about what to do next.

Chapter 16

I didn't leave the house at all that day. I stayed inside, thinking, trying not to think, trying to sleep. Every now and then, I'd get up and go to the window or the door and sneak a look, trying to see if he was out there.

I didn't see him at all that day, but I knew that meant nothing. Maybe he'd been there while I was asleep or was hiding out of plain sight. I kept the curtains closed at all times. The doorbell went once, and I almost jumped out of my skin, but when I peeked out from behind the curtain, I saw someone else, a stranger, most likely selling something. He looked up at the windows, and I ducked away. He probably wondered why all the curtains were closed. Maybe decided to go somewhere less weird.

I finally ate something at tea time, my stomach had been rumbling for a while. But as soon as the food went down, I felt ill, my stomach was in knots.

By seven, I was exhausted and went to bed, the luxury of a real mattress was so welcoming that I fell asleep almost immediately, and I slept through until morning, not even nightmares disturbing my sleep.

I felt better the next day, a good night's sleep in an actual bed does wonders for the state of mind. But I still stayed inside, just in case, as I did the next day and the day after that. At first, it was nice. It was quiet, peaceful. I did as I pleased, ate what I wanted, whenever I chose. Napped on and off throughout the day, and as the days went on, I checked the windows less and less. I didn't see Jacob once.

I started to think that our little encounter that night, as much as it had shaken me, had damaged him more. Maybe my threats of prison had worked, and he'd given up. I started to think that maybe I should go outside again, maybe even go back to work. Maybe Jacob hadn't won at all.

On the fourth day, I opened all the curtains and even some of the windows, letting in some fresh air. It felt good, and I realised how stupid I'd been to think about packing up and going. I could work something else out. It wouldn't be like this forever. Jacob would get tired of it. When had he ever seen anything through?

I decided to do a little experiment. I sat by the window all day, reading a book, looking out onto the street, seeing all the comings and goings. The old woman from next door came out and walked off, slowly, down the street. I watched her for a while, wondering where she'd go, what her life consisted of. I hadn't seen anyone else there, no Mr Old to keep her company. I wondered if she was alone now or if he was in a home like Mum. Or maybe there'd never been a husband. Maybe she'd always been alone.

I went back to my book, but every little sound distracted me, and I'd look up and around the street, making sure that Jacob wasn't the one making the noises. But I hadn't seen him all day, and I was starting to believe he *had* given up, that this was going to work out.

I didn't notice her until she was right there in my face. I let out a little gasp, but she didn't seem to notice, didn't seem to think pushing your face to someone's window would freak them out. I stood up and walked to the door. When I opened it, Mrs Old shuffled away from the window and came to the door.

'I'm Mrs Rodgers,' she said. 'Ethel.'

'Hello,' I said.

'I live next door,' she said, looking at her house. 'I just wanted to introduce myself. As we're neighbours now.'

'That's nice,' I said. 'Very kind of you.'

'I knew Agatha,' she said. 'The lady who lived here before,' Ethel said, trying to angle her head to see inside.

'Oh. Right,' I said. 'What happened to her?'

'She died. Terrible, really. She fell down the stairs. Was never right after that,' Ethel said, and shook her head. 'So sad. How long have you been here?' she asked. 'I saw you the other day, but we didn't get a chance to talk. I didn't see a removal van. Or a for sale sign.'

'It all happened quite quickly, and I didn't have much to bring. Besides, a lot of the furniture was left here. I guess the family didn't want to clear the place themselves,' I said.

'I don't think Agatha had much in the way of family,' Ethel said. 'Her husband died years ago and after that, well, I think she was lost without him. Terrible, really. And of course—'

'I suppose that's how I got it so cheap,' I said, interrupting her before she could give me Agatha's whole life story.

Ethel nodded and then moved a little closer to me. 'I heard some noise the other night,' she said, and I wondered how much she saw, whether she'd seen Jacob, if she'd thought about calling the police.

'It was nothing, just kids messing about,' I said.

'I thought I saw a man. I thought—'

'Excuse me,' I said. 'My phone's ringing. It was nice speaking to you.' I closed the door and went inside, pacing up and down the hallway. I could tell she was still outside, waiting. I wanted her to leave, to stop asking questions. How could I tell her who was out there without her getting suspicious? Without her calling the police? No, I needed to handle things myself.

I caught sight of myself in the mirror in the hallway. I wasn't looking my best. I needed to sort myself out. I made a decision. Starting tomorrow, I was going to get things back on track. I'd get this place looking good, just how I wanted it. The laminate flooring, the chiffon curtains, the accent colours I'd use. A minimalist, stripped back look rather than all this clutter.

I'd get a new job, something better. Something stimulating, better paid. And I'd forget about everything from my past.

Jacob was gone. And so was everything that came with him.

Chapter 17

The other man is bigger than Jacob. Taller, wider. He stands in the doorway, filling it completely. He looks at me with dead eyes, and I can't stand it. I turn back to Jacob. He looks nervous, won't look me in the eye. I can feel my legs shaking like jelly beneath me. I need to sit down. But not here. I need to get out first.

I lift my chin and stride towards Jacob's friend. He doesn't move. 'Excuse me,' I say, and his face changes as a grin spreads across it. His eyes flick over to Jacob and then back down to me. I try to look defiant, show that I'm not afraid of him, but I wonder if he can see me shaking.

'Sit down, Polly,' the man says, and I step back when he says my name. It's not that I'm surprised he knows it, of course Jacob has told him, but it's just the way he says it.

I step back until I hit the table, and I see the cricket bat on the floor. He sees me looking and lurches forward, picking it up before I can. He turns it over in his hand, twirling it and tapping it on his palm.

'Nice,' he says.

'That's mine,' Jacob says from behind me, and his friend looks at him wide eyed.

'All right, mate,' he says. 'Here.' He tosses it towards Jacob who fumbles it and it clatters to the floor. 'Good catch,' the man says.

'Shut up, Phil,' Jacob mumbles, picking the bat back up.

I look back at Jacob who's staring at what he has in his hands, and I wonder if he'll hurt me with it. If that's why he came here.

'So, should we do this?' Phil says, and my head darts around to him.

I see a gap between Phil and the doorway, a gap I could easily get through if I were fast enough. I try to steady myself and then make a run for it. I get out of the kitchen and into the hallway, but then, I feel a hand on my shoulder, pulling at my coat, pulling me backwards.

I try to shrug out of it, but Phil is closer now, is reaching around my neck, trying to get me in a headlock. I throw myself forward, propelling myself towards the front door, but I stumble, tumbling to the floor, Phil on top of me.

The wind goes out of me, and my hip slams into the floorboards. I'd cry out if I didn't have a monster of a man on top of me. He stands up, too fast for his size, and grabs my ankle, dragging me back to the kitchen.

'Get some tape,' he says, and I can hear Jacob rummaging about in the drawers. I kick out at Phil, catching his knee, and he buckles and drops me. I scramble on hands and knees towards the door again, but I can't have kicked him hard enough, and he catches me again far too easily.

'Get off me,' I scream, hoping that Ethel might hear.

'Got some,' Jacob says, and Phil drags me into the kitchen, the loose screws in the floorboard scraping my skin.

Phil pulls me up and sits me on a kitchen chair. He twists my hands behind my back, and Jacob tears some tape off and ties my wrists. I try to struggle, try to make him mess up the tape so that eventually he'll run out, and they'll have to think of something else, but Phil is too strong. I can't move my hands at all, and before I know it, they're tied behind me, looped behind the wooden slats of the chair. I try to stand, but Phil has his hands pressed down on my shoulders, keeping me in my seat.

'Use the rest,' Phil says, and I hear Jacob mutter as he tries to find the end again. 'Come on,' Phil says before snatching the reel from Jacob. 'Hold her still.'

Jacob takes over, and he's not as strong. I can move beneath his hands, but it doesn't matter. Phil tears the tape with a violent rip and starts wrapping it around me. It's tight. Too tight. I can hardly breathe. He winds the whole thing around me so I can't move my arms at all. I'm fastened to the chair completely.

Jacob and Phil take a step back to admire their work. Phil grins again, and I know I'm in too deep. This man is not like Jacob. He's enjoying what he's doing, whatever it is he's going to do. Jacob stands beside him and giggles as if it's all a game, as if that's the only reaction to seeing a woman tied to a chair.

'It's a nice place, this,' Phil says, stepping back, looking around as if he owns the place. 'A bit of paint. Some nice laminate floor in here. It'd be lovely.'

'Why are you doing this?' I say, looking at Jacob. I know it's a stupid question, I know that he believes I've done him wrong, and maybe I have. But if anyone is going to stop this, it's Jacob. I know I can get him to stop. But this other man, this Phil, I don't know him. I don't know what he's here for, what Jacob has promised him.

'Jacob?' I say, my eyes pleading with him.

'You know why,' Phil says and leans into me. 'You're a little cunt.'

I kick out at him, my legs are still free, even if the rest of me isn't. Phil jumps back, a flash of anger across his face before he reverts back to his game face.

'Careful,' he says and walks around the back of the chair, grabbing a fistful of hair. 'Get some more tape,' he says, and Jacob looks around.

'That was all of it,' he says. 'I could go to the corner shop.'

'Never mind,' Phil says, and lets go of me, coming back to where I can see him. As he passes, I kick out again, this time catching his shin. He curses in pain and turns to slap me hard across the face. I cry out.

'Bitch,' Phil says and lunges towards me, his hands going up my skirt.

'Don't. Please, don't,' I say, still fighting, trying to get him to stop.

His fingers dig into my flesh as he gets hold of the tops of my tights and tears them off. I can feel my underwear has pulled down, sitting at the top of my thighs. Phil takes my shoes off and then pulls my tights off while Jacob stands watching, his mouth gaping.

'Hold her legs,' Phil says, and Jacob crouches down, his hands firm around my ankles while Phil ties me to the chair with my own tights. As they stand I try to move my legs, but it's impossible. It's so tight, I can feel it digging into my skin, I can feel the circulation being cut off already.

'You can't do this,' I say, and try to shake the chair, try to do anything to get out of this.

'We can do what we like,' Phil says.

I rock back and forth but nothing happens, nothing moves, nothing comes loose. Jacob stares at me, and I start to beg him. He just stands there, watching me, doing nothing. What he does best.

'Help me!' I scream at the top of my lungs, still rocking, still trying.

'Shut up,' Phil says, but I keep going.

Phil stomps over to the sink. I can't see what he's doing, but I assume it's nothing good. When he comes back around, he has the dirty dishcloth in his hand. 'I told you to shut up,' he says and stuffs it into my mouth.

The taste makes me gag and my eyes water. I can hardly breathe. I'm dying here, and they just stand there. Jacob watches me, but there's no sign of the love he claimed he had for me. Phil looks at me briefly before turning to Jacob.

'All right,' he says. 'What's next?'

Chapter 18

One week earlier

I went to work on the Monday morning, immediately bombarded by people asking me a million questions about my mum, asking if they could do anything, being brought a dozen cups of tea. The rest of the day went past in a blur of phone calls and snippets of overheard conversations about Jill's boyfriend and Claire's birthday party.

I'd hoped that work would distract me from everything else, but it was so dull that there was plenty of space for other thoughts to get in – thoughts about Jacob and Mum and the house and Cathy and Ethel and all the rest of it. I needed to get out, to find something else, something to occupy my mind. I'd known it for a long time but had stayed out of loyalty, and because each time I'd brought up leaving, I'd been offered more money, more responsibility, anything as long as I stayed. But there's only so long that can go on. What else could they offer me?

I let my mind wander. I felt bad about Mum, that I hadn't visited for a while, that I hadn't even called to check she was okay. But I'd had no more calls from Cathy, so I had to assume it was all fine. And it'd been days since Jacob had been around. I chose to think that he'd found someone else, some other woman to depend on, and that our last encounter really had been our last encounter.

So, all that was left was the house, and that wasn't a problem. Not without all the other stuff. Now it was a good thing, something to call my own. My safe place, my sanctuary.

I thought about the old flat, my old flatmates. Wondered if I should invite them round yet, maybe for something to eat. No, it was too soon for that. The place was nowhere near ready; it was still a total tip. What would they think if I they saw the place now? No, I'd hold off on the dinner party, wait until I'd done some work on it, and things were more settled. Besides, I knew they were both busy with their own lives, and it felt as if we'd been drifting apart for a while. Maybe that was one of the reasons I left. But I'd always been the glue that held us together, and maybe without me there, things were falling apart. I wondered how long Kimberley and Sasha would keep living together without me, I worried that I'd left them in the lurch.

I was older than the others, and at the beginning, I'd wondered if that would be a problem. It wasn't. The girls looked to me as, not a mother figure, more of an older sister. They were always wanting to borrow my clothes or wanting me to go out with them. They often had people round at night and would beg me to join them. Sometimes I did, even though what I wanted to do was go to sleep or watch TV. But I hated letting them down.

Maybe I'd pop round after work, get the last of my things, see how they were doing. I bet no one had washed the dishes since I'd left.

***

As I got my things together and said goodbye to everyone, I noticed a bottle of wine on the table in the break room. It was what Janet – or possibly head office – thought was an appropriate bonus for the employee with the best Key Performance Indicators. I had no idea who had won this week, not me, at any rate, I never put in for it, leaving the honour for those who cared. But I figured whoever it was didn't care too much about the wine if they'd abandoned it on the table.

I slid it into my bag as an offering to the girls, planning to replace it the next day, and left, catching a bus to my old flat to catch up with my old flatmates.

I knocked on the door, and some man was standing there. 'Yeah?' he said, and I wondered if he was my replacement or just a new boyfriend.

'I'm Polly,' I said, smiling, and he just looked at me like I was an idiot. I was sure they'd have told him about me. 'I used to live here,' I said.

'Polly,' Sasha said as she poked her head around the door. 'What're you doing here?' She looked up at the man still blocking the door. 'This is Polly.'

'So she said,' the man said, and grinned at Sasha, his hand brushing her waist, and then he walked away, leaving me alone with her.

'What's up?' Sasha asked, stepping aside to let me in.

'I just wanted to say hi. And to get the last of my things,' I said.

'I thought you'd taken everything,' she said.

'Not everything,' I replied.

'There's nothing left in your room. Alex would've found it if there had been.'

'Who's Alex?' I asked.

'I am,' the man said as he came through from the kitchen. 'I'm the new you.'

'Oh,' I said. 'So, you didn't find any of my things? I'm missing some clothes.'

'No,' he said. 'Oh, wait.' Alex pulled the waistband of his jeans and looked down at his underwear. 'No, false alarm. These are mine.'

I looked at Sasha, but she was looking at the floor, clearly embarrassed by him. I wondered who this man was, and why he was being so off with me. I wondered if he thought I was back for my old room.

'So,' I said, pulling the cheap wine out of my bag. 'What's been happening?' I walked through to the kitchen and found Kimberley stirring tomato sauce. She turned and looked surprised to see me.

The table was set for three, almost formally, or as best they could manage with their mismatched crockery and glasses. I couldn't remember us ever sitting down together for a meal, not at the table anyway. I turned to Sasha.

'It's Alex's official moving in party,' she said and looked to Kimberley.

'Not a party, really. Just some spaghetti to formally welcome him,' Kimberley said.

'Cool,' I shrugged. 'Well, I brought wine.' We all looked at the three places set at the table. 'Unless…'

'No, that's okay,' Kimberley said. 'Here. I'll set you a place.'

Kimberley dug out some more plates and a glass, and Alex went off to find another chair, the best he could come up with being a swivel seat from his room. I stared at it, at the stuffing coming out of the back.

'I'll sit on this one,' he said, and Kimberley started dishing up the food.

***

I left soon after we'd eaten, itching to get home. I hadn't planned on staying that long, anyway, but didn't want to be rude. And though Alex had seemed unfriendly at first, he warmed up as we talked and was a really good listener as I told him about Mum and everything that'd happened. He put his hand on mine as I confided in him, and it was around then that the atmosphere changed. I'd seen the way he'd touched Sasha when I arrived and wondered if there was something between them…and now, he was putting his hand on mine. I pulled it away and tried to lighten the mood, changing the subject. I felt bad for Sasha. It wasn't the first time a guy she liked had hit on me, and sometimes I wondered if it was me she blamed, rather than them. Either way, I took the first opportunity I could to leave, promising I'd have them all over to mine as soon as I'd got things sorted.

Kimberley walked me to the door, and I could hear Sasha and Alex's voices coming from the other room, low and taut. I looked to Kimberley, but she just smiled and opened the door.

'It was great seeing you,' I said, and hugged her.

'You too,' she said, and I waved over my shoulder as I left.

'Polly.'

I stopped and turned back.

'You didn't happen to pack up my food mixer when you left, did you? You know, by mistake?'

I shook my head. 'Sorry.'

She paused as if she wanted to say something else and then shook her head. 'Just thought I'd ask. It's probably at the back of a cupboard somewhere.'

'Probably,' I said, and waved again before heading home.

Chapter 19

I walked along the main road and was about to cross the street to get the bus home when I saw a bus pull up heading in the opposite direction. I hopped on, deciding to pay Mum a visit.

The bus was crowded, and I couldn't get a seat. People coming home from work were snippy and kept throwing dirty looks around to anyone who dared brush past them or, God forbid, make eye contact. I kept my eyes on the pavements outside, watching the world pass by, wondering what I'd say to Mum, what she'd say to me. The closer I got to the care home, the more I wondered if it was a good idea or if we'd just wind each other up. I knew Jacob's visit must've upset Mum, that he'd have told her things I didn't want her to know, but it wasn't my fault he'd shown up there. How could I have known?

For a second, I hoped Mum was having one of her turns again, that she wouldn't speak at all, that I could just go and see her without it making me feel bad about myself. *Maybe I shouldn't go*. It's probably best for everyone. For me, for Mum. What if me being there, getting her upset, makes her worse? Brings on another stroke or something. But when I looked up, past the huddle of angry commuters, I realised we were already there.

It'd started raining somewhere between the old flat and the home, which I took to be a bad omen, the dark clouds literally gathering, but I hurried towards the ugly building and went inside out of the rain, shaking my hair, trying to look vaguely presentable.

I found some toilets, and the lights flickered on as I went inside. I was standing at the sink and fluffing my hair, uselessly, when the door opened and a woman came in, herding two kids. We all struggled to fit in the small space.

'I don't even need a wee,' the little boy whined, and the woman pushed him towards a cubicle nonetheless. She closed the door but stayed outside, her foot hooked under the door.

'There's no toilet roll, Mummy,' the little girl's voice said from behind the other cubicle door. The woman sighed and looked over at me. I was expecting a smile, a *what are they like?* expression, but instead, she glared and snarled, 'What the fuck are you staring at?'

I got my bag and left her to it. I was so distracted by her that I just walked towards Mum's room on autopilot, before I'd even decided if I wanted to be there.

As I walked past the nurses' station, I scanned around for Cathy. There was no sign of her. The place was quiet, considering it was peak visiting hours, and as I passed the TV room, I could see images on the screen, but there was no sound. There were two residents in there, both asleep.

I kept walking and passed a room where an old man lived, Barney, I thought his name was, and he was asleep, as usual, his family sitting around him, his daughter at the head of the bed stroking her father's face. I couldn't ever remember seeing Barney awake, and I wondered what was wrong with him and whether it was better to just let him go.

'Hello, Miss Cooke.'

I looked up, embarrassed for staring at strangers, and saw Dean, one of the carers, standing in front of me, carrying a full bed pan.

'Hi,' I said, and couldn't help looking at the dark yellow urine swilling around in his hands.

'Is it raining?' he asked, and I wondered if he was a bit simple, but then he started to laugh, and I realised it was a joke because I looked like a drowned rat.

'Oh, just a little,' I said, unable to think of anything funny in response which annoyed me, but then, "Is it raining?" was hardly comedy gold.

Dean smiled and lifted his bed pan. 'Well, I'd better get rid of this,' he said, and walked on.

I glanced back at Barney's family, and one of the kids, a teenage girl, caught my eye and stood up, closing the door on me. I felt my cheeks redden and pushed away the thought that if Mum was like that, I wouldn't have a problem.

I went to Mum's room and found the TV on without the sound. I wondered if the staff went around muting all the TVs so the babbling noise didn't bother them.

'Hi, Mum,' I said and dropped my bag on the floor. I went and sat on the chair and looked at the TV screen for a moment, trying to work out what was on. Some old western, by the looks of it. I turned back to Mum. 'So, what's this, then?' I asked, meaning the film. But she didn't move, didn't acknowledge me again, keeping her face turned away.

Why was she so upset? What had Jacob said to her? I turned the TV off and decided to find out what it was she was going to say to me the last time, before Cathy had interrupted.

'Mum?' I said, and stood up, shaking her arm. 'Will you look at me?' Nothing. I walked around to the other side of the bed and saw her eyes were closed, apparently sleeping. I sighed and went to pick up my bag, but something stopped me. I needed to know. 'Mum,' I said, and shook her again, leaning closer.

Her mouth gaped, and bits of dried saliva were crusted at the corners of her lips. 'Mum?' I said, quieter this time. Had something happened? Had she had another stroke, or was she just ignoring me?

I looked up at the door before rolling her sleeve slightly. I leaned close to her and examined her face. Her skin sagged just like her mouth. She looked like a fish stranded on land. I reached down to her arm and nipped the skin. She didn't respond, so I did it again, harder this time. She didn't move so I let go of her, realising she wasn't pretending. 'Mum?' I said again, tears forming at the back of my eyes.

This was my fault. I'd done this. But why hadn't Cathy called? Had she thought I didn't care anymore after I ran out the other day? Or had Mum told her not to contact me anymore? Was that what they were whispering about that day?

I shook her gently, and she wobbled but didn't change expression, didn't move herself. She was totally gone.

What had I done?

I grabbed my bag and ran out to the nurses' station. They were all sitting around, drinking cups of tea, giggling. They didn't even acknowledge me standing there.

'Excuse me?' I said, and one of them glanced at me but just went back to her conversation. 'Excuse me,' I said again, louder, and finally, Dean looked at me. He stood up and came to the desk.

'Is everything all right?' he asked.

'No, it's not all right,' I said. 'Have you seen my mum? Have any of you actually been in and seen to her?'

Dean looked over his shoulder at the others and another carer, this one in a different uniform, a uniform that was being stretched to its limits, pushed herself from her chair and came over. 'Is there a problem?' she asked, and I looked at her name badge. Nora.

'Yes, there is. My mum is practically comatose in there.'

Nora just looked at me. There was none of the fake concern or the pointed condescension of Cathy, just pure ambivalence. I could tell she was someone who stopped thinking about her job as soon as she clocked off. Not really the kind of person you want caring for your mother.

'Your mum has an infection,' Nora said. 'She's been sleeping most of the day, probably the best thing for her. If you'd like to speak to one of the doctors–'

'Why isn't she in hospital if she's ill?'

'The doctor has seen her. She's on antibiotics, there's not much else we can do. But if you want to speak to the doc–'

'I don't want to speak to a fucking doctor!'

'So, what's the problem?'

'What sort of infection has she got? Where's she even got it from?' I could feel myself dissolving into tears, the words no longer making sense to me or to Nora. I wiped my nose with the back of my hand. 'She wasn't like that on...' I couldn't remember when I was last there and anything less than saying she wasn't like that yesterday seemed pathetic, like I was as negligent as they were. 'She was fine the last time I saw her,' I said, lowering my voice, trying to act like someone who wasn't feeling guilty.

'I'm sure she was,' Nora said. 'But things can change very quickly. We see it all the time. It's sad, I know. But there's not much we can do about it, I'm afraid.'

'But why didn't anyone tell me?' I said, and realised I was crying now. Real, deep, grieving tears. Why hadn't I been a better daughter?

Nora tilted her head, her best stab at sympathy. 'Do you want to go to the family room?' she asked, wanting to get rid of me.

I shook my head. 'No,' I said. She passed me a tissue, and I blew my nose, feeling stupid crying in front of all those people. I turned and went back to Mum's room and closed the door, just like Barney's girl did.

'I'm sorry, Mum,' I said. 'For everything.'

There was nothing. Maybe this time she'd gone for good. Maybe I was right. Maybe she'd just lie there like Barney, and I'd come and stroke her head like she was a pet, and then, one day she'd just stop being there, and I'd collect her things and go home and that would be it. It would just be me.

As I left, Dean nodded at me, and I gave him half a smile, but I wasn't sure he saw it, having gone back to his card game. Nora was on the phone at the desk and didn't even acknowledge me, oblivious to the fact I'd been so upset less than two hours earlier. She was a heartless cow, and I suddenly wished Cathy was there instead.

They buzzed me out, and I walked downstairs where I ran into, literally, the nasty family from the toilets. Or rather, the little boy ran into me, nearly knocking me over. I looked up at the mother, expecting an apology and then realising that was highly unlikely based on her behaviour earlier. If she recognised me, she didn't show it and just dragged the little girl by the hand towards the door. The boy stayed where he was, glaring at me.

'What?' I said to him, and he punched my leg in response.

'Little shit,' I said and pushed him. Not hard, just enough to show him that he was being rude. He stared a few seconds more and then started to cry. The woman finally turned around, and I expected a showdown, but instead, she just screamed at the boy, 'Get a fucking move on.'

The boy pouted at me, and finally, he went after his mum, stomping his feet. I gave it a few minutes to let them get out of the way before I left, having visions of the woman waiting to have a go at me for assaulting her son.

When I eventually left, I looked around for the Addams family and wondered what time the next bus would be.

And then, I saw him.

My stomach tightened. He was standing in the shadows, smoking, watching. I felt vulnerable there in the dark, the woman and her kids nowhere to be seen. In fact, there was no one else around. Just me and Jacob.

I considered going back inside, asking someone to walk me to the bus stop or even calling a taxi. Maybe Dean could help me. But when I turned around again, Jacob was gone. I looked up and down the street. Nothing. Was I imagining it? Seeing ghosts because I was already wound up?

I stayed where I was a little longer, unsure what to do. And then, I saw movement in the wooded shortcut by the road. I squinted and tried to see what it was, or rather, who it was. Someone was running away through the trees, and I knew it was him.

Before I knew it, I was following, running after him, running to God knows what.

'Jacob,' I shouted after him, but he didn't stop. I kept running, slipping on the wet ground. Finally, I went over on my ankle and dropped to the ground. I could hear my breath, my blood pumping in my ears. But there was no sign of Jacob. He must've made it out onto the road.

I held onto my ankle and cursed myself for being so stupid and chasing him, especially into the woods. I looked behind me, wondering whether to keep going or turn back. In the end, I wandered back towards the home, glancing over my shoulder every couple of yards, hobbling on my sore ankle.

I finally made it into the light, and still, there was no one around. I looked up and down the main road. I didn't think there'd been time for Jacob to disappear completely, and no buses had been past, I was sure of that. So, was he still there, lurking, or had he been a figment of my imagination?

I crossed the road, forcing myself to move faster than was comfortable as I could see a bus approaching in the distance. There was no one else at the bus stop, and I was glad the bus arrived so soon. I was spooked and just wanted to get home.

I wanted to go to the back of the bus, but my ankle was throbbing, so I collapsed on the first seat I found and rested my forehead on the cool window. The bus idled for a few minutes, and I was getting impatient.

Finally, it stuttered to life, and we were moving. I sat up straight, not wanting my head bouncing off the window with every bump in the road. I wiped the condensation away, so as to see more clearly, standing up to look back. We were moving fast – it was difficult to see – yet I was sure now. I was sure Jacob had been there. He'd been waiting outside my Mum's home. He'd run off into the woods. And now, he was standing by the side of the road, watching me go home.

Chapter 20

I ran from the bus stop to the front door, getting inside, behind a locked door as soon as I could. All the way home, I'd been thinking about Jacob. Had he really been there, or was I imagining things? I was convinced it was him. Who else would be lurking outside the home? Who else would run once I'd seen them? And then, once I was on the bus, why would anyone else just stand there looking in at me? It *had* to be him. And yet, I'd run from the bus like a bat out of hell. If Jacob had been standing on that road by the home, there would be no way he could get here before me. If he was there, he wasn't *here*.

But I still made sure all the locks were secure and went through the house closing the curtains and blinds, knowing I was losing it. If he was there, he couldn't be here. I kept telling myself that, forcing myself to calm down.

But...

If I was wrong and it wasn't Jacob at the care home, it was possible he could be here, somewhere. I stopped and listened, suddenly paranoid someone could be in the house already.

No. There's no way he could get in. Only by smashing a window and I'd have noticed that by now. So, he wasn't in the house. Didn't mean he wasn't outside, though.

No. He was definitely at the home. I was positive. But maybe he followed me, got the next bus that came along. He couldn't have got a lift from anyone – who would he possibly call? And a taxi was out of the question, there was no way he could afford it. So, he wasn't here. Yet.

Unless...

What if it *wasn't* Jacob at the home? What if I *was* imagining things? His disappearing act these past few days could've been a way to make me feel safe. I knew I shouldn't have gone out. I should've stayed inside where it was safe, making sure he knew there was nothing he could do to me. I'd let my guard down and look what happened. I didn't give it enough time. He'd been there all along, just out of view, taking his time so I'd think he'd gone, waiting for me to feel safe enough to leave the house. And then…? What? What would he be waiting for? He didn't accost me on my way home, he wasn't waiting on the doorstep to grab me. So what? Was it something else he wanted? Had he been in the house?

I pressed my fingers to my eyes, willing myself to stop. To take a breath.

I walked slowly around the house, checking windows, making sure everything was still there, everything where it should be. I couldn't see anything out of place, but what did that really mean? Maybe he was careful.

I ran up the stairs again and went into the bedroom. Would this be the place he was most likely to come into? I checked the bed for warmth, like Mum used to do when we came home if she wanted to see if the dog had snuck onto her bed while he was alone. The bed was cool under my hand. If he'd been there, he'd gone a while ago. I stood up straight and then bent again. I pressed my face to the duvet cover and inhaled. If he'd been here, I'd be able to smell him. I'd never forget the way he smelled.

Nothing.

I let out a long breath. I was being ridiculous and I knew it. He couldn't get in. It was impossible. He hadn't been here, probably wasn't at the home, either. It was my imagination. I was unsure about him, wanting to believe he'd gone, but couldn't be certain, and so, I'd conjured him up. And I needed to stop. He was gone. He'd given up, given in. There was nothing to worry about anymore.

And then, there was a knock at the door.

Chapter 21

The panic shot through my veins, making me shiver and sweat. I ducked down behind the banister, even though he couldn't see me from the door, my instinct to survive kicking in.

My hands were shaking, and I wished I hadn't turned on all of the lights, letting him know I was here like a lighthouse to a ship.

I'd been right. Whether he was there at the home or waiting here all along, I'd been right. And I'd been stupid to leave. Anything could've happened. But that was it now. No more going outside. I had enough food to last a little while, and you could do anything online these days. Have anything you want delivered straight to your door. But that would require opening the door.

My brain whirred, trying to think of solutions. I could say I was phobic of people, get them to leave it on the back step where I could grab it quickly once I knew the coast was clear. And what about work? I'd have to get a sick note. There was only so much compassion Janet would have. But again, that would require leaving the house, going to see the doctor. Maybe he could do a house call. Did they still do that? Maybe you had to be old and infirm. But what about other people, the agoraphobics and whatnot? I'd find a way around it, I was sure.

He knocked again, louder this time, harder. I wanted to scream, but I didn't want to interact, didn't want him to hear my voice. He didn't get to do that anymore. Didn't get to see me, didn't get to talk to me.

Another knock. I pressed my hands to my ears, blocking him out, wishing him away. Was he going to start making a scene again? Would there be some creepy picture left on the doorstep in the morning? Or something worse? Maybe it was time to call the police? Would they really do that much, other than ask him nicely to stop knocking on my door? Maybe that would be all it took. Jacob was scared of the police. If he saw them pull up to the house, he'd probably run, no words would need to be exchanged. Maybe it would be enough.

I dropped my hands. He'd stopped knocking. There'd been nothing for a while. No shouting, no anger. I stood up and went into the front bedroom. I pulled back the curtain an inch or two and looked down.

What the hell?

Cathy was standing there, trying to peer in through the living room window, despite the curtain being closed. I let out a breath and removed my grip on the curtain, allowing it to fall back into place.

What the hell was Cathy doing at my house? How did she even find me?

I decided to stay hidden. I didn't want to talk to her. But the guilt seeped in. What if it was Mum? What if she'd taken another turn for the worse? What if she'd died? Why else would Cathy come here?

I walked to the top of the stairs and looked down. I could still see her silhouette outside, but it looked like she was turning to walk away. It was now or never.

I ran down and opened the door. Cathy turned and looked surprised to see me. 'I thought you must've been out,' she said, and came back to the door. 'Sorry if I'm disturbing you.'

'What're you doing here?' I said. 'Is it Mum?'

'I wouldn't normally do this. I'm not supposed to. But I tried to call you. A few times,' she said. 'Your mum's been getting herself worked up again. She's convinced herself you're in trouble.' Cathy's eyes flicked to the house behind me before focusing back on me. 'She was trying to get out. She was really wound up, so I said I'd check on you,' she said. 'You haven't been in for a while.'

'I've been there tonight,' I said.

'Oh. Good,' Cathy said, and I could see she was trying to have a look inside, wanting to nose around, wanting to be invited in. I pulled the door closer to my body so she couldn't see anything at all.

'Mum was out of it,' I said. 'Didn't even know I was there, never mind whether I was all right. They said she's got an infection.'

'Oh dear,' she said. 'I've not been in today. I hope it's not too serious.'

'What's it to you? You still get paid, don't you?' I said, and I knew as soon as I said that it was out of line. I looked at my feet, hoping she'd realise I was just tired, stressed.

'Well,' Cathy said, and shuffled her feet. 'I'd better be off. I just wanted to help put her mind at ease.' She half turned away and then stopped, looking back at me. 'Are you all right, Polly?'

'Why wouldn't I be?' I said.

'It's just…' Cathy's eyes drifted to the living room window and then upwards, as if she was looking for something. 'Is someone here with you?'

'No,' I said. 'Who'd be here?'

'I don't know. It's just—'

'What?'

Cathy finally looked me in the eye but said nothing for a few moments, and I wondered what she was thinking. Was she really concerned about me? Was that what this was about? Did Mum think I was in danger, had she seen the bruises on my face the other day? Was that why she'd sent Cathy nosing around?

'Look, I have to go,' I said to Cathy. 'Thanks for coming.' I started to close the door, and Cathy walked off, looking up and down the street as if she didn't know where she was or where she was going.

But I couldn't stop wondering. 'Cathy,' I shouted. 'Wait.'

She sighed and turned. 'What is it, Polly?'

'What did she say to you?'

'About what?'

'About me.'

She looked at her feet, probably cold and wet in her flat, sensible shoes. 'I don't know. I couldn't make head nor tail of it. Gibberish, most of it. But she's obviously worried, wanted to know everything was okay.'

'But why was she worried?' I asked.

'Because she hadn't seen you for days, I suppose,' Cathy said.

'But what did she say, exactly?'

She rolled her eyes this time. 'I don't…if you want to discuss this more, can I at least come in?'

I looked behind me. 'It's really messy. I've just moved in.'

She looked at me like I was something she found on her shoe. 'Whatever. Goodnight, Polly. See you at the home,' she said, and turned again.

'That man,' I said, and she looked back. 'The man who came, who upset her. Jacob. He hasn't been back, has he?' She came closer again, more interested now.

'No, I don't think so,' Cathy said, and waited for me to say more, but I didn't so she shifted her bag again and nodded goodbye.

'How did you know where to find me?' I asked. 'Mum can't even tell you my name half the time. How did she tell you my new address?'

Cathy turned once more, sighing loudly, making a point of looking at her watch. 'Your address is in the file.'

'Oh,' I said, vaguely recalling writing it down. 'Right,' I said, and she nodded and left. I shut the door and locked up before going back upstairs to the front bedroom, wondering if I was being paranoid.

I looked out from behind the curtain, partly making sure Cathy had gone and partly checking Jacob wasn't there. The street was empty once Cathy disappeared from view, and I closed the curtains, then went for a shower. I was tired what with everything that'd happened with Mum and Jacob and now Cathy. I needed to eat and to sleep, but my stomach churned, and I wondered if I'd be able to do either. I let the water get really hot before I got in, and straightaway my skin flushed, and I felt dizzy.

What was Mum thinking, asking Cathy to come to my house? Had she even asked, or was it just Cathy nosing around? No, there had to be more to it. I'd known that when I left that day, when I stomped out of her room. I hadn't wanted to stay and listen, because I was afraid of what would happen. And then, Jacob had shown up at the home, so Mum had sent a spy to check on me. Did she think I was still involved with Jacob? Or was it worse than that?

I ducked my face under the water and held my breath. The water was too hot to stay in very long, so I climbed out, splashing the floor, and stood a moment, enjoying the cool air on my hot skin before wrapping a towel around myself. As I did, there was a noise outside, a bottle being knocked over.

I held the towel tight and ran to the front window, peering out carefully so he wouldn't see me. I saw the movement next door. Only Ethel still got milk from the milkman, still left empty bottles on her doorstep overnight. Someone was putting it back on the step. I squinted and leaned closer to the window when she straightened herself up.

Cathy.

What was she doing next door?

She shifted her bag on her shoulder and looked up at my house. I ducked down, my heart thumping in my chest. Had she seen me?

I waited a minute or so and then moved slowly, raising my eyes to the bottom of the window. She'd gone. I sat up properly and searched the street for her, but she was nowhere to be seen.

Chapter 22

I'd gone to bed without eating, too wound up to have an appetite, but, as I soon found out, too wound up to sleep as well. Somewhere in the back of my mind, I knew I was being silly, but I couldn't stop worrying.

I tossed and turned for hours. Jacob was still out there somewhere, and he'd come back eventually, I knew that much. And why was Mum acting so strangely? And Cathy? Why would she be at Ethel's? What would make her go there?

I was too hot even though it was cold outside. Autumn was turning into winter, and there was more dark than light. But here, inside my house, I was burning up. Maybe I was ill. Maybe I did have a valid reason not to go to work after all.

Work. Stupid, boring work. Another thing getting me down. I needed to find a way out of there too. I needed to stop thinking about the company and start thinking about myself.

I got up and found a book in the spare room, read a few pages, threw it across the room. Tried to sleep again. More thoughts, more pains in my gut. Up again. Down the stairs. TV on. Watched some stupid film that didn't make sense. Started to drift off. Was woken by people shouting outside. Panicked, thinking it was Jacob. Listened intently for the sound of them leaving. Went back to bed where it was safer. Lay in the dark. Felt too hot. Turned on the light. Cried for a while. Sat by the window, looking through a crack in the curtains. Saw a drunk stagger past and dropped the curtain on autopilot as if every passing person was Jacob. Got back into bed. Lay there in the lamplight staring at the ceiling. Turned off the light. Tried to meditate but couldn't stop thinking. Cried some more. Sleep. Finally sleep.

I woke at six and felt like hell. I didn't know how long I'd been asleep but not long. I dragged myself up and brushed my teeth, sticky where I hadn't brushed them the night before. I washed and brushed my hair. Put some clean clothes on. Decided I had to go to work. I felt like I was disappearing.

I was tired. So, so tired.

Chapter 23

As I left the house, I had a quick look around for Jacob, but he wasn't there. Part of me was disappointed. I thought about seeing him out there, thought about what I'd do, but the best I could come up with was handing him the keys to the house and telling him we'd sort things out later. It was sort of funny. But not.

At work, I kept my head down, partly because I was tired, but mostly because I was afraid if someone asked me what was wrong, I'd start talking and tell them everything. In the end, no one spoke to me, but I saw the little glances they gave each other. They probably thought something had happened to Mum. And it had, I suppose.

When lunchtime finally came around, I found a corner of the break room to myself and hoped no one tried to rope me in to their conversation. Usually, I'd be in the middle of things, but today, I just couldn't face it.

After a few minutes, Janet came in. She switched on the kettle and stood with her arms crossed as she waited for the water to boil. I noticed everyone else leave shortly after, and I wondered if they didn't like Janet or just preferred not to take their breaks with their boss.

When it was just me and her, Janet pulled up a seat opposite me. 'I don't want to interrupt your lunch, Polly,' she said. 'But we need to have a chat.'

I looked up from my magazine and found Janet giving me her half-smile that she used when she was in boss mode. I'd always thought Janet was an odd boss. She never really asked people to do things, just sort of suggested them, as if the work was optional.

For a moment, I wondered if she was there to discuss my absences, if there was to be some kind of official warning, but as Janet had practically told me to stay off, I couldn't see how that could be possible. The only other reason for the meeting was to discuss the promotion, and I wasn't really in the mood. I couldn't face telling her I was looking for something else, not now at least.

'Can we do this later?' I asked and stood up, gathering my things. Janet looked confused and shuffled some papers she'd brought with her. 'I just can't do this now,' I said and burst into tears, the weight of everything suddenly too much.

I ran out and into the toilets and sat down and cried, thinking about the house. I didn't want to leave. It was *my* house. I'd worked hard to get it. It was all I'd ever wanted. And now people were driving me out. How was that fair?

'Are you all right?' I could see Janet's feet outside the cubicle.

'I'm fine,' I said.

'Are you sure?'

I wiped my nose and opened the door. Janet looked at me with sympathy and led me to the sink. My face was blotchy from crying, my nose running. I looked at myself and saw what a mess I was. I washed my face in the sink and pressed a couple of scratchy, blue paper towels Janet handed to me to my skin. When I looked up I was still a mess.

'Polly?'

I didn't turn to her, just looked at her through the mirror.

'Is it your mum?'

I started to cry again, and she came over and turned me around, hugging me tightly. 'You shouldn't have come in,' Janet said, pulling back and wiping my face. I missed my mum then, missed who she used to be. How we used to be.

'I'm all right,' I said, and pulled another wad of rough paper towels from the dispenser, wiping my face.

'You don't look all right.'

'I'd rather be here,' I said.

Janet sighed. 'I need some things typing up. If you'd prefer, you could do that, in my office.' I looked up at her. 'I hate talking to people when I'm upset. Especially people I don't know. I always start bubbling again at inopportune moments.' I let out a little laugh-sob, and she put her arm around my shoulder. 'Come on,' she said. 'Let's get you a cup of tea, and then, you can start typing.'

The rest of the day was almost meditative. Typing but not reading the words, just hitting the keys over and over. Janet would probably find a million mistakes when she looked them over, *if* she looked them over, but I didn't care. They probably weren't important, anyway. It was busywork. She was just being kind.

I left the office a few minutes early as I'd typed everything up and only said goodbye to Janet. The bus arrived just as I got to the stop, and I was grateful for small mercies. The weather had taken a turn for the worse. It was cold and windy, the sky threatening rain. I sat at the back of the bus and closed my eyes, trying to work out where we were from the turns and stops. The journey seemed to be much shorter than usual, and as we turned onto my street, I felt anxious, as if I didn't want to get off. I thought about staying where I was, just riding around and around until the driver was done for the day. Then, I could just get off wherever the bus terminated and go from there. See where my legs took me.

But I got off and stood still for a while. I could see my house. I could see the curtains were still closed. I could see there were no broken windows, at least not at the front. I could see there was no one waiting for me outside; no Jacob, no Cathy.

Another bus turned up, and an old man asked me if I wanted that one. 'No, thanks,' I said, and he walked around me. The driver looked at me for a brief moment and then closed the doors, and the bus disappeared.

I should go home.

After a few more minutes, it started raining, and the bus stop filled up with people more concerned with keeping dry than catching a bus. I left them to their small talk about the weather and crossed the road. I could see Ethel peering out of her window.

She stared, and I ducked my head, pretending not to see her. I wasn't sure she'd come out, not in the rain, but I didn't want to take the chance.

My bag clunked onto the floor as I closed the door. There was some post on the mat, all for the dead woman, and it all went in the bin. I turned on the lights and went through to the kitchen. As I waited for the kettle to boil, I couldn't help but look. I opened the back door and checked the doorstep. I don't know what I was expecting to find – another letter, a nasty gift, maybe Jacob himself. But there was nothing there. I closed the door and went back inside, taking my tea to the table.

How long had it been since I'd seen Jacob? If I didn't count last night, because I couldn't truly be sure it was him at the care home, how long had it been? I couldn't remember. Everything was a blur. But it felt like a long time.

I supped the tea, thinking what if he had given up?

I grabbed my bag and found my phone at the bottom beneath the loose tampons and the half-eaten rolls of mints. It rang a few times before someone answered.

'Hello,' I said. 'This is Polly Cooke, I'm just ringing about my mum. Mrs Cooke,' I said. They all called her Mrs Cooke, except for Cathy who used her first name.

'Hang on,' the man said.

There was some scuffling and after a few minutes someone else picked up the phone. 'This is Cathy.'

I felt my stomach drop. I didn't want to speak to Cathy. Of everyone in the world, Cathy was the one I least wanted to talk to at that moment.

'Polly?'

'Yes,' I said. 'I'm here.'

'There's no change. The doctor's been in this afternoon. There's not much we can do. Just wait it out, I suppose.' I heard crackling on the line as if she was moving around, and then, her voice went quieter, as if she didn't want anyone listening in. 'Listen, Polly. I think we need to have a chat. Maybe not here but–'

'About what?' I asked.

'Your mum. It's just... Me and Margaret have got quite close,' she said, and I felt the hairs on the back of my neck stand up. 'I've been spending a lot of time with her, even outside work, and she's–'

'I need to go,' I said. 'I'm sorry.'

I slammed down the phone as if it had scalded me and turned it off in case Cathy tried to call me back. And then, I worried that if I didn't answer her calls, then she'd just turn up at my door again.

Thinking about the night before, about Cathy showing up here, about her intrusive questions, about her relationship with my mother, I felt an anger rise in me. I thought about calling back and asking to speak to the manager. I could put a complaint in about her. She had no right to do what she'd done.

And then, I had a thought. I looked at the time. If she was still at work now, she'd probably finish her shift in an hour or so. I grabbed my bag and headed out again.

***

It was cold hanging around outside the home, lurking in the bushes as if I was some mad stalker. A couple of people passed by and gave me funny looks, but I chose to ignore them and turned away, stamping my feet to keep warm. I could've gone and waited in the bus shelter or even the takeaway just down the street, but I didn't want to miss her, so I stayed put, praying it wouldn't rain.

Thirty minutes later, I was soaking, and Cathy still hadn't emerged. I started to think I'd been stupid coming out at all. And then, the doors opened, and someone came out. Dean. I shrunk back behind the branches and waited for him to disappear. He talked loudly on his phone, oblivious to me, oblivious to the fact I could've been an attacker lurking. I watched him walk up and down the same small patch of the main road, fag in one hand, phone in the other. And then, a car pulled up, and he tossed the cigarette before climbing in.

Alone again, I turned back to the door. Maybe Cathy wouldn't be coming. Maybe she was doing a double shift, do-gooder that she was. Or maybe she was using her own time to sit with Mum.

My hands were almost numb, and I made a mental note to find some gloves when I got home. I was so focused on trying to work out where I'd have put things like gloves that I almost missed Cathy.

Unlike Dean, Cathy's hands were free, and she seemed wary, aware of her surroundings. I ducked down as she passed the end of the shortcut, mud seeping into the back of my skirt, suddenly uncertain of what I was doing. When she'd got a hundred yards or so in front of me, I followed, still unsure exactly what I was going to do.

Cathy kept on walking, glancing over her shoulder every now and then, but apparently not noticing me. I guessed she was looking for something more threatening. I thought about shouting her name, confronting her about what was going on, but I wasn't sure what I'd achieve.

I slowed down, thinking of going back, going home, when something came over me. An urge to see where Cathy lived, to see her life outside of the home. I wondered if she was lonely, if that was why she was clinging on to Mum, getting involved in her life. Whatever it was, I needed to find out.

She walked quickly, so it was easy to stay behind her. I slipped my hands into my pockets and felt my keys, my fingers sliding around them. A couple of kids came out of the corner shop, shrieking and shouting abuse at someone inside, and Cathy picked up her pace. But the kids went the other way, and we were alone again, turning off the main road to a quiet side street, then turning again into a cul-de-sac.

I slowed down as a car pulled out of a drive, and Cathy waved at the woman driving it. I put my head down and pretended to be looking for something in my pockets, feeling conspicuous.

The headlights illuminated me, and I made a bet with myself that that would be the moment Cathy would turn and look. But she kept on walking, rummaging in her bag, only finding what she was looking for as she walked up a drive to a small semi that looked in need of work. I immediately imagined a trellis loaded with Virginia Creeper, perhaps decking over the small front garden. That's what I would've done.

I stopped and watched, my fingers brushing my keys over and over as Cathy opened the front door, light from the hallway spilling out into the night. I saw a small brown dog jumping up and down, overexcited to see her. As the door closed, I thought I saw another figure moving.

Did Cathy have someone to come home to? I tried to imagine who that person could be. Who would fit with Cathy?

I thought about going and knocking, seeing how *she* liked a virtual stranger showing up at her door at night. How she'd feel if I started bothering her neighbours and interfering in her life.

Another light went on upstairs, a shadow moved behind a closed blind. I imagined Cathy getting changed out of her work clothes that stank of urine and fast-approaching death. She'd probably put on pyjamas and go downstairs to her husband, and over a home cooked meal, she'd tell him about her day.

The sadness hit me like a wave, and I had to sit down on somebody's wall, the dampness from the rain seeping through to my thighs. Why did Cathy get this life? Who did I have to come home to? To talk about my day with?

I squeezed my hands into fists. I needed to go home. What was I even doing here? What did I think was going to happen? I turned and walked back to the main road and waited for a bus. I was waiting a long time, getting colder and more frustrated, and was about to get up and start walking when I saw a man and a woman strolling towards the bus stop. I was about to ask if they knew what time the bus was due when I realised who it was.

I ducked behind the shelter as Cathy and her husband approached. They sat down, a foot apart from each other, his hands deep in his pockets, hers clinging to her handbag. I wondered what she'd say if she saw me, if she'd wonder what I was doing there.

But it was starting to rain, and Cathy had come to my home, and I had every reason to be there, anyway, so I moved into the shelter.

Cathy's husband looked up first, giving me a friendly nod before looking back at his feet. Cathy looked up a second later, doing a double take. I wondered if I should say something first, some reason why I was at the bus stop close to her house. But Cathy just turned away as if she didn't know me, as if I was as much of a stranger to her as I was to her husband.

'Should we go to The Swan for one first?' her husband asked, breaking the silence. I noticed Cathy glance at me quickly before answering.

'Can do,' she said, and that was it. No more conversation. I got the feeling that Cathy and her husband had been together a while. Were one of those couples with not much to say to each other. I wondered if she'd told him about me, about coming around to my house. If she'd told him about Mum.

The bus pulled in, and the husband motioned for me to go first. I took a seat in the middle, and when Cathy passed by, she didn't look at me at all. The bus was quiet at that time of night, and though it was hard to tell over the rumble of the engine, it seemed like Cathy and her husband didn't have anything to say to each other at all.

When I finally got home again, I went to bed, pictures of Cathy's life running through my mind, and even though it seemed far from perfect, I wondered if I'd ever have that. And then, I repeated the mantra – *I deserve it too* – until I fell asleep.

Chapter 24

The next day, I didn't cry at work, just took dozens of phone calls and gave pat answers to their queries. I got the bus home, checked the street for Jacob before going inside.

I'd slept better the night before but was still tired, the kind of tired you feel in your bones. There was more mail, which went in the bin, but nothing on the back doorstep. I watched some mindless TV and checked the windows a few times but less than usual. The street was quiet, and no one was hassling me. As I stared into the TV screen, I felt calm, lulled by the flashing images.

I fell asleep on the settee and woke just before my alarm. I climbed the stairs, stiff from the stand-in bed, and went into the bathroom, going through my normal routine. In the bedroom, I opened the wardrobe and pulled out a ratty old dress but put it back and chose something nicer. I realised I didn't feel as tired anymore, and the weight in my guts was missing. I dressed and brushed my hair. I put some make-up on, sure that I wouldn't lose it all to blue paper towels after crying in the toilets.

When I got off the bus at work, I realised I was early, so went into the shop on the corner and bought myself something nice for lunch. I said hello to people as I walked to my desk and got a few smiles. I was pleasant to people on the phone and found myself laughing at one man's joke, which wasn't funny at all, but I knew how to make people feel good about themselves, and I knew I hadn't been doing it enough lately.

At lunchtime I sat in the staff room and listened to my colleagues talking. I promised I'd try to get to Lesley's engagement party, but she told me not to worry too much about it, what with Mum and everything.

'I think I'm on track for employee of the week,' Tom said to Lesley, and we all laughed. Tom won it ninety percent of the time because no one else cared.

'I don't know why you bother,' Lesley said. 'All that work for a crappy bottle of wine.'

'It's not about the wine. It's about knowing I'm doing a good job.'

Lesley rolled her eyes. 'We're hardly doing important work here.'

'I know. But if you're going to do something...' He let us finish his thought as he stuffed some crisps into his mouth.

'Well, I wouldn't work myself to the bone for a three-pound bottle of crap,' Lesley said.

'And neither do I,' Tom said. 'Which is a good job as the stingy bastards didn't even leave one for me last week.'

I realised I'd forgotten to replace the wine, and I scanned all their faces, wondering if anyone knew it was me who'd taken it. But no one looked at me; they were all too busy agreeing how crap management was.

***

On the way home, I stopped at the care home to check on Mum. I didn't see Cathy as I walked past the nurses' station, and I went straight to Mum's room without speaking to anyone, without looking into anyone else's room.

As I got to the door, I could hear a voice. Someone was in there. I leaned in and listened.

'...to the house ... was she? ...yes, she didn't want me to go in though ... spoke to the neighbour ... that's right ... didn't know much ... Jacob ... he'd been there...'

I listened to Cathy's voice, snippets coming through the door, and then, Mum's stilted words interrupting every now and then. I felt sick, wishing I'd confronted Cathy the night before. I pushed the door open, and Cathy jumped.

'Hi, Mum,' I said, and Cathy looked down at her, a question in her eyes. Mum nodded, her head moving laboriously, as if the simple act of saying yes was now too much.

Cathy patted Mum's hand and came towards me. 'I'll be right outside, Margaret,' she said to Mum and then gave me a look. 'I'm sorry about last night,' she said. 'I hope you didn't think I was being rude. It's a confidentiality thing. If I'd introduced you to Steve, it'd mean telling him about your mum and everything so…'

I nodded my understanding. 'Don't worry about it,' I said, and pushed the door closed when Cathy had gone. I left the TV playing and sat on the chair by the bed watching Mum for a while, but she didn't look at me, just kept her eyes on the TV before closing them, blocking me out completely.

'I'm sorry I didn't come yesterday. Things have been busy. But it looks like you're feeling a bit better,' I said finally, and still, there was nothing.

'Lesley at work has got engaged. I'm going to the party,' I said, and still, Mum didn't respond. Saying that, I probably wouldn't have responded, either. It was an entirely dull piece of news.

After a few more minutes, I decided to say something. 'Cathy came round,' I said, and waited for a twitch.

Nothing.

'She said you were worried about me.'

I sat under the flickering fluorescent light that I'd asked them to fix a thousand times, and each sputter of electricity underlined another moment she refused to speak to me. After a while, I couldn't take it anymore.

'Why did you send her?' I turned the TV off. 'Mum? Talk to me.'

Still nothing.

'Why are you being like this? I know you can talk just fine. You're chatty enough with Cathy.' There was a flicker behind her eyes, I could tell she wanted to open them, wanted to say something to me. 'Mum. Why her? Why not me? Why won't you talk to me?'

Her eyes opened slowly. 'You know why,' she said, and I felt a shiver go through me.

I grabbed my things and left, running into Cathy as I did. 'That was short and sweet,' she said, and I thought I saw a smile creep onto her face before I pushed past her out into the fresh air.

Chapter 25

There was no one waiting for me when I got back to the house. No Cathy. No Jacob. Not even any post for the dead old lady. I was leaving the past behind me. It was time to move on.

On the way home, I'd been upset, but between there and here, something had changed. If Mum wasn't going to speak to me, there was nothing I could do about that. Since she'd got ill, things had changed between us. Not only had the court decided to cut me out of any decisions about her life, it seemed Mum didn't want me around either. So that was it. There was nothing more I could do about it. It wasn't what I'd wanted, but I had to accept it. Mum and her affairs were no longer my business. As for Cathy, if she had nothing better to do than run errands for delusional old ladies, then that was her problem. I doubted she'd come back. She got what she wanted. Mum all to herself. I wasn't going to think about them anymore. It was over. Mum was out of my life. Jacob was out of my life. I was starting anew.

I felt lighter than I had in weeks. Years, probably. I put the radio on while I made something to eat and even found myself singing along. After I'd eaten, I found a notebook and started making a list. My new life started tomorrow, and these were the things that I was going to do:

Get my hair cut

Buy some nice new clothes

Start eating properly - maybe join the gym?

Pull the carpets up and get quote for new ones and/or laminate flooring - whole house

Look for a better job

Get new curtains - especially for living room
Get rid of rest of junk from house
Think about home improvements - windows, kitchen, bathroom?
Accept invites - maybe not to Lesley's party though

I kept writing, for pages. It seemed like everything in my life needed changing, which could've been depressing, but I found it exciting. I was starting over. Making things better.

I decided I wanted some ice cream to celebrate my freedom so grabbed my purse and keys and walked out. I stopped on the doorstep, realising I hadn't even checked the street first. A quick glance in both directions told me what my subconscious already knew. Jacob wasn't there because he'd given up. And now I was safe to go out for ice cream whenever I chose.

I practically skipped down to the corner shop and bought a tub of chocolate ice cream and walked home, smiling inside and out. Everything was going to be okay.

I finished off the ice cream and went to bed. For the first time in a long time, I fell asleep quickly without the need for mantras or burying my head beneath the pillow.

***

At work the next day, I went out at lunchtime, buying a paper with job ads and a new house and garden magazine, turning the corner of a few pages where things caught my eye.

When I came out of work, the weather was miserable, the rain made worse by the wind. I ran to the bus stop and saw my bus disappearing around the corner. For a second, I let it bother me, but I chose to use the time to go into the supermarket and buy some delicious hot bread for my tea. There was some soup at home. It would be perfect.

When I got off the bus, I couldn't wait to get home. The wind was getting worse, so I decided to cut across the field behind the house. It was still light, just dull from the rain. I didn't feel vulnerable, even though I probably should've. I walked by quickly, desperate to get home. It'd been three weeks since I moved in and I was still excited by the thought of the house. My own place. My own home.

I risked a blast of icy rain in the face and looked up to the backs of the row of houses ahead. I counted them, in my head. One, two, three, four, five. Five from the end. I kept my eyes on my window. My bedroom window. And something caught my eye. Someone was in my house.

Chapter 26

Phil walks out of the room, to do God knows what, and I'm left with Jacob. He stands there looking at me as if he doesn't know what to do now, as if this wasn't his idea. I should've known from the start that he was capable of something like this. I'd known about things he'd done, known he'd been in prison, but I thought *I* was safe.

I try to talk to him, try to beg him to let me go but the dirty dishcloth in my mouth muffles the words and makes me gag. I can feel vomit sneaking up my throat and my eyes burn. I scream and beg and shout his name, but none of it is intelligible. I struggle against my binds but only make things worse, only cause the nylon tights to cut deeper into my flesh.

I'm crying now, gasping for air, but nothing's getting in. I'm breathing too quickly, and I can feel myself shaking. I'm hyperventilating. Jacob looks at me with fear in his eyes. I can't tell whether he's afraid for me or for himself, but he comes closer, and it looks like he wants to do something…then, he looks back over his shoulder as if he needs permission from Phil.

Do something! I want to scream.

Jacob pulls the filthy cloth from my mouth, and I gasp, inhaling deeply before coughing and spluttering and bringing up some bile that just dribbles down my chin.

'Help me,' I say to Jacob, my throat raw from screaming. 'Do something.'

Jacob looks over his shoulder again. 'Jacob,' I say, softly, not wanting to attract Phil's attention. 'Jacob, look at me.' He finally turns, but his eyes wander, above my head, then to my knees, anywhere but my eyes. 'Jacob, listen,' I say. 'Look at me.' I wait a couple of seconds, and he finally makes eye contact but only briefly. He can't stand what he's done. And I know I can use that.

'Jacob. You know this is wrong, don't you? You know you're going to get in trouble for this.' His eyes settle on mine again. 'I know this wasn't your idea. And I don't know why he wants to do this to me. I don't know what you've told him. But you have to stop it. If you let me go I won't tell the police. I promise.'

I hear the sound of something smashing in the room next door. I can't tell what it is, but it distracts Jacob, and he's no longer looking at me.

'Jacob,' Phil shouts from beyond the wall. 'In here.' Jacob starts to walk away from me, but I need him to stay. I need to get to him, to make him see he can't do this.

'Jacob,' I say. 'Please don't do this to me. I love you.'

He stops and turns to me, and I think I've got him. But his face changes, and he runs at me, pressing his face close to mine.

'Liar!'

I know I shouldn't have said it, but I was panicking. His face is still against mine, he's shaking with rage. I know I've made a mistake. Another mistake. He's breathing heavily, a bit of spit sits on the corner of his mouth. I can smell his breath. It smells of cigarettes and cheap lager.

'What the fuck's going on?' Phil says, charging in and pushing Jacob aside. 'Why did you take this out?' he asks, picking up the dishcloth.

'She was choking,' Jacob says.

'So?'

Phil stuffs it back into my mouth, and I cry out, but it's too late, my mouth is full, and I'm back to where I started, except this time, Jacob isn't on my side. I almost laugh. When was Jacob ever on my side? Phil might be the one giving orders here, the one taking control, but it was Jacob who started this. Jacob, who went crying to this monster because he can't do anything for himself. I try to kick out at them, but the binds are too tight. I am trapped here. At their mercy.

Jacob tries to say something to Phil, but he just pushes him out of the room. I can hear them mumbling in the hallway. What are they going to do to me? I keep trying to move my wrists, to loosen the tape, but it's not working. I look around the kitchen, trying to look for things that can help me, but nothing can help me now, not when I'm like this.

There's a knife on the drainer. I used it for cooking last night. There's the cricket bat on the floor. I could use either to defend myself if only I could get out of this chair. I struggle again, but it's pointless. I'm going to die here. I know I am.

I hear Phil whispering loudly to Jacob. He's angry with him. But I can't hear properly, so all I have is my imagination. I look to the doorway and see Phil staring in at me. He puts his arm around Jacob's shoulder and grins. Jacob smiles slightly and nods at Phil.

What are they going to do?

Phil comes back in, and I can't help myself, my eyes immediately go to the knife on the drainer. He follows my gaze, and his smile widens. He walks over and picks it up, turning it over in his hand. I can still see bits of onion stuck to the knife, and all I can think is that when they do my autopsy, they'll find traces of onion in my skin and wonder how it got there. Or maybe lots of people are killed with the knives they'd made their tea with.

Phil comes and stands in front of me, picking his nails with the knife, something I bet he saw on the telly. He stands there, saying nothing, hoping to scare me. It's working. But I don't let him know that. I try to stare back, but I can feel my head shaking, I can hear my breath struggling underneath the rag in my mouth.

Before I even realise it, I'm begging him to stop. My words are muffled, and Phil laughs and bends down closer to me.

'What was that?' he asks, and winks at Jacob.

I try again, even though I know it's pointless, even though I know he's mocking me. But it's all I have, so I scream and beg.

After I've worn myself out, Phil leans in and pulls the dishcloth from my mouth. I gulp air greedily. He's still right in front of me, and I know he's waiting for me to beg him some more, but now that I can, now that my words are free, I can't do it. I can't beg this man for anything.

'Cat got your tongue, Polly?' Phil says, and presses the knife against my cheek.

'Please,' I say, the word coming out as a stutter.

'Please what?'

'Please don't hurt me.'

Phil laughs. 'Why shouldn't I?'

'Because I've done nothing wrong,' I say.

Phil loses his grin now and presses the knife harder. I can feel it pierce my skin, can feel warm blood dribble down my face. 'You've done nothing wrong?' he says. 'Are you fucking kidding me?' I chance a look at Jacob. He's just standing there, useless as ever. 'Don't look at him,' Phil says, and grabs my face, squeezing hard. 'Don't you dare look at him.'

'Please,' I say, drawing out the word, sounding as pathetic as I look.

'You started this,' Phil says. 'You've got no one to blame but yourself.'

'I didn't–' I start, but Phil squeezes my face harder, and I can feel his fingers leaving imprints on my skin.

'You didn't what? Didn't fuck him over?' he says, and nods behind him at Jacob. 'You need to be taught a lesson.' He lets go of my face and stands back, staring at me. I can hear myself, still begging and pleading, but he's not listening to me anymore. He's already decided what he wants to do and he's going to do it. Phil bends down in front of me again. His hands reach out and pull at my knickers that are halfway down my thighs.

'No,' I say, my voice barely more than a whisper. 'Don't. Please, don't. Not that.'

He rips my underwear with the knife, pulls them off and hands them to Jacob. I'm crying now, deep sobs that blur my vision and close my throat. He's going rape me. They both are. I try to see Jacob's face. He's looking at my legs, won't look me in the eye. He's going to rape me, and he can't even look at me.

I close my eyes and think that I've brought this on myself. I knew what I was getting into. I should've run when I had the chance.

Chapter 27

Three Months Earlier

I'd had one of those days at work. It seemed like the whole world had something to complain about, and they all wanted to take it out on me. And then, there was the new guy, the temp. AJ, he called himself. He'd told Janet he had experience, but it soon became clear he hadn't, and I spent much of the day mopping up after his mistakes, and to make things worse, he didn't even care. He came across as entitled, like he thought he was better than everyone else.

I was already feeling down after Mum had been released from hospital again the night before. She shouldn't have been out; she was ill and needed help. But everything is about money these days and getting the doctors to listen was impossible. I'd lost count of the number of times me and Mum had been to the surgery or to A&E in the last few months. But getting them to believe me was hard, and Mum was always difficult too. I suppose it wasn't her fault, but the doctors must know how it is with these things, the symptoms come and go. Just because she seemed perfectly rational, as she sat across from yet another overworked medical student, didn't mean there wasn't a problem. And if it'd been just forgetfulness, that would've been fine. But it was more than that; they just couldn't see.

But they'd had to listen after she almost burnt down the house. After putting sheets in the oven to warm up, she went for a lie down. It was only because I happened to stop by that it wasn't so much worse. Of course, by the time I'd managed to get inside, she'd woken up, but her lungs were already full of smoke. They had to do something then, shipping her over to the psychiatric ward to assess her. But, once again, they refused to do anything useful. *There's not enough room here*, they said. *She's not high risk, she'll be okay at home.* They were planning to send a social worker out, to do more assessments to see what help she needed. Of course, I could've moved back home, to do what I could, but I had to work. We needed money from somewhere. And what would happen when she set another fire in the middle of the day? Who was going to take responsibility for that?

So, there we were, back at the house, a lingering smell of smoke in the air and me wondering what to do next.

'I think I'm going to go to bed now,' Mum said.

'Don't you want me to stay?' I asked.

She looked at me for a while before answering and then shook her head. 'I'll be all right.'

'What if you have another…' I didn't know how to finish the sentence, at least not without hurting her feelings. 'Let me help you.'

Mum picked up the bag we'd just brought back from the hospital, holding it out to me. 'What's this?' I asked.

'Nighties. My washer's on the blink. If you want to help, you could wash them for me.'

I took the bag of washing and said, 'Will you be okay?'

She gave a slight nod. 'I'll be fine now.'

So, I'd spent the night before at the launderette as Sasha was using our machine, seemingly washing every last thing she owned.

With no more laundry that evening, I was trying to relax a little, trying not to think too much about Mum. I was standing in Tesco, trying to find something for my tea, something I could just take to my room and eat in there because Kimberley had told me that morning they were having a couple of people over for dinner. I knew what Kimberley had meant by a couple of people. She meant there'd be a dozen of them, and they'd be there all night making a racket. Usually, I'd join them, but what with everything going on with Mum, I just couldn't face it. Part of me wondered why Kimberley hadn't been more considerate – she knew how tired I was – but I supposed they couldn't stop living their own lives just because mine was falling apart.

I took the items to the self-serve checkout and got in the queue. It was while I was standing there that I saw him. I did a double take, to be sure it was him. And then he turned and looked right at me, and I knew that it was, even after all those years. He hadn't changed much, older with a little more weight. But his face was the same.

I looked at my feet, feeling his eyes on me. I wondered if I should go to another checkout and just get out of there. I didn't really want to talk to him. What would I possibly say?

I chanced a look up again, and he'd gone back to scanning his cans of lager and microwave meals for one. I started thinking about what that said about him, about his life and how things had turned out for him.

By the time I'd got to the front of the queue, Jacob had gone. I glanced about as I scanned my things and felt relief that he wasn't there, that I wouldn't have to try and think of something to say to him.

As I walked quickly to the bus stop, I was checking my watch to see if I'd missed my bus and didn't notice him at first. He was sitting on the bench, huddled into his duffel coat. He looked up as I approached, and I knew I couldn't ignore him this time. I smiled quickly and hoped he wouldn't recognise me, or at least if he did, he wouldn't want to catch up.

'Polly,' he said. Not a question, a statement. 'It's Jacob,' he said. 'From school.'

I looked up the street for a sign of the bus, but the street was empty. Not even a taxi I could hail. 'Right,' I said. 'I remember.'

Jacob moved his carrier bag from the bench, making space for me to sit down. He smelled of cigarettes, and it caught the back of my throat. He'd smoked for as long as I could remember. Even when we'd first started secondary school, he was out there with the bigger kids, lighting up, and he was always getting caught, always in detention.

'I thought I saw you in there,' Jacob said, nodding back to the store. 'I wasn't sure though, and then my machine went mental.' I frowned at him, not following. 'The scanner thing. I don't know why I bother with them things. They never work right. There's always something won't go through.'

'Right,' I said, and shifted awkwardly, hoping the bus would come.

Jacob didn't say anything for a while, and I didn't want to encourage him, just wanting to get home, and finally, we saw a bus turn the corner and we all got up. A young couple got on first, and I dug around my handbag until I found my weekly ticket before turning to Jacob. 'Are you getting this one?' I asked, the words, *Please don't*, flashing through my mind. I didn't want to spend the whole journey home sitting next to Jacob with his cigarette smell and awkward conversation.

'No,' he said. 'Mine's not due for a bit.'

I nodded and smiled. 'Okay,' I said. 'Bye, then.'

'Bye, Polly,' I heard him shout as I got on the bus, and as I walked to the back seat, I saw him watching me. I could feel his eyes on me right to the end of the road.

***

When I got in, I could hear Sasha talking loudly over blaring music. I pulled my shoes off and left them in the hall. I tried to sneak past without them seeing, but Kimberley saw me and shouted. I stopped and stood in the doorway. Sasha stopped talking, and all their friends turned and looked at me.

'Do you want to join us?' Kimberley asked.

'No thanks,' I said. 'I'm really tired, so I'm going to bed. But have a good night.'

I started to walk away, but Kimberley spoke again. 'Have you eaten?'

I turned back. 'Not yet,' I said. 'I'm just going to…'

'Oh, come on,' Danny said, and reached over to pull me into the room. I rolled my eyes at him. He'd once made a pass at me at one of our parties, but I'd turned him down, partly because he was far too young for me and partly because I knew Sasha had a crush on him. But it didn't stop him from trying again.

'She should stay, shouldn't she?' he said to the rest of them, and they all started egging me on. Danny grabbed my hand, pulling me closer. 'Come and have a drink, Paula.'

'Polly,' I said, wondering just how drunk he was.

'If she doesn't want to, leave her be,' Sasha said, and removed Danny's hand from mine. 'You go to bed, Polly. We'll try to keep it down.'

I thought about it for a moment, wondering if a night of drinking with them was what I needed. But they seemed drunk already, and who likes playing catch up?

'Have a good night,' I said, and walked towards my room, hearing Danny say, 'Spoilsport,' to Sasha as I left.

Chapter 28

I saw Jacob again on the way home from the hospital a few days later. I'd been going around to Mum's every night after work since she'd been released, and each time we ended up bickering about what sort of support she needed. There'd still been no sign of the social worker, and I was insisting on calling them to see what was happening. Mum got upset, and we had a full-on row, and the next thing I knew, she was on the floor, her body twisted, her words stuck inside.

No one could deny it this time. Mum was ill and needed help. There was a flurry of activity as people rushed around, and the following days were full of talk about care plans and long journeys and thinking about the future, while Mum lay there unable to move or speak. I stood and watched her, afraid of what was going to happen, saddened to see her so helpless. I wished they'd listened to me before, that if they'd kept her in hospital where she belonged, then maybe this wouldn't have happened.

People started talking about power of attorney and what would happen as Mum had never signed anything and how I'd be kept in the loop and to keep my chin up. It was all too much, and I'd have to hide in the toilets while I cried, and I wished more than anything that things had been different or that they'd go back to how they were before. I needed someone to talk to and what I wouldn't give to hear Mum's voice, even though she'd often driven me mad before.

'You need to find a better job,' Mum would say.

'Like it's *that* easy.'

'Well, there must be something. You've got a degree.'

'Half the staff in Tesco have a degree. It doesn't mean anything these days.'

'Well, what about Sasha. She's got a good job, doesn't she? Couldn't she put a word in for you?'

'She's a dental nurse,' I'd say. 'I'm not trained for that.'

'You could train.'

'I don't want to be a bloody dental nurse,' I'd say, and Mum's face would change, and she'd fold her arms across her chest in a huff.

'If you don't want me to be interested in your life, you just have to say.'

I hated those conversations. And now, I'd never have them again.

***

I was walking to the bus stop when I saw him. He was sitting on a bench, hunched over, his glasses settled halfway down his nose, smoking a roll up. He didn't seem to see me, and I was relieved, hiding behind an old man to make sure Jacob didn't notice me.

After a few minutes, Jacob stood up and stubbed out his cigarette on the top of the bin. I could see a bus coming up the road and hoped it was mine, rather than his. It was, and I watched him from behind the old man, pacing up and down, muttering to himself. But as the bus pulled in, Jacob pulled a handful of change from his pocket and walked towards it. He was going to get on my bus. I thought about walking away, waiting for the next one. But I was tired and just wanted to get home.

I got on and noticed it was almost full. A couple of people, young lads, were standing at the front, but there were still a few seats towards the back. I made my way down the aisle as the bus pulled away, trying to locate Jacob at the same time as trying not to meet his eye.

The old man took the seat halfway up, and I spotted the last remaining seat. Jacob was sitting across the aisle from it, and I had no choice but to sit alongside him. He looked at me for a few seconds before the realisation hit him, and he smiled. His teeth were bad, and there was a bit of tobacco on his lip.

'Hi, Jacob,' I said as I sat down, and the old woman next to me huffed because she had to move her shopping bags onto her knee.

'Hiya, Polly,' he said, and then shifted his eyes towards the front of the bus. Apparently, neither of us knew what to say. I found it strange that I'd run into him again just a few days later. I hadn't seen him in almost twenty years and now twice in one week.

Twenty years. Christ, that made me feel old. I sneaked another look at Jacob and saw that he looked a lot older than I'd thought. Apart from the rotten teeth, he had lines on his face. A couple were scars, but the lines on his forehead, his worry lines, were deep and constant, and I wondered what had happened to him since we left school that he'd been so worried about. I wondered if I looked as old as he did.

'Have you been to the hospital?'

I focused and realised Jacob had spoken. 'Yes,' I said. 'To see my mum.'

'Is she all right?' he asked, and the lines deepened.

I paused a moment, knowing that *she's fine* was the appropriate answer, that this was just small talk between people who barely knew each other. 'Not really,' I said. 'She had a stroke.'

'Shit,' Jacob said.

'She's not been well for a while. Forgetting stuff, you know?' I shook my head. 'I seem to spend all my time at the hospital these days.' I smiled to let him know I wasn't fishing for sympathy.

'My mum died,' he said, and his eyes swivelled back to the front of the bus.

'I'm sorry,' I said, but he didn't reply.

We were silent for a while, listening to the rumble of the bus and the chattering of a toddler behind us. I glanced at Jacob. 'What about you?' I asked, and he finally turned back to me. 'Where've you been?'

'Just went to get this. It's pretty rare.' He held up a plastic bag but didn't elaborate about what was inside.

We sat silently again, polite conversation exhausted. The old woman beside me leaned over and pressed the bell to get off at the next stop. When she'd gone, I shuffled over into her seat which Jacob took as an invitation, and he moved beside me. I could smell alcohol on his breath as he turned to me.

'Are you going home now?' he asked.

'Yes,' I said. *Please don't ask where it is or, worse, ask to come with me.*

'Me too,' he said. I nodded and couldn't think of anything else to say. Jacob ducked his head and looked out the window. 'I get off here,' he said, and pressed the bell. He stood and looked at me for a few seconds before saying, 'Bye, then,' and walking away, grabbing each pole and swinging on them as if he was a child.

I watched him walk off down a side street, his hands in his pockets, his chin tucked into his coat, even though it was warm outside. I wondered if I'd see him again. Maybe he'd been there all the time, and I was only just noticing.

A couple more stops and I had to get off and change buses, and for a fleeting moment, I wished Jacob had stayed, that we'd gone somewhere together and talked. I got the feeling he didn't like to say much, that he preferred to listen. Jacob was weird, that much was obvious, but I could see something in him. He was the first person who wanted to listen to me in a long time and I started hoping I'd run into him again.

Chapter 29

The next time I saw him was three days later. I'd stopped at the big Tesco on my way home, and his face appeared poking above a self-service checkout machine, again buying cans of lager and a couple of frozen pizzas. He hadn't noticed me, and I decided not to go over. I knew there was nothing I really had to say to him and that it would just be awkward. I'd been down the last time, especially after seeing Mum, and I just wanted someone to talk to. And if I was being honest, I thought talking to Jacob would make me feel better, assuming he was worse off than me.

Jacob had been in the same year as me at school and I guess I wanted to be able to say, look, here's someone who's made even less of their life than I have. Here's another thirty-five-year-old with nothing to show for themselves. I was certain he didn't have a good job or a house. But if I'd reduced myself to this, if Jacob was the barometer I was basing things on, then maybe I was worse off than I thought.

I'd been thinking about him a lot since seeing him the second time. Things I hadn't thought about in donkey's years suddenly came back to me at all kinds of odd moments; as I was on a call at work, as I cleaned the bath, as I walked through the town and saw a kid with snot running down his face.

Jacob had been the weird kid in our year. He was the one who never seemed to have had a bath on Sunday night like the rest of us. His mum didn't come to collect him from school and never came to sports days or anything. Kids picked on him, and he always sat by himself at break time. No one wanted to work with him in lessons because he was a bit slow, and everyone complained that he stank if they were forced to sit next to him during assembly. For a long time, I'd assumed his family were poor. But it turned out that wasn't the case. Turned out his family were just…different.

I suppose I felt sorry for him, but only from a distance. I never spoke to him unless I had to, and I'd laugh like everyone else when someone tripped him up, because if you didn't, it meant you were his girlfriend and everyone knew it. I didn't think of myself as a bully, but I guessed I had been as good as one.

But the thing that stuck out the most when I recalled Jacob was the birthday party he had when he was ten. He'd never had a party before, as I far as I knew, anyway. Jacob had never even been invited to anyone else's party either, unless, of course, he just didn't show up for fear of being abused outside of school as well as inside. I'd had a few parties in my time, certainly before we had to move house, but Jacob had never been invited. I was lucky because I was a girl, and so I didn't have to invite any boys at all.

But for his tenth birthday, Jacob's mum decided to throw a party and invite all the kids from his class. Whether his mum knew what went on at school, I don't know, but it seemed awfully cruel if she did.

Everyone was invited and the week before the party, all anyone could talk about was whether their parents had told them they had to go and what they were going to get him for a present. There were loads of jokes about bars of soap and things like that, and I knew that Jacob must've overheard and probably wished the party could just be cancelled.

In the end, I went because Mum forced me to. She felt sorry for Jacob. There were eight other kids there, presumably all under orders too. Jacob's mum was friendly and fluttered about, bringing out more and more plates of hot dogs and cheese on sticks. She'd made a cake in the shape of a train but someone threw a football inside the house and it landed on the cake and ruined it. Jacob's mum cried, but Jacob just stood there, his face revealing nothing. Once his mum had calmed down, she started the party games and we all sat in a circle and played pass the parcel. Not one person looked like they wanted to be there, least of all Jacob.

After we'd eaten, people started to drift away, making excuses that were weak even for ten-year-olds. I'd gone to the toilet and been appalled at the state of the bathroom. There was mould all around the bath, and the toilet was stained. I didn't dare sit down and left without having a wee. But when I came back down, everyone was gone. It was just me and Jacob and Jacob's mum. I was desperate to go, too, but Mum said she'd be back for me at four so I had to wait it out.

Jacob's mum put the TV on and cleared the plates. Every time she came back in, she'd look at Jacob, sitting there staring through the TV, and she looked like she was going to cry again. Jacob never looked at me once, and finally, I decided to help his mum carrying paper plates into the kitchen. She looked embarrassed when I went in and I knew why. The place was filthy. I knew Mum would die if she saw it. But Jacob's mum tried to smile and told me I was a good girl for helping. The rest of the time was spent awkwardly waiting and pretending to like some ugly paintings that it turned out she'd done herself.

At four, Mum honked the horn outside, and I was relieved I could escape. I wondered if the other kids knew I'd been left behind, and if on Monday, they'd start making up lies about me and Jacob. I felt sick at the thought.

'Thanks for having me,' I said to Jacob's mum as I grabbed my coat and headed for the front door. I looked at Jacob, but he still hadn't moved.

'Wait.'

I stopped, and Jacob's mum handed me another piece of cake in a paper towel. It was mushed up and pieced back together after the football incident. 'For later. Or give it to your mum, if you like.' She smiled down at me, and I took the cake.

When I got in the car, Mum asked if I had a good time. I shrugged and squidged the cake with my fingers, saying nothing until we got home, angry at Mum for making me go. I let her go inside first and then threw the cake over the balcony onto the ground, thinking the birds might as well have it. I went inside and flopped onto the settee, looking around at the cramped flat that'd been our home for the past year.

'It's not fair,' I said.

'What's not,' Mum asked.

'That we have to live here.'

'Don't start, Polly. You think I like it any more than you do?'

'But even Jacob lives in a nice house, and he's weird,' I said. 'Why can't we have a house like that?'

Mum just sighed. 'Well, some people have more luck than others. That's life.'

'But it's not fair,' I said. 'I wish you didn't make me go.'

'Tough.'

'But it was all dirty as well.' Mum looked up and sighed again, and I could tell she'd had enough of me, so I got up and stomped off to my pokey little bedroom. 'It's not fair,' I said again, and slammed the door.

Chapter 30

Phil looks down at me, his face twisted into something like disgust. I don't know why he hates me so much, but it's clear that he does. Maybe he hates everyone. Maybe he's just that kind of person.

I can see Jacob out of the corner of my eye, my knickers in his hand, and my stomach turns. 'Please don't do this,' I say. 'I'll do anything. Just please, not that.'

'Not what?' Phil says.

My eyes go to my underwear that Jacob is mauling and Phil starts to laugh. 'Don't flatter yourself,' he says. 'I wouldn't touch you with his.' He nods to Jacob who suddenly seems aware of what he's doing and throws my knickers onto the floor. 'Can't speak for him, though.'

I look at Jacob, and he just stands gawping. He grabs Phil's jacket and tugs, pulling him out of the room. As they leave I start screaming, trying to take advantage of the opportunity. Even Ethel should be able to hear me.

Phil strides back into the kitchen and punches me in the face so hard that I fall back, the chair slamming into the floor. I hear something crack, and I don't know if it's the chair or me. But either way, pain reverberates up my arms. I think I'm in shock. The pain shoots across my face, and I can feel blood. I guess it's from my nose, but it's hard to tell while I'm lying here as it runs sideways, settling in my ears.

Instinctively, I try to reach up and wipe it away, but my hands are tied, I can't do a thing. And then, I'm lurching forward as Phil pulls the chair upright and I get a head rush, my vision blurring. Jacob is standing there, watching, his hands digging in his hair.

'What did you do that for?' he asks, and Phil wipes his face, some of my blood smearing across it as he does.

'I had to shut her up,' he says, and looks around, finding the dishcloth and stuffing it back in my mouth.

'But…' Jacob starts, but Phil spins to face him.

'But what? You want to do this or not?'

I don't know what they want to do, what their plan is, but I know it won't end well for me. All I can hope is that Jacob changes his mind, that he can't go through with whatever it is.

'Well?' Phil says, and Jacob nods. I see Phil's shoulders drop. He's relieved. He wants to go through with it.

I close my eyes and cry. I don't care if I choke on the cloth, it must be better than whatever they're going to do. I think about the last few months, about how things turned out, about the choices I made, and I wish I hadn't been so stupid, so naive to think that getting involved with him wouldn't end badly.

'Hey,' Phil says, and slaps my face. 'Look at me.'

I open my eyes, and they're both standing there in front of me, and I wish they'd just get on with it. The anticipation is killing me. My imagination driving me mad. But maybe that's what they want. He took my underwear for a reason. To make me think he would rape me. He's messing with my head.

My eyes flick from Phil to Jacob, and I try to work it out. Is that all this is? Messing with my head? Are they really going to do anything to me or just make me think they are?

'You know, you're the worst kind of person there is,' Phil says. 'A bully.'

I try to say, 'I'm not', but my voice is muffled, so it almost sounds like I'm agreeing so I shake my head instead. I know I'm not a bully.

'You disgust me,' Phil says, and I keep shaking my head. 'Admit it,' he says, and hits me again, this time, catching my ear. I cry out in pain. 'Admit you're a bully.'

I keep shaking my head, and he hits me again and again. 'You used him,' Phil says, pointing to Jacob. 'You made him think you loved him. You told him you did, right?' I suck in air through my nose with shuddering breaths, and Phil grabs my hair, pulling my head to the side. 'Answer me!'

'Yes,' I say from behind my gag.

Phil lets go. 'You used him. You played mind games. Well, now it's time for you to see what that's like.' Phil steps back and nods to Jacob. He just stands there, staring at me, and I wish I'd never run into him that day. Wish I'd never met him at all. I hate him. At that moment, I hate him more than anything in the world.

Phil pushes Jacob forward and says, 'Go on. She fucking deserves it.'

'But… this isn't…' Jacob says, and Phil pushes him again.

'Do it,' he says. 'It'll make you feel better.'

Jacob steps back and I think he can't go through with it, but the next thing his arm is swinging forward, his fist coming towards my face, and I feel my skin split where he hits me, can feel my brain rattling in my head. And it just keeps coming. That's the thing with Jacob, he's so easily led.

The chair wobbles again but rights itself in time for another blow. I'm screaming, but the sound isn't going anywhere. No one is coming for me, no one knows what's happening. I am all alone and they're going to kill me.

Chapter 31

Ikept running into Jacob, in the supermarket, at the bus stop. Wherever I went, he always seemed to be there, and I wondered why I was only just noticing him, if he'd been there all along. But it turned out, he'd only moved back to the area fairly recently.

We always talked, and it slowly became less awkward. Maybe I felt sorry for him, but one day, after we'd got on the bus, I realised that there were some nice cafés close to where he lived, so instead of me getting off and changing bus to go home to the girls, I stayed on and asked Jacob if he wanted to go for a drink. He looked confused as if it was the strangest thing in the world, as if I'd asked him if he wanted a quick trip to the moon.

'I'm buying,' I said, in case that was the problem. I'd guessed that he didn't have much money, was probably on benefits.

'Okay,' he said, and flashed a smile before the self-consciousness hit him, and he covered his teeth.

We got off the bus, and I led him to a café on the corner of his street. It was a nice place, clean and friendly with good food that wasn't pretentious. We found a table at the back, and I asked what he'd like before going to the counter to order.

When I brought our pot of tea and cake back to the table, Jacob hadn't taken his coat off, despite the heat inside the cafe. 'Are you not staying?' I asked and nodded to his coat with a smile. His mouth twitched, and his hand went to the toggles on his coat but didn't move any further. I wondered if his coat was some kind of security blanket, if he felt nervous with me.

I pushed the small plate with chocolate cake towards him, and he nodded his thanks and dug in, finishing before I'd even started mine. He had chocolate in his teeth and was running his tongue across them to try and get rid of it. I tried not to look at him and poured some tea instead.

'So,' I said. 'What have you been up to since school?' We'd talked several times now, and I still didn't know much. He only mentioned his mum when I'd talked about mine, but it turned out she'd died just a few weeks before we met. I'd felt a stab of sympathy when he told me, felt awful for thinking bad things about her all those years ago when she'd been nothing but nice to me. I'd tried to find out more, but Jacob clammed up and got off the bus. He wasn't ready to talk about it.

Jacob shrugged and stirred too much sugar into his tea. 'Not much,' he said.

'You must've done something in the last twenty years,' I said. He shrugged again and took a long gulp of tea. 'Did you go to college?' I asked, and he looked at me like I was taking the piss. I wasn't, but when I thought about it, it seemed unlikely. 'What about work?' He looked like he didn't want to talk about that, either, and I wondered if he was embarrassed by some crappy job he'd had. 'My job's not that great either,' I said, hoping he'd feel less intimidated.

'I used to work in a factory,' Jacob said, and I made a face to show I was interested. 'Chickens,' he said. 'Plucking them and that.'

'Oh,' I said. 'What was that like?'

'Shit,' he said, and slurped his tea.

'But you don't work there anymore?'

He shook his head. 'No. I haven't got a job at the moment.'

I nodded. 'It's hard,' I said. 'I keep looking for something better, but there's nothing much out there. Even with a degree.'

'Right,' Jacob said, and started looking out the window.

'So, what else?' I asked, and he glanced back at me, frowning, before looking out the window again. 'Have you been married or had any kids?'

'No. I looked after Mam sometimes,' he said and looked down at the sticky table top, rubbing his finger in drips of tea. I didn't say anything for a while, knowing he was sensitive about her, wondering if I'd pushed the small talk too far. 'I was in prison, Polly,' he said, and his eyes met mine for a second before going back to the tea.

'Oh,' I said, wondering if I should ask what for or if that was rude. I sat and drank some tea, and a hundred things ran through my mind, possibilities of what Jacob could've done to land him in prison and whether sitting here with him was such a good idea, or if I should've found an excuse to go home and stop seeing him.

'I hurt someone,' he said, and I felt my heart thump in my chest. 'Badly,' he said.

'Who?' I asked, trying not to focus too much on what he meant by *badly*.

Jacob looked out of the window again and didn't answer for a while. I thought about changing the subject, but I really wanted to know.

'I got into a fight outside a pub,' he said. 'These blokes were having a go at me all night. I tried to ignore it, honest, but they wouldn't leave me alone.' He sniffed and pressed his finger into some loose grains of sugar. 'I'm not a violent person, Polly. But they started it, and I just lost it.' His nose twitched, and he rubbed it with the back of his hand. 'They were bullies, and I was sick of it and stood up for myself. But it got out of hand.' He sniffed again. 'It was an accident.'

He looked me in the eye, waiting for a response, waiting to see if he'd made a mistake in confessing to me. 'You've been really nice to me,' he said. 'People always keep away from me. It's always been like that, but since I came out of prison, it's worse.' He shrugged. 'It was just me and Mam for a long time, and now, she's gone.' He reached out and put his hand on mine. His nails were filthy. 'I'm glad I ran into you again. You're the first person who's been nice to me since she died,' he said. 'I wasn't even sure you liked me. At school, you know. I remember...' He shook his head. 'I just wasn't sure.'

I knew what he was talking about. After the party, the next week at school, he'd come up to me at break time and thanked me for coming. I could hear his mum's voice behind the words, could tell he was embarrassed to be saying them. But then, he leaned closer and kissed my cheek. You'd have thought he'd hit me the way I ran away from him. I could hear the other kids laughing as I ran inside, tears streaming down my face. I couldn't remember talking to him after that. But then, he probably didn't want to talk to me, either.

I looked down at his hand on mine and wondered what to do. I weighed up the things I knew about him, whether I should continue seeing him. But he seemed genuine about being alone, and I didn't think there was a nasty bone in his body. At least not unless you were a bully.

I squeezed his hand. 'Of course I liked you. And I'm glad we ran into each other too,' I said, and smiled.

Chapter 32

Phil pulls Jacob back, stopping him from hitting me again, maybe aware he's going too far, but he's still laughing. He's enjoying watching Jacob go crazy. My vision blurs, and I can't tell if it's from the tears or the blood or if something in my brain has been shaken loose. For all I know, I could be dying.

Phil comes over and sweeps the hair out of my face. He wants me to look at him, but I can't focus, I can't even keep my head up without his hand on my face. 'Get some water,' Phil says, and clicks his fingers at Jacob before pointing to the sink.

'Thank you,' I say, but I don't know if I say it out loud or just in my head. I can hear the tap running, and then, Phil lets go of me and my chin drops to my chest.

'No,' I hear Phil say. 'Here, use this.'

I can see their feet moving about. I see a cupboard door closing. What's in that cupboard? I can't remember. I can't think straight. His feet are in front of me, and then, I'm shaken into real consciousness by the cold water thrown over me. Phil stands there with the bucket in his hand.

'That's better,' he says.

The dishcloth soaks up some water, and it goes down the wrong way, sucked in by my gasping. I'm choking, and I can't do anything about it. They don't do anything, either, just watch me. Jacob comes around and pulls the cloth out, and some air gets in, but nothing is helping. I can't breathe properly.

'Do something,' Jacob says, and Phil comes over, knife in hand, and I wish he would just end it. He slices the tape from my wrists and chest and slaps me hard on the back. I fall forward, but my legs are still bound to the chair so I just hit the ground, coughing and spluttering. After a few seconds, I seem to be getting some air to my lungs, and I calm down a little. *I can get through this. I can if I'm smart about it.* Phil crouches and cuts the tights with the knife, and suddenly, I'm free. I want to run, but I can't move at all. My legs feel numb. My body aches. I'm free, but I can't do a thing about it.

Someone lifts me up. I turn my head, causing a pain to shoot through my skull. I see Phil behind me, holding me under my arms. He drags me to the living room, and I let him. I can't bring myself to fight anymore. He throws me to the floor, and I lie there on my side, waiting to see what he'll do next.

'Please, let me go,' I say, my voice as feeble as my body.

'We're not going to do that,' Phil says and looks at Jacob. 'Not yet.' He crouches down in front of me and looks me up and down. 'So, what are we going to do now? What would be a suitable punishment?'

'Please,' I beg. 'Please, let me go.'

'I can't do that, Polly. Because I don't think you've learned your lesson yet. I don't think you're sorry.'

'I am,' I say.

'You are? What are you sorry for?'

I look at Jacob. *I'm sorry I ever met you. I'm sorry I ever thought you were harmless.*

'I'm sorry I hurt Jacob,' I say, and Phil laughs.

'That's pathetic,' he says. 'You did more than hurt him. This isn't about some fucking break up, is it?' He grabs my chin and makes me look at him. 'Is it? You chose Jacob because you thought he was vulnerable. That he was some sort of spaz. But what would make you vulnerable, eh?' He pulls at my shirt. 'Maybe I could strip you, throw you outside. Let the neighbours have a good look at you. Would that do it? Or I could empty your bank account. What about that? Or maybe I could do something to your mum.' He stands up, looming over me, looking for a reaction. 'No. 'Cause you don't care about other people do you? I bet if I did something to your mum, you wouldn't give two fucks.'

'That's not true,' I say.

'How often do you visit your mum, Polly?' Phil asks.

'What?' I ask, wondering what that has to do with this.

'You're a selfish cunt, aren't you?' he says. 'That's why you need to be shown. That's why we need to hurt you, just like you hurt other people.'

'I don't,' I say.

'Liar!' Phil says, and boots me in the guts. I double up and feel like I'm howling inside, but nothing is coming out. When I open my eyes, Phil's boots are right in front of me. 'You pick on vulnerable people, because you think no one cares about them, and no one will stop you. But you were wrong about Jacob. You tried to fuck him over, because you thought no one would care. But *I* care,' he says. 'I care about Jacob, and that's why you're here.' He pulls me up by my hair again and pushes his face into mine. 'Who cares about you, Polly? Who's going to come and help you?'

He drops me back to the floor, and my face presses into the carpet. *No one. No one is going to help me.*

Chapter 33

When I got home, the flat was empty, and I felt my shoulders drop in relief. I dropped my bag by the front door and went and flopped on the settee in the living room, relishing the peace and quiet.

Something had changed lately. I'd always liked living with the girls, but I was starting to feel like I'd outgrown them, that it was time for me to move on. I'd been thinking about it more and more, and what had previously been a fantasy, nothing but wishful thinking, was now becoming something else. I'd always enjoyed looking in the windows of estate agents, sometimes even going in and taking some information and spending the night working out what I'd do with the space, dreaming of how much better my life would be in one of those houses. But it had been a fantasy and that was it. I couldn't afford the kind of places I was looking at, and even if I did think more realistically, two bedrooms instead of three or four, a small garden instead of large, even if I did choose something modest and in need of work, I knew it was unlikely anyone would give me a mortgage because I was on my own. Deposits were so much these days that hardly anyone I knew stood a chance of buying whether they were a couple or not. It wasn't fair, but that was how life was.

But recently, something had shifted in my thinking. I was tired of living in one room, tired of being a loser. It was all right for Sasha and Kimberley, they were younger than me, it wasn't so weird for them to still be sharing. But I was in my thirties. I needed to do something – be pro-active. And a few months back, I thought I'd found a way to get my own place, but it had fallen through, as these things inevitably do, so I was back to square one, thinking it was never going to happen.

Maybe it had something to do with Jacob, maybe seeing him and remembering how people used to treat him made me realise that I had to stand up for myself and make something happen. I always remembered listening in to Mum and Joan talking after Dad had left, and Mum always said the same thing – you've got to look out for yourself because no one else will. It always stuck with me, so once I'd made the decision, I knew I was going to get my own place, whatever it took.

I heard the key in the door and Sasha's voice bellowing down the hall. I sat up to say hi and realised she was on the phone. She waved but continued her conversation.

I sat for a few minutes, listening to Sasha's side of the conversation, but she was giving me a headache, so I got up and went to my room. After a while, I heard the front door as Kimberley came in, and thirty seconds later, the TV was on. After listening to a game show compete with Sasha's giggles for a while, I stood up and grabbed my bag. I wanted to come home to quiet or at least to civilised conversation, not this. But if I had to stay, I was going to need some paracetamol.

'I'm going out,' I said as I passed the living room.

'If you're going to the shops, can you get some more milk. Ta,' Sasha shouted.

I was going to say okay, but something stopped me, and I turned back to the living room, wondering if that was the only reason they liked having me there, that I was the responsible one, the one who worked hard, who'd mother them. Sasha looked over her shoulder at me. 'I'll pay you later,' she said.

'I'm not going to the shops,' I said.

'Oh. Where're you going?' Sasha asked.

'To meet someone. Jacob.'

Sasha and Kimberley exchanged glances, and a smile spread across Kimberley's face. 'Who's Jacob?'

'Is there something you're not telling us,' Sasha said, sitting up straight. 'Have you got a boyfriend?'

'Yes,' I said.

I don't know why I said it, what on earth possessed me, but something in me snapped. I didn't want Sasha thinking I was a threat to her, to the endless parade of unreciprocated crushes she brought home. And maybe there was a part of me that just resented running errands for her. But why tell them that? I could've said anything, anything else at all. I could've just said no, told her to go to the shop herself. But I didn't.

Sasha and Kimberley looked at each other before they looked at me. 'Since when?' Sasha asked.

'Since a few weeks ago,' I said, and wondered why I was still talking.

'What's he like? Have you got a picture?' Sasha asked.

'No,' I said. 'And I have to go. I'm going to be late.' I walked out and slammed the door behind me. Why didn't I just say I was meeting a friend? Why was I even lying to them at all? They were my friends.

I ran down to the main road, out of view, in case they were looking out the window hoping to catch a glimpse of Jacob. I had no idea what I was going to do now. I couldn't go straight home after getting some paracetamol, not without looking like an idiot.

I looked up and down the street and headed right, towards the library. I could go and sit there for a few hours, knowing it was the last place the girls would ever come to.

Inside, there was a book group meeting, and a bunch of old ladies were arguing the merits of *Olive Kitteridge*. I worked my way through to the back of the library where they kept the newspapers. There was an old man sitting at the table, several papers spread out in front of him, but he appeared to be asleep.

I took a seat opposite him and found a copy of the local paper. I wasn't really interested and couldn't focus on the words. I turned the page without knowing what I'd just looked at, and the old man woke up with a start. He glared at me and got up and left, leaving behind the property supplement. I reached over and took it and started looking through, staring intently at houses I could never afford, and some I would never want to.

After half an hour, I closed the newspaper and my eyes. I thought about my dad and how after he left, me and Mum had to move to that crappy little flat on the edge of town. I thought about how hard Mum worked and how long it'd taken her to get something better and how, after all of that, there were now strangers talking about long term plans and selling the house to pay for full time care.

I wiped a tear that had escaped and hoped that none of the book group ladies were watching me. I pulled all the papers the old man had been hoarding towards me and flicked through, searching for the jobs pages. I knew there had to be something out there. I checked every last advert, but there was nothing. Anything that looked good, required experience I didn't have. There were plenty of intern positions, basically slave labour, but even they were out of reach to me. They either wanted kids or someone with a degree in the right subject. Mine was always the wrong subject.

I shoved the papers back across the table, and a few pages fluttered to the floor. One of the librarians passed at that moment and tutted at me, bending down to retrieve the stray pages and tidying the table, glaring at me all the while, as if I was solely responsible for all the mess in the whole place. I got up and moved to a chair in the stacks, sitting amongst the crime novels. I picked one at random and flicked through until the lights dimmed a couple of times, announcing it was almost closing time.

As soon as I got outside and the fresh air hit me, I realised how stuffy it'd been in the library, and the cool air helped me to think clearly. I didn't need to go home and confess to the girls I'd lied about Jacob. I *did* have somewhere to go.

I walked quickly to the road, trying to recall what time the buses went. I was in luck, and one was pulling in just as I got to the stop. I sat down at the back of the bus and finally felt like I had purpose. I knew what to do, where to go.

Chapter 34

I knocked on Jacob's door and felt butterflies in my stomach. All of a sudden, I doubted my being there and wanted to run away. It was a stupid idea. Sitting on the bus or in a cafe and chatting was one thing. Turning up at his door because I didn't want to go home was another altogether. I turned to walk away, but the door opened, and Jacob stood there apparently not recognising me.

'Hi, Jacob,' I said, and it dawned on him who I was, but he seemed, probably quite rightly, confused as to why I was there. He frowned at me and came out, pulling the door behind him so there was only a little gap. I couldn't see inside, but I could hear voices, and at first, I thought he had people round, and I was about to make a complete idiot of myself, but then I realised it was the TV.

'Hiya, Polly,' he said, and blinked slowly, pushing his glasses up.

'Sorry for just turning up,' I said. 'I was just...' I didn't know what to say, what story to make up. I could hardly tell him the truth.

'Are you all right?' he asked.

I looked at the ground and nudged a piece of glass with my foot. 'I'm okay,' I said, and looked back at him.

Jacob looked behind himself at the front door before turning back to me. 'Did you want to come in?' he asked, and I nodded. 'It's a bit of a mess,' he said.

'That's all right. So is mine,' I said, which was a lie.

Jacob opened the door and led the way. I followed him through, and he muted the TV. The curtains were closed, and the only light was a dim lamp in the corner. Jacob looked embarrassed, and his eyes darted around the room, possibly looking for things he'd want to hide. I thought about asking to use the bathroom so he could do a quick tidy but guessed it would be just as bad in there.

'I can go if you're busy,' I said, and regretted it because it sounded sarcastic.

'No, it's all right,' he said. 'Here.' He moved some empty crisp packets from the settee and indicated I should sit. 'Do you want a drink?'

'Tea would be nice,' I said, and he nodded and left me alone in the room.

I looked around at the place as my eyes adjusted. There were piles of papers and magazines stacked sloppily around the edges of the room, and dozens of small cardboard boxes lined the top of a sideboard. I looked over my shoulder before stepping closer, realising the boxes were model trains. I flicked through the magazines at the top of one of the piles – *Model Rail, Collector's Gazette, Model Railroader*. I shook my head. I'd forgotten Jacob was a train enthusiast. I had a sudden memory of him doing a presentation at primary school, talking passionately about his trains as the rest of the class sat there half bored, half stunned. No one had ever heard Jacob talk so much. But after Lee Palmer called him Thomas the Wank Engine and the whole class laughed, he never spoke about trains, or much else, again.

A few minutes later, Jacob returned with a mug of tea, and he put it on the floor beside the settee, and I took a seat. He sat at the other end of the settee, as far away as he could get without sitting on the arm, and he nodded to the TV. 'Have you seen this?' he asked, and I looked at the screen and tried to work out what it was. I shook my head anyway, and Jacob turned the sound back on. I wasn't sure what the film was, but every now and then, Jacob started laughing, even though I couldn't work out what was funny. I wondered if I was missing something. Finally, I looked over to him, and he looked so happy I couldn't help but laugh too.

When it was finished, Jacob looked uncomfortable, as if he was unsure what to do now the distraction of the film was over.

'Do you want to watch the second one?' he asked. 'I think I've got the DVD.'

I noticed his eyes drift to his trains and wondered if he wanted me to go. But then, he was the one who suggested another film. I glanced at the clock. It was still only just gone nine, and I wasn't ready to go home. 'Sure,' I said.

Jacob smiled and put another disc in. 'I could make you something to eat, if you like?' he said. My first instinct was to say no, but I realised I hadn't eaten since lunch time and how bad could it be anyway? Jacob fed himself all the time, presumably, and he wasn't dead yet.

'Okay,' I said. 'That'd be nice.'

'Okay,' he said, and turned and went to the kitchen. I was going to follow, offer a hand, but decided it might be better not to see the kitchen. Instead, I stayed in the living room and looked around some more while I waited. The room was cluttered, and it appeared it hadn't been decorated in a decade or more. But it was nicely proportioned and south facing, and if it were painted a lighter colour – like antique white – it would look great. I moved to the window and ran my hand along the heavy curtains, thinking if it was my place, I'd throw them away and get some nice warm oak wood blinds.

Half an hour later, Jacob came back in with a pizza. It was obviously one from the freezer, and I wondered why he'd stayed out in the kitchen while it cooked, if he was just nervous, or if he wanted me to think he'd made it himself. 'Thanks,' I said. 'It looks lovely.'

We sat in silence again, watching the film and eating the pizza, and this time, I found myself laughing as much as he did. By the time it was over, I felt relaxed, happier than I had in a long time, and as I got my bag and made my way to the door, I thought that maybe this hadn't been such a bad idea at all.

Chapter 35

I was spending more and more time with Jacob, going to his house almost every evening after work. When I did go home, Sasha and Kimberley would ask me more questions about my mystery man, but I refused to answer and played along as if it was all a big game.

But the thing was, I kind of enjoyed Jacob's company. It was easy just sitting there night after night, watching something mindless with someone who didn't judge me. The time I spent with him, at his place, was the happiest I'd been for a long time, as surprising as it seemed. Maybe it was just being somewhere new or getting out of the flat that was starting to suffocate me. Me and the girls had been living on top of each other for too long, it was nice to have some space. Or maybe it was the feeling of purpose I had at Jacob's. I started to think maybe Jacob could offer more than just somewhere to go when I wanted to hide. Besides, Jacob needed the company as much, if not more, than I did.

I'd offered to cook, an actual home cooked meal for a change, instead of something from the freezer, the night I planned to stay at Jacob's for the first time. I thought it might seem odd to Sasha and Kimberley that I never spent the night with my boyfriend, so I figured a sleepover would get them off my back. I was pretty sure Jacob wanted me to stay, there'd been signals for a while, even if he never said anything outright. And while I'd been there the last few times, I'd tidied up a bit here and there, cleaned the bathroom while Jacob went to the shops for wine because I'd refused to drink his cheap lager, and, while he showed me the elaborate toy railway he had set up in his bedroom, I accidentally dropped orange juice on the bed so I had an excuse to change the sheets.

That night, as we sat at the kitchen table, Jacob told me about the meals his mum used to make for him, that her Sunday dinners were the best thing in the world. 'I miss her,' he said, and then shovelled a roast potato into his mouth. I leaned across the table and put my hand on his. 'This is the first proper dinner I've had since she's gone.'

'I remember your mum,' I said. 'She was really nice to me when I came to your party. Do you remember that?'

Jacob's face darkened, and I wondered if it'd been a mistake reminding him of that awful day. It couldn't have been a good memory for him. But he smiled slowly and said, 'You were the only one who stayed. I never forgot that.'

I didn't tell him that I only stayed because I was trapped there, waiting for Mum to come and get me, or that I'd hated every minute of it. And I didn't remind him about what'd happened at school afterwards. Instead, I piled more food onto his plate, and he nodded his thanks.

'It's so hard, isn't it?' I said.

'What?'

'Looking after our parents.' I sighed and put down my knife and fork. 'It's awful seeing my mum like that. Sometimes I can't even bear to go and see her.' I looked him in the eye. 'Is that a terrible thing to say?'

'No,' he said but looked down at his plate and forked a carrot.

'Do you get lonely?' I asked, and he shrugged. It was like getting blood out of a stone at times. I wanted to know all about him, about his life, his friends, where he went, who he saw. As far as I could tell, or as far as he'd let on, there was nothing in his life.

'Maybe you need to do something,' I said, and Jacob looked across the table at me.

'What do you mean?'

'I mean, I know you looked after your mum for a while. But she's not here now, so maybe you need to get out and do something. Find a job. Something to take your mind off things.'

Jacob looked down at his plate and pushed some carrots around in the gravy. 'Like what?'

'I don't know,' I said. 'What do you like doing?'

'My trains.'

'There must be something else.'

He shrugged. 'Watching films,' he said.

'Okay. What about the cinema, then? You could see if they have any jobs going there.'

'Maybe,' he mumbled and stuffed some more meat into his mouth.

'What about friends?'

'What about them?'

'You must have some. Do you go out with them at all?'

'Not really,' he said. 'I used to go down the pub a lot, but I don't really see anyone these days. You're the first person I've talked to for ages.'

'You must talk to other people.'

'Not really,' he said. 'Everything's online these days. All my bills and that. Even at the shops, you don't have to see anyone, just go on them machines and you're done. I don't even go to the post office anymore for my giro, it goes straight into my bank.'

'But you must go to the job centre, right. To sign on.'

'Yeah, but they don't talk to you. They just talk *at* you.'

I couldn't tell whether Jacob was sad about all this, or if he was glad of the lack of human contact, that he could just disappear into his own world which revolved around watching film after film or staring at model trains.

'What about your neighbours? Do you see them?'

'Not really. I never talk to them, anyway,' he said.

'Have you thought about moving?' I asked.

'Moving?' he said as if it was the strangest thing on earth. 'Why would I move?'

'I don't know,' I said. 'For a change of scenery.' I put my knife and fork down and took his hand again. 'Maybe we could...'

'We could what?'

I watched him carefully, trying to work out what he was thinking. 'No, it doesn't matter,' I said, and he frowned. I started eating again.

'What were you going to say?' Jacob asked, and I shook my head.

'Nothing. Eat your tea.' We sat in silence until we'd finished eating, and then, I moved the plates, rinsing them, hoping that Jacob would see that was a better idea than leaving them to fester. When I was done, we went through to the living room, and Jacob dug through his DVD collection finding something to watch that night.

'How would you feel about me staying tonight?' I asked while his back was turned. He stopped rummaging and looked at me.

'Here?' he asked.

'Yes,' I said.

'You want to stay here. With me?'

Yes,' I said, and wondered what he meant by *with* me.

Jacob put down the DVDs and came over to me. 'I'd really like that,' he said.

'Me too,' I said, and we stood there in front of each other, neither of us knowing what to do next. I wondered if it was a good idea suggesting I stay over, if he was going to get the wrong idea. I needed to set boundaries. But Jacob was already on the wrong track. He pressed his body into mine, his hand went to the back of my head and pushed my face back into his, his tongue forcing its way into my mouth.

The taste of cigarettes was so overpowering, I almost gagged, but he let me go, and I took a breath of clean air. 'Jacob, I have to go to the bathroom,' I said, and left the room as quickly as I could, slamming the door behind me.

I stared in the mirror and saw how red my face was. How had I let this happen? How had I not considered he might react like that to me saying I wanted to spend the night? Just because Jacob never had a girlfriend at school, it didn't mean he was asexual. He was a grown man. Why wouldn't he think I was coming on to him? I needed to leave.

There was a knock at the door. 'Are you all right, Polly?' he asked.

'I'll be out in a minute.'

I waited until I heard him walk away, and then, I tried to remember where I'd left my bag, if I could get to it easily. I left the bathroom and snuck to the kitchen without him seeing me. I found my phone and took it out, walking back to the living room with it in my hand. I stopped in the doorway.

'I have to go,' I said and he looked confused. 'The hospital rang. It's my mum.'

He stood up and came over to me. 'I can come with you.'

'No,' I said, and started walking to the door, pulling my coat on. 'It's okay. I'll speak to you later.' I pulled the front door open and felt Jacob's hand on my shoulder. 'I'll see you later,' I said again, and he leaned down and kissed me, this time more gently.

I rushed away down the street, and as I got around the corner, out of his sight, I stopped and sat on a wall, gagging at the lingering taste of cigarettes in my mouth. I suddenly hated myself for getting into this, hated Jacob for what he'd done. I hated everyone at that moment and knew that Mum was right, and I had to start looking out for myself. Whatever it took.

Chapter 36

Phil starts picking things up, showing them to Jacob, and then smashing them, tearing them, doing whatever he can to destroy my belongings. I lie there, listening to the destruction, wishing for the millionth time I'd never met Jacob, that I'd never been so stupid to feel sorry for him. Not back at school and certainly not now. He was a monster, and I should've seen it.

I see Phil is by the window with his back to me. Jacob is staring at his friend. I try to work out how long it would take for me to get to the door, if I could stand up and make a run for it before they got to me. But I'm hurt. I can barely feel my legs, my ribs are sore, maybe even broken, my face is throbbing and my vision blurred. How likely is it I can even get up without them noticing, never mind make it out of the room, down the hall and to the door, which I try to remember if I locked when I came in.

I still try though, thinking it can't get any worse. I get to my knees and start crawling to the door. I get barely six inches before Phil turns and sees me.

'No you fucking don't,' he says, and strides over, his heel of his boot slamming into my back, forcing me to the floor again. He bends over and picks me up as if I'm a rag doll and throws me onto the settee.

I start laughing. I'm hysterical now. I can't believe this is happening to me, that I'm trapped in my own home with these men intent in hurting me, and yet I know I'm not dreaming because the pain is too real, the fear is too strong.

'Shut up,' Phil shouts at me, but I keep laughing and it seems to freak him out. He turns to Jacob, who comes over and looks at me like I'm some exotic animal in a zoo. He's unsure what to make of me.

'Stop it, or I'll really hurt you,' Phil says, and I laugh some more.

'You've already really hurt me. Maybe you should just kill me instead,' I say, and he looks at Jacob again. He's starting to look worried, and I think maybe this is it. Maybe they'll stop if I keep going. I laugh louder, forcing it out. Screaming it at the top of my lungs.

'Shut up!' Phil shouts again and then storms out of the room, leaving me with Jacob. I wonder if I could overpower him now he's alone, but I know I can't. I've felt his strength before. I can't overpower him, but maybe I can force him to leave. I stand up, legs unsteady, and get in his face. He steps back at first, looking out of the room, hoping Phil is coming back to sort his problems for him.

'What's the matter?' I say, forcing him into a corner. 'Can't handle me on your own?'

I realise I'm right. Jacob doesn't know what to do. I don't need to be physically stronger than him I can beat him with my words, with my brain.

'You need your little friend to help sort me out because you're scared of a woman?' I say, and shove his chest.

And then, he grabs the tops of my arms, squeezing until it hurts. 'Stop it,' he says.

'Make me,' I say, and he does.

He lets go of my arms and aims his fist towards the centre of my face.

***

I wake and find myself lying on the floor in the living room. My head aches, my jaw feels funny. My tongue explores my mouth and finds a gap where a tooth used to be.

'Look who's awake,' Phil says, and crouches in front of me. I reach up to my face. It feels swollen, tacky with drying blood. 'I don't know what you said to him,' Phil says with a smile, 'but he really went to town on your face.'

I turn my head slightly, seeing myself in the reflection of the TV cabinet. The glass distorts my image, but I can see the damage anyway. I can see what Jacob has done to me. I look to my right and see Jacob sitting on the settee, head in his hands, his knee bouncing up and down.

'You should know better than to get on the wrong side of Jacob,' Phil says, and looks at his friend with pride.

'Just let me go,' I say. 'You've got what you wanted.'

'Have we?'

'Just let me go,' I say. 'You'll never see me again.'

Phil sits back and spreads his arms wide, taking in the room. 'You're damn right. You're out of here. This is gonna be my home, ain't that right, Jacob? It's gonna be me and you. Just like the old days.'

Jacob looks at his feet, and I wonder if that was the deal – come and help me terrorize my ex and you can have a roof over your head, rent free – or if Phil is just being presumptuous. He looks to Jacob again. 'So, what do you say, mate? You want to keep her a bit longer, or do you think she's got the picture?'

I look at Jacob, too, and he finally looks up at us, and I think he looks guilty for what he's done, that he knows he's gone too far. 'Please, Jacob,' I say, and he stares at me, at the mess he's made of me. 'Please. Why are you doing this?'

He jumps off the settee and is in front of me before I know it. I try to move back, but I'm against the wall. 'Because this is my house, Polly!' Jacob says. 'You stole it from me!'

Chapter 37

Jacob seemed surprised to see me when I showed up at his place the next night. I'd been ignoring his calls, unsure what to do next. I'd been so sure the night before that I should go ahead with it, that moving in with him was the right thing to do, but every time I thought about him, every time I pictured his hands on me, I felt sick, a creeping dread wrapped around me like poison ivy.

But by the time I'd finished work, I knew I had to do it, I had to go and see him and make things right. It wasn't ideal, it wasn't the way I'd always dreamed of, but desperate times and all that. I had a choice between going home and staying a renter forever or going to Jacob's and putting up with him. Jacob might've felt like the worse option at that point, but he was also a way out, a stepping stone to something better. The only way to make things better.

I bought a couple of bottles of wine on the way over and then stopped at the pizza shop closest to his place. I couldn't bear another one of his own inventions, usually something involving tinned spaghetti on top of something else. I had to draw a line somewhere.

I knocked, shifting the pizza box to the same arm as the plastic bag with the wine. The plastic dug into my hand, the heat from the pizza started to burn my wrist. Finally, Jacob answered and picked up the pizza box, leaving the wine for me to bring inside. I followed him to the living room, trying not to step on the trains which were spread out across the floor. He stood there, holding the pizza box against his belly. 'I didn't think you'd come,' he said, and I wondered if he realised he'd done something wrong the night before. 'Is your mum okay?'

'She's fine,' I said.

'You didn't answer your phone today. I thought maybe something had happened to her.'

He put the pizza down and came over, putting his arms around me. His clothes smelt musty, as if they hadn't been washed in a long time, and my stomach turned, though I doubted it was all down to the smell. I wondered again whether it was all worth it in the end.

I backed out of his embrace and picked up the pizza box. 'I'll get some plates,' I said, and carried it out to the kitchen. Jacob had thought it was odd that I wanted to eat takeaway pizza from plates the first time I suggested it. But he'd come around to my way of thinking soon enough. He was malleable in all sorts of ways.

We sat and watched a film as we ate, even though Jacob had obviously seen it a hundred times and I didn't care. When we were done, I took the plates and started the washing up.

'You don't need to do that,' Jacob said, but I ignored him and continued. If I did the dishes as soon as we finished every meal, perhaps he'd respond like Pavlov's dog and start doing it himself.

When I'd finished with the dishes, I took another glass of wine through to the living room, and Jacob searched for another DVD. As he did, I looked around, thinking again of what I would change, the few things I might keep the same if I lived there. 'What about this one?' he asked, and I nodded without taking any notice of what it was. They were all the same to me.

He came over and sat closer to me than he normally did. I made sure I never put down the wine glass, but I could tell he was wanting to move in closer, was wanting to pick up where he'd left off the night before.

About halfway through the film, I realised he'd edged right up to me, his arm had gone around my shoulder, inch by inch, as if we were teenagers on our first date. It almost made me laugh. My wine glass was empty now, so I had no reason to keep hold of it, but I clung on anyway. I could feel the warmth from Jacob's body, I could hear his breath close to my ear. I didn't turn to him or respond in any way. My eyes were fixed on the TV.

Jacob leaned in closer, one hand resting on my shoulder. He tried to kiss me, but I refused to turn my face to him, thinking he'd get the hint. But subtlety wasn't Jacob's strong point and he kept on trying.

Finally, I gave in and turned. His lips brushed mine and I thought about getting up and refilling my glass but instead I decided I needed to take charge of the situation before it got out of hand. 'Jacob,' I said, and pulled back as far as I could.

'What's wrong?' he asked.

'It's just…' I wriggled free of his arms and put the glass on the table. 'It's just…' I turned and faced him and looked him up and down. 'You smell.'

He frowned at me and said, 'I smell? Of what?' He lifted his T-shirt to his face and inhaled. 'Fags?' he asked.

'No,' I said. 'I think it's your clothes. When did you last wash them?'

He shrugged. 'I don't know.'

'Well, maybe it's time they went in for a wash,' I said.

He looked a little hurt but nodded. 'I'll do it tomorrow,' he said, and reached for my hand.

'Maybe you could do it now. Put a wash on and then have a shower,' I said, wondering if he'd understand the implication. Although that was all it was. I had no intention of following through.

Jacob looked behind him, as if he could see through the wall to the kitchen, to the washing machine. But he didn't move. I started wondering if he even knew how to use it.

'Do you want me to do it?' I asked, and he looked at his feet, embarrassed. 'I don't mind,' I said.

'Okay,' he said and started to strip. 'My mum used to do my washing.' I nodded and wondered how long it'd been since he'd had anything cleaned. He was down to his boxers but seemed reluctant to take them off in front of me, suddenly shy. I gathered up the pile of clothes and smiled.

'Go and get in the shower,' I said. 'Leave your pants outside the door, and I'll put the washer on.'

I waited until I heard the bathroom door close and then went to his bedroom and dug around, finding dirty clothes thrown all over the place. I picked up as much as I could, knowing it'd take a few washes to get it all done.

I could hear the shower running and guessed that Jacob probably didn't take long showers, a quick rinse would be enough. I knew I should get the washing in quickly so I could go back to the living room. But the temptation was too much. In all the times I'd been to his place, I'd never had the chance to really snoop around.

I opened a door and found the bedroom of an elderly lady, perfectly preserved, not a thing seemed out of place. I wondered if she'd died there. I couldn't remember Jacob telling me exactly what'd happened, only that she'd been ill for a while. I could smell a hint of perfume, preserved, thanks to closed windows and doors and a lack of cleaning. It was the same perfume she'd worn all those years ago.

The water stopped running, and I took the washing and ran down the stairs, stuffing it into the machine, scrambling around for washing powder. Once it was in, I lay down on the settee and closed my eyes, listening to Jacob move about upstairs. I wondered if he'd actually have anything clean to put back on, but for now I didn't care. He wasn't going to touch me again tonight. Instead, I just lay there thinking about the house I was in, the house I'd visited all those years ago and coveted with a vicious envy. I'd thought back then that people like Jacob and his mum didn't deserve such a place, and maybe it'd been wrong, maybe I'd been too judgemental. But things were different now. His mum was gone, and Jacob couldn't take care of himself. So, really, it was for his benefit as much as mine.

I heard him come into the room. Could tell he was standing over me. 'Polly,' he said softly.

I ignored him, pretended as best I could to be asleep, the same way I used to do when Mum would come in my room when it was time for something I didn't want to do. Pretend to be asleep and if that didn't work, pretend to be ill.

'Polly,' he said again, this time putting his hand on my shoulder and shaking me. I let out a little moan, a sleepy acknowledgement. He sighed, and I heard him walk away. I opened one eye a crack and saw he was naked. Not shy anymore. I closed my eyes again and lay there, praying he wouldn't keep trying to wake me. I heard his foot fall on the creaky floorboard by the door and knew he was back. *Leave me alone.* And then, he draped a blanket over me. It smelled musty too but more like it had been stuffed in the back of a cupboard too long than unclean.

'Night, night,' he whispered and turned off the light.

I heard him climb the stairs and felt relief wash over me. I knew I might as well stay there, that lying on the settee, unmolested, would be all right. I wondered if I could do it forever, just never go back to the flat again. I didn't want to be there anymore, didn't want to be part of that childish group, couldn't stand the way Sasha looked at me every time some bloke she fancied flirted with me. It was hardly my fault, was it?

I lay there in the dark, thinking of good excuses for not letting him touch me again and how I could reconcile that with getting what I wanted. Because one way or another, I was going to be living in the house.

Chapter 38

The next morning, I left before Jacob got up, leaving him a note apologising for the night before, saying how tired I was what with work and Mum and all that. I said I'd come over again that night if he wanted me to.

When I turned on my phone, I had a couple of messages from Sasha telling me that the rent was due and could I transfer the money as soon as possible as the landlord was giving her grief because he couldn't get hold of me. I put my phone back in my bag and headed out. I'd cancelled my rent payment as soon as I knew I'd be moving in with Jacob. It just seemed easier than trying to get it back later.

I walked to the bus stop thinking I'd have to stop by the flat on the way home from work to get some clean clothes. But going after work would mean seeing the girls, and I didn't want to get into an argument about rent, so I crossed the road to get a bus in the other direction.

As I stood at the bus stop, I called work, telling my boss I had an emergency dentist appointment and would be a little late. I said I could always make up the time later, but I knew I never would. Janet was soft. Too soft to be a manager. People were always taking advantage of her.

***

I crept in to the flat just in case one of the girls was skiving off work, but it was all quiet, the only thing I could hear was the buzzing from the fridge and the annoying drip from the kitchen tap that no one had bothered to fix. I went to my room and found a bag, stuffing in enough clothes, underwear and toiletries for a few days away. I made sure I took some tampons too, just in case. Before I left, I looked around, making sure there was nothing I'd forgotten. I checked the mail from the day before but there was nothing interesting, just a letter to apply for a credit card that I couldn't afford to get.

I checked the fridge and found a bottle of wine chilling. I took it out and put it into my holdall and then rummaged in the cupboards and found a new bottle of ketchup. I hated the stuff but knew Jacob had run out so I slid that in, too, to save me going to the shops later.

***

After work, I got the bus straight to Jacob's. I was starving as I hadn't eaten much all day after someone asked me about the dentist, and I'd had to keep up the charade by remembering to stick to yogurt and cups of tea and rubbing my jaw constantly.

I considered stopping at the pizza shop again, but I was tired of pizza and wanted something different. Instead, I got off and walked to the corner shop, buying everything I'd need to make coq au vin. It cost a fortune, but I knew Jacob was unlikely to have any of the ingredients already. I knocked on the door and he took a while to answer. When he finally let me in, I handed him the bags of shopping and my holdall to keep his hands busy.

We walked through to the kitchen, and I started unpacking the food. Jacob stood watching, fascinated. 'I'm going to make coq au vin,' I said. 'Go and sit down.'

'I can help,' he said.

'No. That's okay.' I leaned over and kissed him on the cheek. He stood a moment longer and then left the kitchen. When I'd finished and there was nothing to do but wait, I poured two glasses of wine and went through to the living room. He was playing with one of his toys and looked engrossed.

'Here,' I said, and he took the glass but looked at it suspiciously. I went back to the kitchen and got my holdall and brought it through.

'What's that?' he asked, the glass of wine abandoned on the table, untouched.

'I just thought I'd bring a few things, some fresh clothes, toiletries. You don't mind, do you? I just thought if I'm going to stay over...'

'I don't mind,' he said.

I gulped half of my wine and nodded to his. 'Don't you like it?'

He picked up his glass and sipped some, his face creasing. 'No, it's nice,' he said, and put it down again. He was a terrible liar.

After we'd eaten, Jacob made another move, draping his arms over my shoulders. I smiled at him and then asked an inane question about the film he'd put on, distracting him for a few minutes. Then, I went and refilled my glass. After that, I excused myself to go to the toilet. I stayed up there a little while, cleaning the toilet and sink as best I could while I waited. He came up and knocked on the door after ten minutes and asked if I was all right.

'I'm okay,' I said. 'I've just got a bit of an upset stomach. I'll be down in a minute.' I heard him go downstairs, and after a few more minutes, I followed him. 'I hope I haven't poisoned us,' I said with a smile but still clutching my guts.

'I'm all right,' he said.

I sat down beside him and held a cushion to my belly, excusing myself a couple more times, spraying air freshener after each visit. 'Maybe I should go,' I said after my third trip to the toilet.

'No,' he said. 'Stay.' Then, he jumped up and grabbed his jacket. 'I'll go and get you something for your belly.'

'You don't need to do that,' I said.

'I don't mind,' he said, and then he was gone, returning ten minutes later with some Imodium.

'Thanks,' I said, and took the packet to the kitchen, taking a couple out of the packet and slipping them into my pocket. 'I might go to bed,' I said as I went back in to Jacob. 'I don't feel so good.'

'Okay,' he said, and turned off the TV.

'You don't have to come,' I said.

'I don't mind.'

As I turned and headed up the stairs, I rolled my eyes. He really couldn't take a hint. So, I went in to the bathroom and brushed my teeth and then took off my trousers but left everything else on and lay down on the bed, clutching a pillow to my guts.

'Poor Polly,' he said, and rubbed my back which, I had to admit, felt nice.

***

I guess I fell asleep quickly, and when I woke I realised it was after eight-thirty and I was going to be late for work.

'Shit,' I said, and jumped out of bed.

'Where are you going?' Jacob asked.

'Work,' I said.

'But you're not well.'

Any other time I would've just called in sick, but I'd already called in the day before, and besides, the other option was to stay there all day with Jacob.

'I don't feel so bad now,' I said, and found some clean clothes in my holdall. I took them into the bathroom and had a wash and got changed. When I was ready, I went back into the bedroom and kissed Jacob on the top of his head. 'I'll see you later,' I said, and rushed out, thinking it'd be tough to keep this up, but it'd be worth it in the end.

Chapter 39

The next few days went past in a blur of excuses and avoidance. *My stomach still hurts, I've got my period, my mum's taken another turn for the worse.* Jacob was patient and didn't force himself on me, but I knew it would only last so long. I'd used the period excuse the night before so figured I could draw it out for a week at least. But while I was on the bus, I realised I was actually due on the week after and wondered if Jacob would believe I had two-week long periods. It was possible, I supposed.

But other than avoiding intimacy, staying with Jacob wasn't so bad. I'd trained him to clean up a bit more, had taught him to use the washing machine. I was helping him as much as myself really. I even convinced him to look at job adverts.

I didn't go home to the flat for three days and then only because I needed more clean clothes. I didn't really want to see the girls, Sasha had been calling non-stop about the bloody rent. But I knew I couldn't slip out of work again so had to face seeing them.

'Hi,' I said from the doorway. They both looked up.

'Where've you been?' Sasha asked. 'I've been trying to get hold of you.'

'I'm fine,' I said. 'I've been at Jacob's.'

A look passed between them. 'The landlord's going mad,' Sasha said.

I rolled my eyes. 'I haven't even been here most of the time,' I said, and went to collect some things. I could hear the girls talking in low voices out in the living room, and I got the feeling they were talking about me. I put down my bag and snuck out into the hall, pressing myself against the wall.

'You tell her,' Kimberley said.

'She's your friend,' Sasha said.

'We can't just ask her to go.'

'She's hardly here, anyway.'

'I know, but...'

'So, we'll just say he's going to stay for a while, on the sofa, if he has to. And he'll chip in with the bills,' Sasha said. 'Which is more than she's doing.'

***

'I hate them,' I said through my tears, wiping my nose with the back of my hand and pouring more tepid wine into my glass. Jacob sat there watching me but didn't speak, just let me rant. 'Anything could've happened to me and they don't even care, all they care about is getting money off me. And they're always talking behind my back. They think I don't know. And I think they've been in my room again. They just take all my things and treat me like shit. I can't stand it anymore. I don't want to be there anymore.'

'So, don't go back,' Jacob said, and I looked up.

'It's not as easy as that, Jacob.'

'It is,' he said.

'I've got a crappy job,' I said. 'I can't afford to move, certainly not somewhere by myself.'

'So, live here,' he said, and I looked up, eyes wide.

'I can't,' I said.

'Why not? You're always over here. There's loads of room. And you wouldn't have to pay rent anymore. I don't pay anything, just bills. Here,' he said, and went out into the hallway, returning with something in his hand.

'A key?' I said, and he nodded.

'Now you can come and go whenever you like. And you can stay forever,' he said, and leaned over and kissed me. I hugged him tight and said thank you over and over. 'You're welcome,' he said and pulled back, brushing my hair from my eyes. And then, he kissed me, his tongue searching around my mouth as if he'd lost something. I wanted to stop him, say, 'I've got my period, remember,' but at that moment, I didn't feel ill at the thought, it even – almost – felt right. Or maybe it just felt necessary to keep up the charade. Either way, I let him continue.

As he ran his hands over my breasts, kneading them rather than caressing, I let my mind wander. Maybe I should've just made it clear from the start that this was a friendship, nothing more. I bet he still would've let me stay. But it was too late for that now. I'd made my bed, and now he was unzipping my jeans.

I let him fuck me, right there on the settee. It didn't last long, thankfully, and wasn't as bad as expected. He looked so pleased when he was done and asked me if I liked it. 'Yes,' I said, and excused myself to the bathroom, scrubbing myself until I felt almost clean.

Jacob was still smiling when I went back down. He looked like the cat who'd got the cream. But I knew it was the first and last time it was going to happen. I had a key now.

Chapter 40

It'd been weeks since I moved into the house, and I didn't think I could take it anymore. I'd barely let Jacob touch me since he invited me to stay, the excuses came thick and fast, more often than not about my mum who always gave me an out if I needed some time alone. I was suddenly finding myself at Mum's bedside more than ever, especially as she was now in the home and the visiting hours were less strict.

It seemed like everything concerning Mum was now out of my hands. The powers that be made the decisions, and what they decided was that Mum needed full-time care, care that I couldn't provide. Suddenly, everything that'd happened before her stroke was considered important; her state of mind, the fact I thought I was unable to provide care. So they decided on a place and informed me that to pay for such good care, the house would have to be sold, and there was nothing I could do about it. I often wondered if Mum was aware of what was happening, even if she couldn't communicate much of anything, and if she blamed me for letting them do it to her.

But there was nothing I could do now. Besides, now, I had bigger problems.

Before I'd moved in things were fine, I could cope with sitting there night after night watching stupid films and drinking too much. And I'd made some changes too. I'd cleaned the fridge, throwing away all the disgusting things that'd been festering there for God knows how long. I bought proper food, things humans eat. I scrubbed everywhere from top to bottom, let air in, made it habitable. I was an unpaid cleaner, really. I also convinced Jacob it would be a good idea to start sorting through his mum's things that were cluttering the place up. I had plans for that room.

I still hadn't managed to get Jacob off his arse and into a job, though, and maybe that was what bothered me the most; that he was there all the time, that he was so needy, so dependent on me. In a lot of ways, I'd become his surrogate mother and though that was preferable to the other option, it was driving me slowly mad.

'Why are you wearing the same clothes as yesterday?' became a frequent question, along with, 'Can you please tidy up a bit while I'm at work,' and 'Can we do it tomorrow, I have a headache?'

Even though we weren't having sex, it was on my mind all the time. I could tell Jacob wanted to, and again, I wondered if he'd ever had a girlfriend before or if this was all new to him. He'd sit staring at me while I was trying to watch TV or he'd come in the bathroom while I was brushing my teeth. Where anyone normal would come up and put their arms around me, press their face to my neck, their body to mine, Jacob would just stand there and watch, and when I finally turned around, he would reach for my breasts like a baby needing milk. I'd try to smile and walk away, leaving him to brush his teeth – something else I'd had to train him to do every day – getting into bed and praying for sleep.

He often spent the first few minutes after we turned off the light edging closer and closer to me, maybe hoping I wouldn't notice if he was stealthy, but eventually, he'd be up against me, rubbing himself, and I'd lie there, ignoring him, hoping he'd quickly finish and go to sleep.

Some nights made me so uncomfortable that after work the following day, I'd be reluctant to go home, wandering around trying to kill time. I hadn't been back to the flat for a while, and when I did, my visits were fleeting. I never told the girls I'd overheard their conversation, that I knew they were plotting against me. If I mentioned it, they'd overreact and blame me for eavesdropping. I never saw the man they'd been talking about getting in to replace me, but I noticed traces of him; a pair of trainers here, an extra mug on the drainer there. I wondered if they'd let him sleep in my bed while I wasn't there, but I couldn't find any proof, so I decided not to mention anything. Besides, I didn't want to burn my bridges with the girls in case things didn't work out with Jacob. I hadn't told them I was planning to go for good, but I figured if things went to plan they'd realise sooner or later.

I visited Mum a lot, of course, but visiting hours only lasted so long, and it was hard work sitting there all night, talking to myself for hours. Sometimes, I'd take a book with me and just sit in the foyer outside, killing time before I could face another visit.

Once, I even got the bus home, getting off a stop early and sat in the bus shelter for almost two hours, reading a book by the dim neon of the streetlight. In the end, I got tired of people asking if I wanted this bus or that bus, so started ignoring them, and finally, it got past eleven, and there were no more buses anymore, but I still sat there, my resentment for Jacob simmering.

When I finally walked home, I could see the light on in the living room through a crack in the curtain and decided to walk around the block a few times instead of going inside. After a few goes round, I knew it was useless and that Jacob would never go to bed without me, that I was stuck with him. I unlocked the door and went inside, going straight to the kitchen rather than saying hello. I resented the fact he made me lurk outside my own home because I was afraid to go inside, afraid of what he would want from me.

'I was worried,' he said.

I'd heard him come into the room behind me, but I kept my back to him, drinking water and refilling the glass from the tap before finally looking at him.

'Why?' I asked.

'It's almost midnight. Where've you been?'

'I'm a grown up, Jacob. I don't need to tell you every little thing.'

'But–'

'But what?' I said, itching for a fight. 'It can't be like this if we're going to keep living together.'

'Like what?'

'You checking up on me all the time, wanting to know every last thing. I can't stand it, you're suffocating me,' I said.

'I was just asking–'

'Exactly. Always asking, always needing to know. It's too much, Jacob,' I said. 'I have a life outside of these walls, you know. I have my mum, I have work. I have friends. It's not all about you.'

Jacob looked hurt, but I didn't care. I was being smothered by him, but he was too stupid to see it.

'Have you got another boyfriend?' he asked, and I wanted to say, '*Another?*' but instead, I slammed the glass down on the worktop.

'How could you ask me that?'

He shrugged. 'You seem different,' he said.

'I'm just tired,' I said. 'Tired of work, tired of seeing Mum like that. And you don't make things easier for me. I mean, look at the state of this place again. You promised you'd clean up. What do you even do all day, apart from play with those bloody trains? I have so much on my plate, and you do nothing. You have no responsibilities, nothing to do, no one to see. You're driving me insane.' I stormed past him and ran up the stairs to the bathroom, locking the door behind me.

'Polly,' he said as he tapped on the door. 'I'm sorry. I'll do better. I will.'

I didn't speak for a while, but when I finally came out, he was sitting at the top of the stairs, scratching at his arm like he did when he was nervous.

'I'm tired,' I said. 'I just want to go to bed.'

'All right,' he said and stood up. I put my hand out and stopped him as he came towards me.

'I think maybe you should sleep in the other room tonight.'

Jacob looked puzzled and then over his shoulder at his mum's bedroom. 'In there?'

I nodded. 'Just for tonight.' I put my hand on his cheek to let him know it was all right and then went into the bedroom and closed the door. I got into bed and spread my legs out, relishing the space, the freedom of being alone. But I could smell him on the sheets, so I got up again and changed the bedding before getting back in and sleeping better than I had in a long time.

***

When I got up the next day, Jacob was asleep on the settee, the TV still playing in the corner. I left him where he was and made some breakfast, eating it in the kitchen, guessing he wouldn't wake up if I was quiet. But I guessed wrong. He came into the kitchen, rubbing his eyes before scratching his balls. 'What time is it?' he asked, and I put the rest of my toast in the bin and started gathering my things.

'Time to go to work,' I said. 'For some of us, anyway.'

Jacob didn't respond to this, it was obviously too subtle. I pulled my coat on and made sure I had my keys. He just stood watching, and for a moment he looked like a child, that poor, bullied kid from school.

'You slept on the settee,' I said. 'Were you watching something on TV?'

'No,' he said. 'I just can't sleep in Mum's room.'

'Why not?' He looked away, his eyes darting about, his nose twitching. 'She wouldn't let you?'

He shook his head. 'She died in there.'

I walked over to him and touched his face, hugged him tightly. 'I'm sorry,' I said. He just shrugged again, and I picked up my bag that'd slipped down my arm. 'I'd better get going,' I said, and he nodded and watched me leave, waving from the door like my gran used to do, just kept on waving until she couldn't see me anymore.

As I sat on the bus, I started wondering if things had got out of hand, if it was time to put a stop to it. I couldn't pretend any more, I couldn't fake being Jacob's girlfriend. I couldn't bear him touching me, couldn't take his company for longer than a few minutes at a time. How was this ever going to work?

I thought about leaving, just walking away and not going back. There was nothing there that I couldn't live without, really, most of my things were still at the flat. I knew the girls would welcome me back as soon as this misunderstanding with the rent was sorted. They needed me there. Was this new guy going to cook for them? Give them advice? Provide them with tampons because they'd forgotten to buy them again? I doubted it.

But the flat. The girls. I'd be going backwards. I'd worked so hard to get where I was, to move on and make life better for myself.

I got off the bus and walked the short distance to work. I knew I had to make a choice. I really didn't want to go back to the flat. My only option was going to Jacob's. But I was starting to hate him, and we were making each other miserable. It might've been a big house, but there wasn't enough room for the two of us. One of us had to go.

And as I got to the office and climbed the stairs, I realised it wasn't going to be me.

Chapter 41

All day at work, my mind was somewhere else, trying to think of the best way to get what I wanted, the things I could do to drive Jacob away. I wondered how I could manipulate him, how easy it would be. I thought of a few ways to push him out but maybe they would just make him hate me, that he'd just throw me out instead of making him want to leave. I needed to be more imaginative.

At lunch, I started making a list and figured it would take some time. I didn't know if I could wait that long, but I was going to have to suck it up. You don't get anything for free or without working for it. And this was no different. It would be hard, but it would be worth it.

***

I started things that night. I went home straight from work, and Jacob was there at the door waiting, annoying me already. He was grinning, desperate for me to go inside. And when I went in, I knew he was going to make this hard for me.

The living room was spotless, no empty cans or wrappers were littering the place, the carpet was hoovered, even the air smelled fresh. Jacob took my hand and led me to the kitchen. There were no dishes piled up, the bin was empty. 'And look,' he said, and opened the fridge. 'You like these, right?' He'd bought some M&S meals, all my favourites.

'How did you afford these?' I asked.

'Got my dole today,' he said. 'And I got you these too.' He opened the back door and pulled a bouquet of flowers from the bucket he'd been keeping them in. 'I'm sorry, Polly,' he said, and kissed my cheek.

I took the flowers and started to cry. *Fucking arsehole*. It was like he knew, like he was playing his own game, trying to win for himself.

'What's the matter?' he asked.

'Nothing,' I said. I gave the flowers back to him and ran up the stairs, shutting myself in the bathroom again. And this time, he didn't even come up and pester me. He knew what he was doing, and it wasn't going to work. I was still going to do this, I couldn't stop now.

I had to get him out.

Chapter 42

That night, I wriggled away from him as he tried to cuddle me. This wasn't so out of the ordinary, so was unlikely to mean anything to Jacob. But the next day, over dinner, I stared at my plate, making hardly any eye contact with him at all, making non-committal noises as he mumbled on about trains. Then, I left him on the settee halfway through a film he was desperate to watch while I went to bed. I pretended to be asleep by the time he joined me.

The next day, I crept out of bed, dressing quietly in the bathroom so as not to wake him and left before he got up. I didn't answer his texts all day and didn't bring home the bottle of milk he'd asked me to get.

This went on for a few days but seemed to have little effect, and again I realised that I was being too subtle for Jacob. Whereas any normal person would see something was wrong, Jacob just carried on, oblivious.

So, the next day, I stepped it up a little and found the collection of tokens he'd been carefully cutting from packets of cereal to claim a free set of bowls. I scooped them up and threw them in the bin and then took the bin bag and put it outside ready for the bin men to pick up later that morning. Jacob didn't notice immediately, it was a couple of days later when he had another token to add to the pile that he realised his collection was gone.

'Where're my tokens?' he asked, looking around the kitchen as if tokens could get up and walk. I shrugged and drank my tea, watching him lift things to check beneath and check the mug they'd been stored in over and over again. 'They were in here. Loads of them,' he said, and finally, I gave in.

'Oh, those things. I didn't realise you were keeping them. I put them in the bin when I tidied up.' He started rifling through the bin, and I waited a moment before continuing. 'I've emptied it since then. They'll be long gone.' I stood up and rinsed my mug. 'Sorry,' I said, and left him to it. But two minutes later, he'd followed me upstairs where I was sorting out more of his mother's things when he came in and apologised to me.

'I shouldn't have got upset with you,' he said. 'You didn't know.'

He kissed me, and I wanted to slap him. First of all, he hadn't even got upset and second of all, I *did* know and he knew it. He'd told me over and over and over about those stupid bloody tokens. I needed to step it up some more.

Late in the afternoon, after I'd spent all day sorting through the old woman's things and listened to Jacob playing with his toys, I dragged a couple of bin bags full of stuff down the stairs and left them by the door. I poked my head around and said to Jacob, 'I'm just going to the shops.'

'Okay,' he said, barely looking up.

I took the bags, heaving them down the road. Thankfully, there was a charity shop around the corner. It was supporting some church or other, but I didn't care; I just needed to get rid of the junk quickly. I left the bags with an ungrateful woman and then browsed for a while before going to the corner shop and then finally did a few laps around the playing fields. I knew Jacob wouldn't have moved from the settee and even if he had, it was unlikely he'd be looking out the window, wondering why I was wandering around as if I were homeless.

When I got back, Jacob *had* moved from the settee, and I could hear him moving around upstairs. I left him to it and wondered if he'd noticed. I let him come to me.

'What've you done?' he said.

I frowned, not understanding. 'What're you talking about?' I'd started making tea and held up his favourite mug, waving it in his direction. He ignored the implied question. He was angry. Finally.

'Mum's stuff,' he said.

'What about it?' I continued making the tea, pottering about as if nothing was wrong.

'What've you done with it?'

'I've just taken it to the charity shop, like you told me to.'

It was Jacob's turn to look confused. 'I never said that.'

'Yes, you did,' I said, and put the kettle down, turning to him now the conversation was heating up. 'When we started cleaning up the other day, I asked if there was anything you wanted to keep. You took a few of the photos and a couple of the paintings and said the rest could go.'

'I didn't.'

'Jacob, you did.'

'I would never say that.'

'Well, I'm sorry, but you did,' I said, and turned back to my tea, stirring it up.

'That's my mum's stuff,' he said, raising his voice, and when I didn't reply or look at him, he came over and grabbed my arm, spinning me around to face him. 'I wouldn't say that, it's all I've got left.'

I sighed and put my hand on his cheek. 'I'm sorry, Jacob. I wouldn't have taken it if I'd known, but you *did* tell me to get rid of it.'

'I *didn't*,' he said, his voice getting louder and louder.

'Look, maybe you can get it back. If we explain to them what happened,' I said, and Jacob let go of me and walked out, pulling his coat on. 'It'll probably be closed now,' I said, knowing full well it was.

'I'm going to have a look,' he said. 'Which shop?'

'The one on the High Street. The cancer shop,' I said, just before he walked out, slamming the door shut.

The house was quiet with him gone. I sat at the table and drank my tea, enjoying my time alone, and then I got up and wandered through the house, imagining what it would be like to live there alone, the things I could do with it, the person I could be.

I lay back on the bed feeling anxious to get to the point I could call it my own place, where Jacob was no longer a problem. I was pleased with how today had gone, not only had I got to Jacob, but I'd also got rid of some of the junk that'd been clogging up my space. I just needed to keep going, and he'd be gone in no time. That was the secret, getting into his head.

***

He came back forty minutes later, slamming the door behind him again. I left him to stew for a while before going down. 'Any luck?' I asked, and he shook his head.

'It was shut.'

I sat beside him and rubbed his back. 'I'm sorry,' I said. 'Maybe tomorrow.'

'Tomorrow's Sunday.'

'Right,' I said. 'I forgot.'

'I can't believe you threw my mum's things away.'

'I've said I'm sorry. But you did tell me to.'

'No, I didn't,' he said, and jumped up.

'You did, Jacob. I don't know, maybe you forgot or something.'

'I wouldn't tell you to do it in the first place, so I can't have forgotten.'

'I shouldn't have asked you when you were upset. I should have waited.'

'You didn't ask me at all!'

'How can you not remember?' I sighed. 'Come here,' I said, and beckoned for him to follow me up the stairs. I led him into his mum's bedroom where I'd left a pile of photographs and two of the least offensive paintings leaning against the wall. 'This is what you wanted to keep. Remember? We'd been going through some of it. You took those photos out, and we talked about putting the paintings up on the wall somewhere. Then you got upset about the rest of it, and you said it could all go. I guess you were upset and not thinking, but you *did* say it. I should've known better, I suppose,' I said.

He stood there, shaking his head for a while, pacing up and down, and I could almost see his brain working. He was trying to remember it, trying to work out if I was right, if he'd made a mistake.

'Why would I have kept these things and thrown out the rest, unless you asked me to? It doesn't make sense.'

'I wouldn't have said it,' he said finally, his voice quiet now as if he knew he was defeated anyway.

'All right,' I said, making sure my tone said that I still didn't agree. 'But you know I don't think it's healthy hanging on to all that stuff, anyway. I mean, what're you going to do with a load of old clothes and bottles of talcum powder? It was all junk, really.'

'You got rid of her jewellery, her paintings, stuff that was important to her. To me, too. They were my memories.'

'Not all the paintings,' I said, and wondered if I should go back to the church shop and retrieve some of the stuff. But it wouldn't help me in the long run and that was what I needed to remember. Besides, they'd probably taken one look at the awful paintings and tossed them in the nearest dumpster. Who'd even buy those things?

I remembered seeing some of them on the walls when I went to Jacob's party all those years ago. I remember staring at one of them, a particularly ugly one of three angels playing harps on a cloud. His mum had caught me looking and told me she painted it herself. I smiled and said nothing more about it, aware of being diplomatic even at that age. I wondered if she gave them as gifts to friends and family, and if there were hundreds of them disgracing walls all over the place. But Jacob said he didn't have anyone else, no more family, no friends. So maybe her entire oeuvre was now in the charity shop on the corner.

'I'm sorry,' I said again, and went back downstairs. I could tell from the noises above my head he was in his mum's room, probably lying on the bed, because now, that was all he had left. The bed where she'd died.

I sat down and turned the TV on, watching a cooking programme until Jacob stopped sulking.

Chapter 43

Jacob being Jacob forgave me for throwing his mum's things away, even after he'd been back to the cancer shop, and they couldn't find the stuff, saying it must've sold quickly, if it'd been there. He'd gone to all the others on the High Street too, just in case I'd been mistaken, but none of them had what he was looking for. He obviously didn't know about the shop around the corner. Or didn't believe I would lie blatantly about where I'd gone.

He was slumped miserably on the settee when I came home from work, and I was expecting another row, but he just smiled sadly as he told me all was lost.

'It's not your fault,' he said, and I could tell he meant it, that he'd started doubting himself, that in some moment of madness, he'd given the okay to throw everything away. But he moped for days, regardless, and it was hard to make any more in-roads with my plan.

On Wednesday, he had to go and sign on, something he hated, something that always put him in a mood. Not only did he have to get up early, but the staff at the job centre were rude, he said, and treated him like a piece of shit on their shoe.

'They're not nice to anyone, I don't think,' he said, 'but they're especially nasty to me.'

'Why?' I asked. 'Don't you think you're just being paranoid?'

'No,' he said. 'It's coz they can't put me anywhere. No qualifications or anything. Prison. Thick. They don't like people like me. They probably wish they could just shoot us all. Get rid of us.'

I laughed, but Jacob was serious. I looked at the clock. 'I'd better go,' I said, grabbing my bag and heading to the door. 'And you should get a move on too.' I went to the door and stood, waiting to see if he'd notice, or if I'd have to wait until I came home from work to find out what happened.

'Shit,' he said, and I walked back into the living room.

'What's up?'

'I can't find my dole book,' he said, rummaging around on the dresser. 'I keep it in this drawer. It's always here.'

I went to the dresser, standing beside him as he searched. 'Did you put it away after last time?'

'Yes! I always put it back. Mum said always put important stuff away in the same place so you don't lose it. It should be here. I know I put it here the other week.' He tossed things about, getting more and more wound up by the second.

I checked my watch. 'I'm going to be late for work,' I said.

'And I'm going to be late to sign on,' he said. 'What am I going to do?'

'Can't you tell them you lost it? Can't they give you a new one?'

'No. It's got my log in it. They'll think I'm making it up, that I haven't looked for any jobs.'

'But you *haven't* looked for any jobs,' I said.

Jacob ignored me and continued searching the drawer for the tenth time. I sighed and put my bag down, not really caring if I was late for work. 'I'll help you look,' I said.

'It should be here,' he said, digging amongst a load of old bank statements and other useless things.

'But it's not. Obviously,' I said, and made a quick sweep of the living room, then checked the drawer in the hall, before going into the kitchen. I waited a few moments and then pulled the little plastic case out of the drawer where he kept tools and loose screws.

'I've got it,' I said, walking back to the living room, holding up the booklet for him to see. He took it from me and looked it over as if it couldn't be true.

'Where was it?'

'Kitchen drawer,' I said, and picked up my bag again. 'Right, I'd better go.' I kissed his cheek and left him standing there, puzzling over how it got it in the kitchen when he could've sworn he put it away where it always lived.

When I came home that evening, he was still wondering and wouldn't shut up about it while we made tea. 'I always put it in the dresser,' he said for the hundredth time that day. 'Always.'

'Well, obviously you didn't,' I said and chopped an onion.

'Why would I put it in the kitchen, with the screwdrivers and stuff?'

'I don't know. Maybe you were distracted or something. Did you need to fix anything that day?'

'No,' he said.

'Well, I don't know what to say,' I said. 'It's just one of those things.'

***

Those things kept happening for the next week or so until Jacob didn't know if he was coming or going. I could see the confusion all over his face every time something moved or disappeared or he forgot a conversation we'd had just hours earlier.

'Don't you ever listen?' I said as he told me he didn't know what I was talking about again. 'I told you this morning.'

'Did you?'

'For God's sake,' I said. 'We were sitting there, at the table. You were eating your breakfast, and I told you that the home had rang, that Mum had had a turn.'

'I don't remember,' he said. 'I'm sorry, Polly.'

'Never mind,' I said, and shrugged away from him, leaving him sitting alone to think it over.

***

The next day, we went shopping, stocking up on food for the week. When we got back, I pretended I'd had a call from the home and left him to unpack the bags. Later that day, when he was engrossed in a new train magazine, I went into the kitchen and rearranged his unpacking, so that when it was time to make dinner, we couldn't find half the ingredients.

'We definitely bought tinned tomatoes,' I said, and searched the tins cupboard, pulling everything out, one by one. 'What's this doing in here?' I held up a pack of cheese. 'Jesus, Jacob, it'll have gone off if it's been in here all afternoon. What were you thinking?'

Jacob didn't answer, just took the cheese and looked at it like he'd never seen such a thing before. I let out a big sigh, and Jacob turned to where I was standing, holding open the cupboard under the sink where the cleaning products were kept. 'I've found the missing tomatoes,' I said, and picked up a couple of tins. 'I'm getting worried about you,' I said, and went through the other cupboards and drawers, retrieving the mislaid items.

'But...' he said, cheese in one hand, tin of tomatoes in the other. 'I'm sure I put it away properly.'

'Clearly not,' I said, pretending to be angry for a moment before giving him my most sympathetic face. 'Are you feeling all right?' I held my hand to his forehead like my mum used to do when I was little.

'I think so,' he said. 'I just don't understand it.'

'Go and sit down,' I said. 'I'll finish up here.'

***

After dinner, Jacob was quiet, barely taking an interest in the night's film. I knew he was thinking about the shopping and probably all the rest of it too. Apart from all the things being in the wrong place, there were the conversations he'd forgotten, the things he couldn't remember saying to me. And then, of course, there was the sex that he couldn't recall.

I looked down at Jacob asleep on the bed as I came in from the bathroom. I climbed into bed and put my arms around him. 'That was good,' I whispered into his ear, and he muttered something. I nipped his arm to wake him properly and said it again.

'What was?' he asked.

I looked at him for a second and said, 'You didn't enjoy it?'

'Enjoy what?'

'Don't be mean,' I said, shoving him playfully.

'No, I...' he said, that sweet, puzzled look on his face again. 'I don't remember.'

'Jacob, what's the matter with you? It was ten minutes ago. You're just taking the piss now.' I stood up and put my clothes back on. They were still warm, having just come off a few minutes earlier.

Jacob watched me, his eyes darting about, worry creasing his face. 'We didn't...'

I stormed into the bathroom. When I came back into the bedroom, I held the condom up to Jacob. He looked from me to the condom, sticky and full. He didn't try to look any closer fortunately or else he'd have smelled the rose scented hand cream I'd dolloped inside.

'I don't remember.'

I sighed and walked over to him, cupping his face. 'Jacob, you need to see a doctor. There's something really wrong. It's like you're blacking out or something.'

He shook his head and sat down heavily on the edge of the bed. 'What's wrong with me?' he said, and started to cry. I stood over him for a second before going to him and holding him, pressing his head to my chest.

'We'll sort it out,' I said. 'It's probably just stress. You're still not over losing your mum. It's normal, Jacob.'

He looked up at me and said, 'I don't feel normal.'

'I know,' I said, and stroked his hair. 'I know.'

Chapter 44

I held Jacob all night, listening to him talk about his mum, about how everything had changed when his dad had died. I remembered asking my mum over and over why someone like Jacob could have a house like his when we had to live in a grotty flat. Even before my dad left, the house we'd had wasn't as nice as Jacob's. And his mum didn't even work hard, not like mine.

'Life isn't fair,' was all Mum used to say.

'What did your dad do?' I asked Jacob as he lay there in my arms, his tears damp on my sleeve.

'He worked at British Steel,' he said. 'I don't know what he did. I don't remember much about him at all. I was only seven when he died.'

I remembered Jacob being absent from Mrs Ray's class just before the Christmas holidays. I'd seen the headmaster come in not long after register and whisper something to her, her hand coming up to her mouth, her eyes surveying the rest of the class. No one else seemed to be aware that anything was happening, but I'd seen it. I'd seen the sadness in my teacher's eyes. We weren't told, of course. That fell to our own parents after school. I didn't know if the secretary had called them all while we had story hour or if the rumour had just circulated itself. But that afternoon when Mum picked me up, she was quieter than usual, held onto my hand a little tighter.

When we got home, she told me that Jacob's dad had died. A car accident, she said. She had tears in her eyes when she said it, and I wondered if she knew him. I remember Dad being there and them whispering in the kitchen, hugging in front of the oven, the smell of roast chicken drifting down the hall to where I was sitting, listening in.

We'd put the Christmas tree up a couple of days before, and every day for the next week, Mum would come in, take one look at the decorations and start to cry, saying, 'That poor boy. That poor family.'

Jacob had always been the odd kid at school and always would be. But until his dad died, he'd been clean and mostly tidy apart from the odd spell of unbrushed hair or muddy trousers. But after the accident, bit by bit, things changed for Jacob and his mum. Much later, maybe when I was a teenager, Mum told me that Jacob's mum had always been a bit scatty, a bit unreliable. She was a painter. She didn't work, other than as a housewife and an artist. It'd been his dad who'd looked after things; sorting the bills, sorting Jacob. So, after he died, things fell apart. She did the best she could, Mum said, but her creative temperament alongside her grief made her batty. She stopped cleaning the house, barely cooked, left Jacob to his own devices. I wondered how this tallied up with the birthday party she threw for him, the sadness in her eyes when she realised what sort of kid her son was. Maybe she realised then how she'd failed him, how disappointed her dead husband would've been. People in the street looked down on them, they were one of those families. But they had the house. Jacob's dad had been smart enough to pay off the mortgage on the beautiful house, and no one could take that away.

So, they were the weird family with the nice house. And we were the respectable family with the crappy flat because my dad didn't have the decency to die, he just left and ran off with some woman he'd met in the pub one night. There were days after he'd gone that I wished he'd died, not that he would've left us anything – he'd frittered away any inheritance, if there ever was any, in the pub. And me and Mum, who worked so hard, got stuck in a dump just because life was unfair. Because Jacob's dad wasn't my dad, and mine wasn't his. A simple twist of fate.

***

I woke before Jacob and left him on the bed, going downstairs to make some breakfast. I went to the corner shop, sneaking out, trying not to wake him, and bought some bacon and eggs.

As I stood in front of the pan, watching the bacon sizzle, I thought about the night before and if I should send Jacob to the doctor. I'd been trying to keep our relationship under wraps, at first because I was embarrassed, but then because I'd thought the best way to do this was by keeping it as quiet as possible. But what if a little outsider help was what I needed?

'Morning,' he said, and I turned around, spatula in hand.

'Did I wake you?' I asked. He shook his head.

'I could smell bacon,' he said, and sat down at the table.

'It'll be a few minutes,' I said. 'I thought it'd be a nice treat.' Jacob nodded and sat with his head in his hands. I left the fry-up cooking and went to the table. He looked up as I sat down. 'How are you feeling?' I asked.

'Stupid.'

I tilted my head and made a face. 'You don't need to feel stupid.'

'Do you think I'm mental?'

'No,' I said, and reached for his hand. 'But maybe you should go and see the doctor. If you're worried. Maybe he can help.'

'Maybe.'

'Do you want me to come with you?'

Jacob paused for a moment before nodding. 'Do you mind?'

'Of course not,' I said, and got up to turn the hob off, dishing up a pile of bacon and eggs for Jacob, a smaller portion for myself. 'I'll call the surgery after breakfast, see if we can get you in today.'

We sat and ate, Jacob stuffing it down like he'd never been fed, making it impossible to speak. Which was good because I didn't want to talk, I wanted to think. I had to make sure I remembered all the occasions when Jacob forgot or mixed things up or was otherwise crazy. The doctor needed to know it all.

***

We got an appointment that afternoon, and all the way there, Jacob asked me if it was a good idea. 'What if they think I'm going mad?' he asked, his voice loud in my ear, trying to be heard over the noise of the bus.

'Then, they'll help you,' I said.

'But what if they lock me up or something?'

'Of course they won't.'

'But–'

'Just tell him the truth, tell him what's been happening. He'll tell us what to do, what's best for you. They don't just lock people up these days.'

I could tell Jacob was scared and wanted to keep asking, 'but, but, but' – but I didn't want to talk about it anymore, so I changed the subject. 'Did you think those tomatoes tasted odd?' I asked.

'What tomatoes?'

I turned to Jacob, incredulous. 'The ones we had for breakfast,' I said. 'They seemed funny to me.'

'We didn't have tomatoes,' he said, and then, his voice wavered. 'Did we?' I did the head tilt again and squeezed his hand. 'It's happening again,' he said, panic all over his face.

'Don't worry. We'll sort it,' I said.

***

'And how long has this been going on?' Doctor Turner asked, fiddling with his pen, not looking very interested at all. I'd started listing the incidents, all the times Jacob had acted strangely, but after three or four examples, the doctor put his hand up and stopped me, turning to Jacob instead, getting him to follow his finger with his eyes.

'A few weeks,' I said, and Turner looked from me to Jacob again.

'Jacob?' Turner asked, and he nodded.

'Yes, a few weeks. I think.'

'And you haven't started drinking more than usual? Taking drugs?'

'No,' Jacob said.

'You haven't sustained a head injury of any sort?' Jacob shook his head. 'And when did your mum pass away?'

'Three months ago,' he said.

Turner nodded and sighed. 'I think it's probably just stress. Losing a parent is hard. Very hard. Do you have any support?'

Jacob started to shake his head but stopped when I said, 'He has me.'

Turner looked at me again, and I could feel his dislike of me, even though I was the one looking out for Jacob, even though I was the one who'd convinced him to see a doctor.

'I meant more in the way of professional support. A social worker or—'

'He doesn't need a social worker,' I said, thinking that was the last thing I needed, someone poking around our business, around the house. 'He needs medical help, if there's something wrong. Isn't there some sort of test you can do?'

Turner sighed again and dropped his pen on the desk. 'We could do a scan, make sure there's nothing physically wrong.'

'Like what?' Jacob asked.

'Well, it could be a number of things, something in the brain.'

'Like cancer?' Jacob asked.

Turner cleared his throat. 'Well, that's a possibility. But a very small possibility. But for your peace of mind and mine, we'll get you in and make sure nothing's going on up there.' He swivelled his chair and tapped at his keyboard.

I looked around the room as he did so, wondering if I'd made a mistake taking Jacob there. I'd hoped for a more sympathetic doctor, or someone who knew psychological disorders when they saw them. He didn't seem to know what he was doing at all. And I'd forgotten just how hard it was to convince them of anything.

There were posters on the magnolia-coloured walls. One about the risk of diabetes, another about the sexual health clinic. On the other wall, a graphic picture of a lung after thirty years of smoking stared out at me, alongside one for a helpline for abused women.

'Okay,' Turner said. 'You should get a letter with an appointment at the hospital. Come back to see me after the scan, and we'll take it from there.'

Jacob stood up and thanked the doctor and headed for the door. I collected my things slowly, and when Jacob stepped outside the room, I told him I'd be just a second. I closed the door again and Doctor Turner looked annoyed that I hadn't left.

'Is something wrong?' he asked.

I moved closer to the doctor, lowering my voice. 'I didn't want to say this while Jacob was in the room,' I said. 'But I thought you should know, in case it's relevant.'

'What is it?'

'Well,' I said, bowing my head, biting my lip, acting like it was so hard to say. 'Jacob hit me.'

'Hit you?'

'Yes,' I said, and looked up. 'It's happened a few times. I mentioned it once, I was angry, asked how he could do it, but he didn't know what I was talking about.' I looked over my shoulder again, lowering my voice further. 'I thought he was lying at first, covering himself. I thought this whole thing was made up, that he was just pretending to forget things so he wouldn't have to do them.'

'But?'

'He seemed genuine. When I told him he'd hit me, he was upset. Really upset, crying and begging forgiveness. So, when it happened again, I couldn't bear to tell him.'

Turner frowned, looking concerned and more reasonable than he had five minutes earlier. 'What's your name, again?'

'Polly,' I said.

'Polly. You're his girlfriend, yes?' I nodded. 'How long have you been together?'

I wanted to say a long time, but I knew I'd be caught in a lie, so had to stick to the truth. 'A few months,' I said. 'But we've known each other all our lives. We went to school together.'

'And has Jacob been violent before now?' I took a deep breath.
'Polly?'

'He was in prison,' I said. 'He hurt someone. Badly.' Turner's
eyes widened. 'It was an accident though,' I said quickly. 'He's not
a violent person really.'

'But he hits you.'

'But not all the time,' I said. 'It's just when he goes into these
states, like a blackout or something. He doesn't know what's
happened. He wouldn't hit me any other time.' Turner rubbed
his forehead but didn't speak, didn't tell me this changed things,
that Jacob would be committed at once.

'Perhaps you should go to the police,' Turner said.

'No, no, I can't,' I said. 'He didn't mean it. I know he didn't.'

'This is an abusive relationship. Even if there is some medical
or psychological explanation for Jacob's behaviour, it's not safe for
you to be there. Is there somewhere else you can go?'

'No,' I said, and heaved my bag onto my shoulder. 'I'm not
leaving.'

I heard him call to me as I walked out the door, but I didn't
turn around. I found Jacob in the waiting room, and he stood up
as I came out. 'What's going on?' he asked.

'Nothing,' I said, and pulled his arm, leading him outside.
'Let's go.'

Chapter 45

I felt slightly uneasy after speaking to Doctor Turner, wondering what would happen next. Would Turner send the police around? Could he even do that? Or arrange a social worker to come and speak to Jacob. I was starting to wish I'd never taken Jacob, that maybe Turner would be more trouble than good.

But Jacob was quiet all night, a welcome relief, and when we went up to bed, he told me he didn't want to go for the scan, that he was scared of what would happen, scared of what he would find out.

'But it might help,' I said, not really caring one way or the other. I wasn't sure if the scan would do me any good. It wasn't going to show any illness, unless there actually *was* some problem, a tumour growing slowly that would kill him at any minute. But that wouldn't do me any good at all. The house would be taken from me immediately. There'd be someone who came out of the woodwork, claiming they had more rights than me.

On the other hand, if it showed nothing, if all it proved was Jacob's problems were in his mind, then maybe when it came to it, the world would be on my side.

'I don't want to go,' Jacob said, sounding like a spoilt child.

I sighed. 'Well, you'll have to cancel the appointment, then,' I said, and rolled onto my side, away from him. I didn't care. The seeds were sown. Doctor Turner would've made notes saying not only was Jacob forgetting things and blacking out, he was also violent. As long as he didn't send anyone round, it could work out. When the time came and I needed Jacob out, I could use that medical history, use Turner's corroboration, to my advantage.

'Night, Jacob,' I said, and closed my eyes, knowing it was going to work out one way or another.

***

Jacob cancelled his appointment for a scan, preferring not to know if there was something wrong with his brain. If Doctor Turner found out about it, he either didn't care or didn't have time to follow up and nothing more was done. I'd spent days waiting, expecting a phone call or a visit from someone. Some nosy social worker or a friendly police officer who'd been trained in dealing with abuse. But no one came. No one cared enough about Jacob, or me, to come knocking.

I'd toned things down in the aftermath of our trip to the doctors, but as soon as the scan was cancelled and forgotten, Jacob went back to normal, seemingly unconcerned with anything except watching films and playing with his trains. He still refused to look at job ads and rarely left the house.

I knew I had to step things up again or else I'd be trapped in this hell forever. So, I started up with the old tricks of moving stuff around and making him think he'd forgotten things we'd talked about. But he seemed to care less and less, not really bothered anymore that he might be going mad.

I started arguments about it, tried to provoke a reaction, wondered if he actually *would* hit me. But he'd just walk away and then apologise later. Even when I said things about his mum, about her paintings, about her neglecting him as a child. Even when I could see he was so angry with me that he was shaking, he never lifted a finger to me. He wouldn't. He wasn't a violent man. Not with me, anyway. He would never hurt me.

He was driving me mad.

Chapter 46

It was AJ who got it for me. AJ the temp. And even though I hadn't liked the look of him from the moment he started, even though I knew he wasn't a nice person, I knew he could be useful. I'd overheard him talking about drugs, about his crazy weekends, and knew that he'd be able to get me something. So, I followed him into the break room one afternoon. I took a pound coin out of my purse. 'Did you drop this?' I asked and held the coin out to him.

He paused for a second and then smiled. 'Yeah,' he said. 'Thanks.' He took the money, and I could feel his hands were sweaty. I didn't like him at all, but I needed him.

'So, you're a temp, right?' I said.

'Yeah,' he said, and started making a cup of tea. 'Want one?' he asked and held up a mug. I nodded and waited until he came to the table to continue.

'How are you liking it?'

He shrugged. 'It's a job, innit?' He slurped his drink, and my toes curled. 'How long have you been here?'

'A few years,' I said.

'Shit,' he said, and I could tell he thought I was some loser who couldn't do better. I wanted to throw my drink at him and tell him that I'd been offered a supervisory position but had turned it down and that I had a degree and that I was waiting to hear back from better jobs anyway. I wanted to say at least I wasn't a temp doing a shitty job to support my drug addiction. But instead, I smiled at him and took a sip of tea.

'So, you're the one I should come to if I get stuck, then? You must know every trick in the book,' he said.

'I do,' I said.

'I'm saving to go to Thailand,' he said. 'Six months with my mates. It's going to be mint.'

'Sounds great,' I said, and then listened to his drivel until our break was over and had to sit through the same spiel the next day at lunch. The third day, I asked him if he could get me something, and he looked surprised but agreed anyway.

'Tomorrow?'

'Perfect,' I said.

***

The next day, AJ walked past my desk and winked, sliding something under my phone. It was Halloween, and the whole office was covered in ghosts and ghouls and people were handing out sweets left, right and centre. No one suspected a thing.

AJ walked away, and I sneaked a look when no one was watching. The little squares had strawberries printed on them, and my heart raced a little as I stuffed them into my bag.

I avoided AJ as much as possible after that, and by the end of the week, he was gone. I wondered if he was in Thailand and if he'd get arrested on his way back six months down the line, a load of drugs smuggled into his suitcase. He'd deserve it.

***

I had no idea how much it would take to have an effect on Jacob, where the line was between making him feel he was losing his mind and it actually being dangerous. So, I started him off with half a tab. I watched him carefully as he ate the dinner I'd prepared for him. But forty-five minutes later, nothing had happened, and I wondered if the effects of LSD were diluted when ingested with mashed potato. Or maybe AJ had sold me duds.

An hour later, I noticed he'd been staring at the wall for some time, but it wasn't clear if this was normal behaviour for Jacob or the effects of the drug. I was about to ask when he started giggling.

'What's up?' I asked.

Jacob didn't answer, he just sat there laughing at whatever it was he was seeing on the wall. He didn't seem concerned by it, didn't seem to think anything was wrong, and after a while, it became too annoying to listen to, so I went to bed and left him there enjoying himself.

In the morning I found him asleep on the settee where I'd left him. When he woke up, I asked about his night, what he'd been laughing at so hard, but he just shrugged. If he thought anything was wrong, he was keeping it to himself. So, over the following week, I upped his dosage day by day until he finally started to behave correctly. At night, he'd be on edge, twitchy and distracted, even gasping and shouting once or twice, and then the next day, he'd be quiet, nervous, confusion etched on his face. I could tell he wanted to say something, but he always held back.

I upped the dose further. I needed him to confide in me, for him to admit that he was losing it. Finally, Jacob asked me if I saw it too, reaching out to touch something or someone before snatching his hand back, shaking and muttering.

'Don't you see her?' he asked me over and over until it started to grate.

'There's no one there,' I said. 'What's the matter with you?'

Jacob kept pacing, talking nonsense, speaking to the walls, and all the while, I held up my phone and made a record of his latest episode, trying not to laugh until finally, it wasn't funny anymore. Jacob clawed at the wall, screaming, smashing things up – even his precious trains - begging me to tell him what was going on.

Three hours later, I was almost climbing the walls myself, desperate to calm him down, wondering if I'd gone too far.

'It's okay, Jacob,' I said, over and over, stroking his cheek, trying to stop what was happening.

The next morning, Jacob was quiet. He knew something was wrong but refused to talk about it. 'Maybe we should go back to Doctor Turner,' I suggested.

'No!' he snapped. 'Just leave me alone.'

I grabbed hold of his arm, and he flinched, pulling away from me. 'You can't just ignore this, Jacob. Something's wrong. Really wrong.'

'I'm not going back to the doctor. I'm not mental.'

'No one's saying you're mental but this…this isn't normal. You need help.' I took my phone out and found the video footage of the night before. 'Look.'

Jacob turned away from me until he heard the sound of his voice, screaming. He looked over his shoulder, and I held up the phone for him. His face dropped. He looked like he might start to cry.

'I don't know what happened–'

'Exactly. You've been like this for weeks. I can't stand it anymore. It's not just losing things, forgetting everything. You're getting worse. You don't even remember hitting me.'

'What? No,' he said, and tried to touch me, but I pulled away. 'I wouldn't do that.' He shook his head. 'Have I hurt you?' His voice was tinged with tears.

I shook my head. 'You don't remember, do you? You don't even remember talking about it.' I sat down. 'I don't think I can take this anymore. I really don't.'

'Polly, you have to believe me. I don't know what's going on,' he said. 'And I don't remember hitting you. But I wouldn't do that. I know I wouldn't.'

'You did, though.'

'But–'

'What would your mum think? What would she say if she knew about all this? She'd want you to get help.'

He looked like he wanted to cry. 'I'm scared.'

'I know. But you need help.'

Jacob turned away from me again, and I sighed. 'Maybe you should just go, Jacob,' I said.

'Go where?'

'I don't know. A friend, maybe? Just not here.'

'I don't understand.'

'I'm scared, Jacob. I know it's not your fault, but we can't go on like this. *I* can't go on like this. If you won't get help, you need to leave.'

'But this is my house,' he said.

I tilted my head again and touched his face. 'Oh, Jacob,' I said. 'You really don't remember, do you?'

'Remember what?'

'That you gave the house to me. You wanted me to buy it from you.'

Chapter 47

I showed Jacob the letter he'd composed declaring he was signing the house over to me for a large sum to be paid off monthly for as long as it took. I was aware when I wrote it, carefully rewording it over and over to make it sound less formal, less educated, more like something Jacob would say himself, that it wouldn't hold up in a court of law. But it was something, and if things went as I'd hoped, there would be no need for a court of law.

Jacob looked at the sheet of paper, the short paragraph explaining the situation, the scrawled signature at the bottom. The signature was perfect. I couldn't count the amount of times I'd practised it.

His forehead creased again, and I could hear the cogs turning as he desperately tried to remember doing it. But like so many other things recently, he had no memory at all. 'I don't…' he started, his fingers brushing the words on the page. 'I can't remember doing this.'

'Does this mean you don't want to go through with it anymore?' I asked. 'Because if you don't, that's okay,' I said, keeping my voice calm and neutral, 'but I'll have to get my money back.'

'What money?' he asked.

'The money I've started paying you for the house.'

Jacob put the contract down and rested his head in his hands, rocking gently. I left the paper where it was, not afraid that he'd destroy it as I had plenty of copies elsewhere. 'You still have it, don't you?' I said, and he looked up.

'I don't know, Polly,' he said. 'I don't remember. I don't even remember you giving me any. Where did I put it?'

'It went into your bank account,' I said. 'I'm supposed to pay you every month.'

He shook his head violently, maybe trying to shake some sense into himself. 'I don't think I'd do this,' he said. 'This was Mam's house. I wouldn't give it up. I wouldn't.'

'You're not really giving it up though, are you? You're selling it to me. You said you wanted me to have it, that I could look after it better than you. You said you needed money.'

'No!' he said. His eyes snapped open and he stared at me. There was anger in his glare. 'I don't believe you,' he said, his voice low and taut.

'What don't you believe?'

'Any of this. The house, the money. None of its real.'

'But it *is* real, Jacob. It's right here in front of you.' I nodded to the sheet of paper with his signature. I could see his hands turning into fists and momentarily thought I should stop and just walk away. But I couldn't. I'd got this far. I'd put so much into it, worked so hard, I couldn't give up now. I was owed.

'Look, I think you need to go back to the doctor—'

'No,' he said, shaking his head. 'I'm not going. There's nothing wrong with me.'

'Go back and see Doctor Turner. Go and get the scan,' I said.

'No!'

'Jacob, there's something wrong with you. You keep doing things and then forgetting them. It's not normal.'

'Stop it!'

'There's something really wrong.'

'No.'

'You're blacking out, you're forgetting things, you're doing things and don't know why.' I pointed to the mess from the night before. 'You did that and don't even know why.'

'No.'

'Maybe there's something really wrong with your brain. You need help.'

'There's nothing wrong with me!' he screamed and launched himself at me, pushing me to the floor. He stood over me, shaking with rage, his fists clenched, and I cowered and waited for the rest, but he just stood there doing nothing and all I could think was, *At least I wasn't lying about him hitting me.*

'I just want to help you,' I said, and reached up to his hand. He pulled away and walked over to the window.

'No, you don't. You're like all the rest. You think I'm stupid. You're lying to me.'

'I'm not. I'm worried about you. But if you won't let me help you, then maybe I should go. But I need my money back.'

'There is no money. You're lying.'

I walked out, returning a minute later with my laptop. 'I'll show you,' I said, and opened up my online banking. 'Here,' I said, and pointed to the screen. 'I paid you £150 last month, I didn't have much to spare, then. But here, two days ago I sent you £500 when I got paid. See?'

Jacob stared at the screen, at the two payments I'd pointed at. He took the laptop from me and stared closely. 'How do I know where it went?' he asked.

'Because that's your account number. There, look.'

'I don't know my account number.'

I went and found some paperwork in the dresser, rifling through for a bank statement. I pointed to the information on the letter. 'That's you.' He sat there looking from the statement to the computer screen for a long time, uncomprehending. After a while, I was losing patience. 'Get your coat,' I said, and stood up. 'And your bank card.'

I dragged him down the street to the cash point and made him check his balance. He hadn't spent the money I'd sent him, probably because he hadn't known it was there. I nudged him over and pressed the buttons so the machine spat out a mini statement.

'Look,' I said. 'Here's the £150 and here's the £500. You believe me now?'

Jacob took the flimsy piece of paper from me, and his face dropped. He couldn't deny it now. It was all there in front of him. Same as it would be for anyone who started asking questions.

'So, what's it going to be?' I said. 'Are you going to change your mind? Because if so, you'd better withdraw the money now, and I'll get my things and go.'

He looked at me, tears settled on his eyes. He didn't want me to go, I knew that. He needed me. He couldn't cope without me. He had no control of anything anymore.

'No,' he said. 'I don't want you to go.'

'All right then,' I said, and retrieved his card from the machine.

We headed back in silence, and I knew it was going to be okay. Jacob believed it. I could tell him anything now, and he'd believe it. And so would everyone else. I had the contract, which wasn't legally binding, but it would cover me in case anything happened, proving I hadn't really done anything wrong. I wasn't taking advantage of him, I was trying to help an old friend. A man who couldn't bear to live in a house haunted by memories of his mother.

I'd tell them that I was allowing Jacob to stay there as long as he wanted, but his behaviour had got out of control. He'd leave for days at a time, and when he returned, he'd be angry and violent.

I'd tell them that, yes, we had been in a relationship for a while, and I'd have witnesses who could verify that – Sasha and Kimberley, Doctor Turner – and wouldn't they think I was a good person for being with him, for taking a chance on a man like Jacob? A woman like me, a responsible, hardworking, respectable woman, risking it all to be with Jacob.

I'd tell them he sucked me in, got me to agree to buy his house and – due to desperation and my love for him – I agreed. I'd started paying him my hard-earned money in good faith and look what happened. Who wouldn't take my side?

I had things under control. And when the time was right, I'd tell Jacob to leave and he'd go and that would be that. Because who was he going to turn to for help?

Chapter 48

The next few days were calmer, more like the early days of our relationship. There were no arguments, no fights. Jacob was quiet and even let me choose the films we watched. He didn't ask for sex, he didn't seem to care about anything at all. He just ate what I gave him and helped with the dishes. I considered confronting him with the drugs, having something else to dangle over him, to make him do as he was told. If he was caught with drugs, he would likely go back to prison, and I knew he feared that more than anything. But I held on to that as a last resort, knowing the mind games were enough for now. I hadn't wanted to drug him again, not after the last time. But I realised that in order to keep up appearances, he'd have to have a little episode now and then.

In a lot of ways, it was like he wasn't there. He certainly wasn't in mind, even if his useless body was still taking up space on the settee, stinking because he'd stopped washing again. Part of me wondered if it could work like this, the two of us co-existing. I could move into his mum's room. I'd got rid of most of the junk, and it was almost aired out now. There wasn't so much as a trace of the old woman or her slow death.

The house was big enough that if I didn't want to, I wouldn't have to see Jacob much at all. I could get a TV for my room so I'd no longer have to sit through a Bruce Willis triple bill or sit and listen to him witter on about trains. I could make my own dinners and leave Jacob to his ready meals and takeaways. I could even redecorate things around him. Let him keep his revolting bedroom but change the rest.

But it wouldn't be the same. I wanted my own place. It was all I'd ever wanted. And that couldn't happen with Jacob there. There was nothing for it. I was forced into a corner, I had to stick with the plan.

So, after a few days of playing nice, I made my last attempt. I knew he was broken enough to go for it, it was just a matter of doing it well, doing it properly to make sure he was gone for good.

***

I knew he was asleep in front of the TV, I'd heard him snoring when I went down for a cup of tea. It was as good an opportunity as I'd ever get.

The first time didn't hurt so much, and I knew it hadn't worked. But hitting yourself in the face is extremely difficult. There must be some sort of defence mechanism built into your brain to stop yourself from doing real damage. I checked in the mirror and couldn't even see a mark. It was pathetic.

I looked around the room for something to use, something that would do real damage without trying too hard. I picked up the big mug that Jacob liked to drink soup out of, the one that annoyed me because of the slurping, that he'd leave somewhere for days so that bits stuck to the side and were impossible to get off. I knew I'd be killing two birds with one stone as I swung it at my face. I caught my nose and it hurt like hell, but I did it again just in case, and this time, the handle broke off and the mug fell to the floor, shattering into enough pieces to make it impossible to glue back together.

I could feel blood trickling from my nose, and my cheek throbbed. I ran through to the hallway and checked in the mirror where I could see the damage. It was perfect. I ran back to the kitchen, sliding down to the floor amongst the broken ceramic and waited for Jacob to wake up.

***

I was starting to lose the will to continue when Jacob finally came wandering in. He looked at me sitting there, his face confused from sleep, not really taking in what was happening, until something clicked in his little brain. He moved quickly and bent in front of me, reaching for my broken face. I jerked away from him.

'Don't touch me,' I said, and he pulled back.

'What happened?' he asked.

I scowled at him and clutched my cheek, which was burning beneath my hand. 'You happened!' I struggled to my feet and moved away from him. 'You need to leave. Now,' I said.

'But–'

'Get out!'

'Polly, what's going on?'

'You fucking hit me. You threw that at me,' I said, pointing to the mess on the floor.

'No,' he said. 'I was asleep.'

I forced a laugh. 'This has to stop,' I said. 'I'm not taking it anymore. You think you can do this to me and then pretend you don't remember? You're a fucking psychopath. I wish I'd never met you.'

'I didn't do this. I wouldn't,' he said, and tried to come towards me, but I moved behind the table and looked around for a weapon to protect myself. 'I was asleep,' he said again, but I could see the doubt creeping over him. He was certain he'd seen dancing badgers in the living room a few nights earlier.

'I want you to leave. Now,' I said. 'Or I'm calling the police.'

'But I didn't do anything,' he said. 'I didn't do anything.'

'You'll go back to prison,' I said, picking up a knife from the drainer which made him stop where he was. 'I'll call the police, and they'll see what you did, and you'll go to prison.'

'But I didn't do it.' He paced back and forth, hand rubbing at the same spot on his forehead. 'I didn't do it,' he said again, his voice stronger this time, surer.

'You'll probably get a few years. Is that what you want?'

'Polly, why are you doing this?'

'If you don't leave me alone, I'll call them, I swear I will,' I said, waving the knife towards him, showing how serious I was. 'Just go, Jacob. Just leave me alone.'

'No,' he said. 'I'm not going. I didn't do anything wrong. I didn't hit you. I know I didn't. I know it.'

'So, who did, then?'

'I don't know,' he said.

'You think I did it to myself? You think I go around hurting myself and trying to blame you? I'm not the crazy one. You are,' I said, and jabbed the knife in his direction.

'There's nothing wrong with me,' he said.

'That's not what the doctor says. You know what Doctor Turner said to me that day when you went outside? He said you were insane, that you needed help and that he wanted to lock you up. It was only because I said I'd look after you, that you're still here. And now, I wish I hadn't bothered.'

'You're lying,' he said.

'Am I? You really think you're normal? You've *never* been normal, Jacob. You're just like your mum. You're both crackers.'

'Stop it,' he said.

'I'm just being honest. You said people lie to you all the time, well, I'm telling you the truth. If it wasn't for me, you'd be in the loony bin right now.'

'Liar!' he said, and shoved the table at me. 'You're lying, about everything. So, you leave. You get out of my house.'

'It's my house, Jacob. You sold it to me, remember.'

'No, I didn't. You're lying.'

'You can leave now, or I'll call the police and you'll either end up in jail or the mental hospital. Your choice.'

Jacob ran around the table and grabbed my arm, trying to get the knife from me. We struggled and he pushed me into the fridge, but I refused to let go, bringing my knee up and catching him in the balls. He let go of me and bent over, clutching himself.

'I'm giving you one last chance,' I said, and looked at the knife.

He ran from the kitchen, down the hall and out the door. I watched him run down the street, not even looking back. He was gone.

I closed the door and locked up, went into the kitchen and realised I was still holding the knife, so I wiped it down and then tidied up the rest of the mess. Then, I made a cup of tea and had a sit down, wondering what to do with the rest of my day.

Chapter 49

I walked down the hallway at the home, past other visitors, past the carers, and not one person asked me what'd happened. No one blinked at the mess of my face, no one cared enough. They were all too busy. But I was glad. I didn't want people asking questions.

In Mum's room, I pulled up a chair beside the bed and watched her face as she lay there, half propped up with lumpy pillows. She was asleep, her mouth open, her skin sallow. She looked like the living dead, and I wondered if she'd ever be right again. At least she couldn't see me. Couldn't see what I'd done.

'Hi, Mum,' I said, and buttoned up her bed jacket in case she was cold. 'How are you feeling?'

I knew she couldn't hear me or respond, but I didn't know what was worse, sitting there talking to myself or sitting there in silence. So, I told her about work and how boring it was, about the temp who'd been a drug dealer and that he got sacked for doing his business in the break room. That wasn't strictly true, but it made for a better story.

I told her that Sasha had been dumped and that she'd put on a lot of weight, which wasn't true either, as far as I knew, but it was just something else to tell her. And then I was running out of things to say, and all I could think about was Jacob. I wondered if he'd gone for good, if I was that lucky, or if he'd come crawling back when he thought I'd calmed down. I wanted to talk to someone about it. But I knew I couldn't. I had to keep it to myself. About the house at least.

'Do you remember Jacob? The weird kid I went to school with? You made me go to his party when I was little?' I asked. 'I hated it, and I was so angry that his family had that nice house. And you always said life wasn't fair and that was it. But I knew you were jealous too. I knew you wanted that house as much as I did. And you always said you had to look out for yourself, didn't you?'

Cathy popped her head in the room, and I stopped talking.

'Everything all right?' she asked, and I turned and nodded, forgetting about the state of my face. Cathy gasped and stepped into the room. 'What happened?'

I shook my head and looked away. 'Nothing. I'm fine,' I said, and she stood there gawping at me until I stared back, wide eyed. She got the hint.

'Anyway,' I said when Cathy had left. 'I ran into Jacob one night. I knew it was him straight away, he looks almost exactly the same. I didn't really want to talk to him, but he saw me and started talking, and you know what people are like. And then I kept running into him. To be honest, I'm not sure if he was following me or something. I felt sorry for him, so I talked to him. I guess it was the same as when we were at school and I was the only one who'd stay at his party. I'm a sucker, I suppose.

'So, anyway, we started seeing each other a lot, and then, he told me his mum had died so it's not like I could just walk away, could I? But he's so needy.'

I looked at her, but there was nothing. Not even a flicker of life or a twitch of a muscle. She was just lying there. She didn't know what I was saying at all.

'I wish I hadn't let him touch me,' I said, my voice even quieter now. I didn't want the nurses to hear this. 'But I suppose we both got what we wanted in the end. He got me. I got the house.'

Chapter 50

When I got home, I unlocked the door and went inside, and I just knew he was there. The TV wasn't on, there was no smell of burnt food, but I could tell he was in there, somewhere. His presence somehow announced itself. Maybe I'd known deep down he'd come back, that I was naive to think he'd just go like that, without a fight, without more of a struggle. I certainly wouldn't have.

I walked through to the living room and found him sitting on the settee in the almost dark, no TV to distract him, nowhere for his thoughts to be directed except at me. He turned to me as I went in, but his face was blank, and I couldn't tell if he was angry or if he'd forgiven me again, that he'd thought the events that took place earlier were just another little squabble. A lover's tiff.

I put my keys in my pocket and wondered why he hadn't changed the locks. Wondered why *I* hadn't changed the locks when he ran away. Had I been so confident I thought I didn't need to take precautions? Was Jacob so stupid that he thought things would be okay between the two of us when he came back? Maybe he was just too stupid full stop. Doing something like changing the locks would be beyond him.

'What're you doing here?' I asked as he stood up, my words stopping him from coming any closer.

'I live here,' he said, and from anyone else it would've sounded sarcastic, but from Jacob, it was just a plain fact. A straight answer to a straight question. But it also meant he hadn't taken to heart anything I'd said or done earlier. That all my efforts were for nothing. What was it going to take to get him to go and leave me alone?

'We've been through this,' I said. 'You can't stay here anymore.'

'I can,' he said. 'I'll give you the money back.'

'No,' I said. 'It's too late for that.'

'Here,' he said, handing me a wad of notes. 'You can go home.'

'*This* is my home,' I said, and took the money anyway.

'It's my home,' he said, sounding like a child. 'My mum wouldn't want you here. She wouldn't want me to leave.'

'Your mum is dead,' I said. 'It's got nothing to do with her.'

'It's her house. My house.'

'Not anymore,' I said, and walked away from him, into the kitchen.

'You have to go, Polly,' he said, and came up behind me, pulling at my sleeve. I spun around, and he moved back, startled by my anger.

'I'm not going! And if you don't get out of my house, I'm calling the police.'

'You can't,' he said.

'Watch me,' I said, and pulled my phone from my bag. 'Who are they going to believe, Jacob? We've been through this. I've got proof you sold the house to me. I've got proof you hurt me. Do you really think some policeman is going to walk in here and take a look at both of us and throw *me* out on the street? You're pathetic, Jacob. You always have been. Even your mum thought so.'

'She didn't,' he said, and suddenly, he was the ten-year-old boy that no one wanted to play with.

'Do you know what she told me when I came to your birthday party? She said she wished she hadn't bothered spending money on someone that nobody liked. That she was embarrassed you were her son, and she wished she'd had one of the other boys, one of the kids who played football or could read and write properly. She wished *I* was her kid. When everyone else had gone and there was just me left, she told me she wished I could stay, and you could go home to someone else, that you could be somebody else's problem instead. Because that's all you are Jacob, someone's problem. So, don't think your mum would care for one second whether you stayed here or not, she'd probably be glad to see the back of you.'

I saw it coming, but I didn't flinch, didn't try to move away from it. He was fast and used his whole body, all thirteen stone was behind his fist, and it felt as though my skull had shattered, and I fell to the floor, blinded for a while, my ears ringing, blood flowing.

I could hear him, but he wasn't really speaking, or if he was the pain in my head was distorting things so it just sounded like noise. Angry, feral noise, like a wild animal loose in the house.

When my senses returned, my faculties more or less intact, I cowered, did what I could to defend myself from him, but I was on the floor, and he was over me, his fists swinging randomly, hitting whatever they found nearest. I could feel pain shooting up from my ribs, my legs, my arms, my face. I couldn't tell one body part from another after a while, I felt like one giant bruise forming beneath his hands. A mass of bones just waiting to crack and crumble.

I was curled up in a ball when he stopped, the ringing in my ears constant. I could hear him breathing, heavy sobbing gasps for air. I knew he was still looking at me, standing over me, staring down at the mess on the floor, the mess he'd made.

My eyes were closed, but I could feel him there, feel his body heat that mixed with my own and was making me burn. My skin ached and throbbed, it hurt to move, to breathe.

'I'm sorry.'

At least that's what I thought he said, but when I finally opened my eyes, at least the one that wasn't swollen shut, all I saw was the back of his heels running out of the kitchen. He thundered down the hall and out of the door, slamming it behind him, and all I was left with was the ringing in my ears and the pain in my bones.

***

I'd thought twice about it, but I guessed that in the short term, it would at least keep him away and maybe, hopefully, even get rid of him for good.

I tried to stand up but everything hurt, and walking, even to the kitchen table, was a struggle. He'd really done some damage, and I couldn't help but laugh. I'd imagined having to inflict something on myself, some measly little shallow scratch with a knife or another mug in the face. But this was better. There was probably even some forensic evidence. His knuckles had likely left an imprint on my skin.

I managed to drag myself to the mirror in the hallway and looked at the damage, at the blood and the bruises and the way my body curled in on itself. And then, I called the police.

***

Two officers called to the house; one man, one woman. When they'd come to the door they didn't seem interested, offhand almost, as if I'd interrupted their tea break. But then they came in and saw me under the florescent lights, and they changed. They got out their notebooks and pens and scribbled things down as I told them what'd happened. They asked too many questions, and I had to tell them things I didn't really want to get into, about our relationship, and whether this was my house and if I had somewhere else to go, as if I should be the one to leave after what'd happened.

But they took it seriously, and the woman took some photographs of my injuries as evidence of what Jacob had done. They wanted me to go to the station and to the hospital, but I refused. I wasn't leaving the house. Never again. They looked at each other, a sneaky glance that I saw easily, even with my swollen eye. *She's mad*, their glares said. But I didn't care. I wasn't leaving and letting him back in.

'Do you have any idea where he might've gone?' the male officer asked. 'Any friends or family he could've gone to? Any favourite pubs or places he might be hiding at?'

'I don't know,' I said. 'He's got no family. I don't know his friends. He never mentions anyone. He'll probably come back here.'

'And you're sure you don't want to leave?' the woman asked. 'We can find somewhere for you. A hostel or shelter, if you don't want to go to a friend.'

'No,' I said. 'I'm not leaving.' They both sighed and stuffed their notebooks back into their pockets. 'So, what happens now?' I asked.

'We'll look for him,' the man said. 'If he comes back here, give us a call immediately, or if you hear from anyone about where he might be.'

'That's it?'

'There's not much we can do until we find him,' he said, and they turned towards the front door.

'I need to change the locks,' I said, and they looked at each other again, and the man nodded slightly.

'I'll call someone,' the woman said, and went outside to use the phone. She sounded tired, and I wondered if they were nearing the end of their shift or if she was just constantly bored in her job.

She came back in and said someone was on their way and that they'd wait with me until the job was done. I offered them a drink, and they accepted, but the man got up and said he'd make it. The woman sat there on the settee and looked around, probably judging the state of the place, making assumptions about me from the house and from what'd happened.

I ignored her and stood by the window, looking out for the locksmith arriving, wanting it done as soon as possible so they'd all go and leave me alone. I just wanted to sleep.

And then I saw him.

Jacob was standing on the other side of the road, his hands in his pockets, his hood pulled up. He was staring at the house, but I wasn't sure if he'd seen me yet. He was looking at the police car parked in front of the house, and I knew he'd be terrified. His eyes left the car, then, and he started to walk away, but he noticed me standing there and stopped. We gazed at each other for a few seconds, and I wondered if I should tell the police officer sitting behind me that the man who'd beat the shit out of me was standing across the street, that he was there just waiting to be arrested. But I decided not to. There'd be time for that later. Instead, I smiled and gave a little wave, knowing that was enough.

Jacob took off down the street, faster than I'd ever seen him move. And I knew he was gone for good this time. It was over. I'd won.

Chapter 51

By the time the locksmith and the police had left, I was exhausted. I went into the kitchen and took a few Ibuprofen with a glass of water and then dragged myself up the stairs to bed. I wanted to collapse beneath the covers and sleep for a long time, knowing that Jacob was gone, that he couldn't get in anyway, even if he was stupid enough to come back.

But the smell in the bedroom reminded me of him, and I just couldn't bring myself to stay in that room. I knew I'd never sleep, and that if I did, his face would haunt my dreams. So I limped to his mother's bedroom and climbed onto the mattress where she'd died and pulled the bare duvet over myself, aching for sleep.

I somehow slept without any trouble, the memories and fear fading out as I drifted into sleep. There were no bad dreams, no good dreams, either, just a long nine hours of sleep that did me the world of good.

When I woke, I felt refreshed, and though I still ached and things still hurt if I put pressure on them or moved too quickly, I felt much better. But I knew I couldn't go to work, not in this state. Instead, I made an emergency doctor's appointment, making sure I saw Turner so that he could see just how bad things had got.

The look on his face said everything. As I walked in, his mouth dropped, and before he'd even taken a look at me, he was talking about the police.

'I've already spoken to them,' I said. 'I just need a sick note.'

'You'll need more than that,' he said. 'Have you not been to the hospital? Had any x-rays or anything?'

'No,' I said. 'I'm fine. I just can't go to work like this, so a sick note would be helpful.'

He looked me over, saw the way I clutched my side. 'You should've had stitches,' he said. 'And your ribs could be broken. You really need an x-ray to make sure.'

'But there's nothing you can do about it if they're broken, right?'

'Well, no, but—'

'So, there's no point.' I sighed. 'I just want to go home and rest. So, please,' I said as he let out a long breath and sat at his desk. He typed quickly, pausing occasionally to think before going back to the keyboard. I wondered what he was writing but didn't care too much as long as I got what I came for.

'It's for a week,' he said. 'Come back and see me after that.'

'Fine,' I said and took the note from him, leaving without another word.

***

I called work and told Janet I'd been assaulted and would be off the rest of the week. She asked a million questions, and I could hear the others in the background, desperate to know too, but in the end I told her I needed to go, that the police were waiting and hung up.

I went home, careful to check the street for Jacob before going to the house, although I knew he wouldn't be brave enough to risk coming and getting caught by the police. I knew I had nothing to worry about once I was inside the house.

I made myself a cup of tea and took a packet of biscuits into the living room. The kitchen was still a mess from the night before, but I was too tired and sore to do anything about it. I didn't even move the cups the police had left on the table, which were now crusted with dried tea. I didn't care about any of that, I just wanted to sit and rest and enjoy my new home.

I spent the day watching endless reality TV shows about junk and cooking and coach trips and sick animals. I knew it was pathetic, that I should be doing something, cleaning or getting rid of junk, but I felt like I was on holiday, so I tried to push all the *should do* thoughts to the back of my mind and focus on recuperating.

I'd barely moved by the time the clock struck four p.m., and I wondered if I should call the home and tell them I wouldn't be in for a while. But Mum had been vacant last time I was there, so she probably wouldn't know or care whether I visited, and the staff probably wouldn't notice, except for Cathy, who couldn't keep her nose out of anything.

In the evening, my eyes were blurring either from my injuries or from watching TV all day, so I turned it off and lay back on the settee, thinking about what I needed to do, what my next steps would be. I wondered if the police were going to be a problem, whether they'd keep showing up at the door, updating me on their case. Or if they did find Jacob, what he'd tell them and whether they'd believe any of it, whether they'd have to dig into our affairs to show they were looking into things properly, and if they did, if they'd find anything suspicious. Part of me hoped they didn't find Jacob. I knew the threat of being arrested would be enough to keep him away and that was all I needed really.

After I'd had something else to eat and a few more painkillers, I sent Kimberley a text telling her I was moving out of the flat, that I'd be collecting my things when I could. She mentioned the rent, but when I told her I'd been attacked, she dropped it.

I fell asleep on the settee that night and slept well again, even if I did have a crick in my neck the next morning to add to my injuries. But I was feeling better, my eye had opened up, my bruises were changing colour, and my ribs didn't hurt so much when I moved. I doubted they were broken at all. Jacob couldn't even get that right.

***

By mid-morning, I was bored of TV and sitting around, so I walked to the corner shop for some supplies, ignoring the stares from people in the shop and strangers on the street. I went home, dumping the food in the kitchen before calling a taxi and picking up some of the money Jacob had brought back.

The driver was friendly, too friendly really, wanting to chat constantly, asking me if I was all right, and wanting to know the details of what happened to me. I was annoyed to start with but found it cathartic somehow to be able to tell someone, someone who didn't matter. I told him about Jacob hurting me and that I was going to get my things from the flat so I could move to a friend's house where I'd be safe. The driver looked suitably shocked and said if he ever ran into Jacob, he'd break his neck.

Once we got to the flat, I asked him to wait, said I'd probably be a while coming up and down with my things, but that I had money, as long as it wasn't more than fifty quid. The driver shook his head and waved the money away.

'This one's on the house,' he said, and offered to come up with me, to help cart my things down to the car. Thankfully, Sasha and Kimberley were out, so I didn't have to explain anything, didn't have to try and match up the things I'd told the driver to the things I wanted them to know.

We found some bin bags in the kitchen and tossed everything from my room into them, and he'd take them down to the car a few at a time while I packed more up. There was some junk I no longer wanted, so I left that for the girls as they'd probably need it more than I did, and then, I went into the kitchen and found bits and pieces that belonged to me in there.

I threw the last few things in a bag, and the driver came up and took it from me. 'All set?' he asked as I looked around the flat. I didn't feel anything, really. I knew I wouldn't miss the place. I was moving on.

'That's it,' I said, and we went to the door. He started down the stairs, but I had a thought and went back, opening the fridge. I piled a few of the better items into a carrier and took them with me, saving me a job of shopping for a day or two. Besides, Sasha was always wanting to lose weight, so really I was doing her a favour. Then, I left, taking the keys with me in case I needed to come back for anything else.

The driver dropped me back at home and kindly helped me take my things inside. When he was done, he stood there with his hands on his hips as if he was waiting for something. *The money*, I thought, *his 'it's on the house' was rubbish*.

'Here,' I said, taking the money from my pocket, but he shook his head again and held up his hands.

'No, I told you. It's on the house.' He smiled at me, and I wondered if he wanted something else. If he was some kind of pervert, that I'd been fooled into thinking he was a nice guy. But then he nodded and turned to the door. 'I hope things work out for you,' he said. 'And if you're ever stuck, call the taxi number and ask for Kev. I'll make sure you're all right.' He walked to his taxi and got in, waving as he drove away.

I went back inside and looked around at the mess, the piles of bin bags with all my things in, the cups and plates littered about the place. And, of course, the blood and broken things. I had a lot to do, but I was happy. Because I finally had a place of my own.

Chapter 52

I didn't go out much over the next few days, what with having the sick note letting me off work, and I knew I should spend the time sorting things out in the house. I started scrubbing and cleaning. Tearing at wallpaper, pulling at carpets, trying to see what was underneath. I filled endless bin bags with junk. I tossed all of Jacob's trains into bags and put them by the bin, but then changed my mind. There was probably some poor kid out there who'd love them.

Sasha had called a few times, but I ignored her. In the end, I decided to change my number and get a new phone. Not because of Sasha, but because Jacob had started calling, and it was starting to get on my nerves.

The first call had been the day after he'd left. I hadn't answered, and he didn't leave a message. He didn't bother for a day after that, but then, he'd tried again, this time letting it go to voicemail. But instead of speaking, of telling me he was sorry or even threatening me, he just let it play out, just breathing down the phone like a lunatic. I didn't know if that was meant to be some sort of intimidation or if he was just too dense to realise it was recording, but either way, it was just irritating rather than upsetting. But after he'd called a dozen times, a few times simply shouting my name down the phone, I decided I had to make a fresh start.

So, I went to town, found the cheapest phone I could get and dumped the old one. It wasn't worth anything, so I didn't care too much. And really, who else was going to try and call me on that number? Who in the world had my number that I actually cared about?

When I came back from the shops with my new phone, I decided to do a bit more cleaning, a bit more putting things away, but it was a long process. I had to empty cupboards and drawers of Jacob's things, even some of his mum's things were still hanging around. It didn't seem to matter how much I threw away, I always found more hiding in corners and clogging up space.

I was thankful for the furniture, for the white goods, even if a lot of them were filthy. At least I didn't have to buy my own, what with paying Jacob some money and the locksmith, I was low on funds and knew I'd have to make do for a while.

I thought about the money I'd been sending to Jacob and wondered if I should send some more to keep up appearances in case anyone came asking. But after what'd happened, I didn't want to give him anything and figured that if anyone asked, I could always say I forgot after the incident or that *because* of the incident, I was planning to leave and forget about the deal, I just needed to find somewhere else to go. But what I was really hoping for was that no one would do anything. And if I kept my head down, maybe that would be possible.

I sat on a chair in the kitchen, exhausted from cleaning. I was feeling better, even if the external signs of Jacob's anger were still visible. And I was getting bored of being in the house all the time. I only had a day left on my sick note but knew I wouldn't return to Doctor Turner for another. I'd go back to work the day after next and let them see for themselves what'd happened, let a little sympathy brew because it could come in handy later on.

I made a cup of tea and decided to call it a night with the cleaning and sorting. I needed to give myself a break. I was working too hard. I went through to the living room and lay back on the settee, thinking about the house, my plans. I thought about Mum and how I hadn't visited for a little while. But I looked at the clock and realised visiting hours were almost over, and it would have to wait.

I got up and went to the window, seeing it was dark, so closed the curtains. The whiff of stale smoke made me nauseous, and I noted that new curtains should be top of my list.

And then, I saw him.

He was standing across the street, smoking. His face was in the shadows, but it had to be him. Didn't it?

I squinted, trying to see, trying to work out where his eyes were pointed. Was he looking at me? At the house? He moved slightly, and I knew he'd seen me. I ducked behind the curtain.

He wouldn't come back, would he? He wasn't that stupid. He had to know the police would be looking for him. I could call them easily, tell them where he was. He *had* to know that. So why was he here?

I took a breath and realised that I had the upper hand. I was the one in the house. I was the one with the keys. I was the one who the police believed.

I wasn't afraid of him.

I moved back in front of the window and stared across the street, defiant. I wasn't afraid of him. I wanted him to know that. I wasn't afraid and never would be. I stared across the street, and he slowly moved from the shadows, his cigarette glowing in the dark.

And then, he walked away.

Fuck you, I thought. *I win.*

Chapter 53

'All right, Polly, time to go,' Phil says. 'I think she's learnt her lesson, haven't you?'

'What're you doing?' Jacob asks.

'She's had enough,' Phil says. 'She's gonna go. Aren't you?' I nod and rub my wrists where they were bound. 'And you're not gonna go to the police, are you?'

I shake my head, and Jacob looks at Phil and then at me and something comes over his face, a dawning realisation of what he's done, of what he's got himself into. Hadn't he thought about the consequences? That as soon as I walked out that door, I could go to the police and tell them what these monsters did to me? Or wasn't he concerned with that? Did he just think they'd have a laugh, mess with me a little and that would be it? Then, he and Phil could just move in and live happily ever after?

'I won't. I promise. Just let me go,' I say, but Jacob doesn't look convinced, and now Phil is looking like he has doubts too.

'So what? You think we should kill her?' Phil says, grinning. He wipes sweat away from his forehead, wiping it on his jeans. I notice the knife in his hand and wonder if I could try and get it.

'You said yourself she hadn't got anyone, that she's a miserable cow nobody likes. So, who's going to come looking for her? Especially here? Eh?' Phil laughs and turns the knife in his hand. I don't know if he's joking, and worse, I can't tell if Jacob knows, either.

He hands Jacob the knife, and he stares at it as if he's never seen a knife before, as if he doesn't know what to do with it.

'Put it down, Jacob,' I say. 'This isn't you. Just put it down and I promise I'll go, and I won't tell anyone what happened. You'll never see me again.'

Phil leans close to Jacob and whispers something, something I can't hear, but I can see Jacob's face change, and I'm desperate to know what he said.

'Please, Jacob,' I say. 'Just let me go. Don't listen to him.'

I can hear Jacob's breath even above my own. I'm trying to judge the distance between here and the door. Maybe I should just go for it. I should at least *try* to get away. I can scream and run and make a scene, and someone will help me. Someone out there will hear me and come rushing in and find these bastards, and they'll be locked up forever.

I don't know if it's me or Jacob who moves first, but I'm on my feet, and Jacob is in front of me. I can hear him but not the words. I don't know what he's saying, it's all a blur, just noise. But I can hear something else too, a knocking from somewhere. Phil is looking at the door, his face drops.

And the knife is there, in my eye line, and I'm reaching out for it. I can feel the cold blade, it slices my hand. And then, the hot handle, warmed by Jacob's hand.

I can hear shouting, maybe from me, maybe from Jacob, maybe from Phil. Maybe from all of us.

I have the knife in my hand, and Phil is lurching forward, and Jacob is standing there.

I have the knife.

I can feel the warm liquid seeping over my hand, and I think I've really hurt myself by grabbing it, but it's better than the alternative.

I can still hear knocking, though I can't tell where it's coming from.

And then, it feels like my hands are full of blood, and I look down and there's so much of it, but it doesn't seem to hurt as much as it should. It doesn't seem to hurt at all.

Chapter 54

Jacob slumps to the floor, the blood is coming from him, somewhere in his guts. He's still alive, I can hear gurgling, can see blood coming out of his mouth. He looks small and fragile, and I think *I can't have done this*. I can't have. I wouldn't do something like this.

I look at Phil. He looks smaller too. His face is frozen in horror, his eyes glued to Jacob. He knows this is his fault. *He* was the one who brought Jacob here, who started all this. *He* hurt me. *He* started waving the knife about. *He* killed Jacob.

Except he's not dead. He's not dead.

He has hold of Phil's arm, pulling him down, grabbing at him for help or to keep him there so he can be punished for what he's done.

There's a noise at the window, a scream, and I see the back of someone running towards the door.

I drop the knife and look at my hands, covered in blood, mine, his, who knows. I look back to Phil. He's trying to help Jacob now, pressing his hands into his exposed insides, his blood covering him too.

'Help me,' Jacob gasps and looks at me. I can see the life going out of him, the light in his eyes dimming.

'Do something,' I shout at Phil, but he just sits there, his hands inside his so-called friend.

And then, the door opens, slamming into the wall. Phil looks at me. I look at him. Someone can help us. Can help Jacob.

'Help me,' I scream at the top of my lungs. 'He's killed him.'

Phil lets go of Jacob and stands up, looks around the room like a trapped animal. He runs out to the kitchen and tries the back door, but it's locked. I'm still screaming, begging for help as Cathy comes in, her face pale before she's even got to Jacob.

'He killed him,' I say again, and Phil runs back from the kitchen, almost into Cathy, knowing it's too late, and he's trying to blame me, telling her it was me, over and over.

Cathy looks down at Jacob, kneeling over him, looking for a pulse. Then, she has her phone in her hand.

She's going to call the police.

'Cathy, look at me. You saw him, didn't you? You saw what happened?'

Cathy stares at Jacob's lifeless body before turning to me, her eyes brimming with tears. 'I saw,' she says quietly, and Phil lunges at her, grabbing her arm.

'Liar!' he shouts, and Cathy cowers, her eyes still fixed on me.

'I saw you,' she says, her chin trembling. 'I saw you. I know what you did.'

Phil lets go of her arm, and Cathy comes towards me but thinks better of it and steps back, phone in hand.

'I know what you did, Polly,' she says, and I shake my head.

'It wasn't me. It wasn't my fault,' I say.

'You killed him. You did it to him, like you did to her,' she says.

'I didn't do anything,' I say, moving towards her.

'She did it,' Phil says from behind Cathy, but she seems to have forgotten he's there.

'I know what you did,' she says, tears streaming, spit flying. 'All for a fucking house!'

'I don't know what you're talking about.'

'She told me. She told me what you did. About the fire.'

'She's lying to you,' I say. 'She doesn't know what she's talking about. You know she's delusional.'

Cathy shakes her head. 'No. She told me. She wrote things down,' she says. 'You're going to pay for it.' She starts to dial.

'It was him. Can't you see what he's done. What he's done to me?'

Cathy shakes her head, raising the phone to her ear. Phil stands behind her, and I wonder why he's still here. If he's just making sure she tells on me, like some pathetic little kid. I wonder how he's going to explain his role in all this, or if he'll just blame my injuries on Jacob.

'Cathy, please,' I say as I hear the tinny voice on the line.

'You killed him. Like you killed her,' she says, and I find myself moving. My hand is on the knife. I'm running. I see Cathy's face drop, the phone spills from her hand. Phil lets out a cry and then I'm standing over Cathy, the knife in her chest, her blood on my hands.

Phil turns and runs out the front door. I think I can hear his feet slamming into the pavement, but it could be the blood rushing in my ears.

I can hear the voice on the line, and I don't know what to do. I think about hanging up. But what would I do then? Run away like Phil?

I pick up the phone, gasping, and tell the voice that he's killed them both. That he tried to kill me too. Send help. Please.

I disconnect and look around the room. I pick up the discarded tights and wrap them around my neck, pulling tightly until I'm dizzy. I lie down beside Cathy, my hands on her chest as if I was trying to save her. And then, I wait for help to come.

Chapter 55

I lie there on the floor, thinking. I have to get things clear in my head for when the police ask. Phil broke in, he hurt us. He killed Jacob. Maybe he knew Jacob, wanted revenge for something. Or money, maybe. And then, I guess Cathy showed up. My friend Cathy. She must've seen me and Jacob on the floor, thought we were both dead. Called the police. But Phil was still here, and when she confronted him, he killed her too. I woke up as he ran away. I crawled to Cathy and got the phone. I tried to help them, but it was too late.

And what about the house? What do I tell them about the house?

And what if Phil shows up again? Will they believe what he tells them? No. He's a criminal. No one will believe him. Besides, why would I lie about all this? What reason would I have to lie? Unless they can work things out through science. They can do all sorts these days. But why would I still be here? Why would Phil run away if he hadn't done anything wrong?

I can hear a siren. I don't know if it's the police or the ambulance, but there's a blue light outside. It's giving me a headache.

I see someone come into the room. Paramedics. Two of them. They look at Jacob and Cathy and then at me.

One of them squats in front of Cathy and says something, gives a shake of the head. He moves to Jacob and does the same as the other man leans over me. I'm alive. This one's alive.

The paramedics talk to me, but I say nothing, and they move me as the police come in. There's lots of talk, but I can't focus enough to hear what they're saying, because Jacob is dead and

Cathy is dead, and how did it come to this? I just wanted them out of my life.

One of the police officers is talking. I hear the word murder, and I think I better tell them about Phil so they can find him. So this can be over.

***

I'm taken to the hospital. They take my clothes, take swabs. They ask me a few questions, but the doctors tell them to back off.

I wonder when it will be a good time to ask about the house. I guess not yet. And besides, the police might not know. And I don't want to seem like I'm money grabbing, some sort of gold digger.

'I'm going to send you for some x-rays,' the doctor says, interrupting my thoughts. 'You've really taken a beating. You're lucky you got out of there alive.' He stands and leaves the cubicle, and I'm alone for the first time since this morning. This morning when I was happy. I was positive everything was going my way.

I wonder if I'd been right to go into the house when I saw him in there. If I'd been stupid to put myself at risk. But I needed to stand up for myself. I couldn't let him think he could treat me like that. And how was I to know he'd have someone with him, especially a murdering psychopath like Phil.

It was his fault really. Him and Jacob. He's got no one to blame but himself. And Cathy. Why was she even there? If she hadn't poked her nose in, none of this would've happened.

Chapter 56

I constantly shake with the police in my presence. I gave them a description of Phil last night, and they seemed content to leave me alone and go off and find him. I thought that would be the end of the questions, but it's not.

The detective who comes to ask me questions is kind. He's older than all the other officers I've seen by a long shot, almost too old to be still working is what I think when I see him, but he has a kind face and he's gentle with me. Part of me suspects it's an act, to try and get me to confess something or trip me up, but the other part of me wants to believe he wants to help. I want to believe he's a good person. He wants to find Phil and punish him for all he's done.

'We've found CCTV footage of him fleeing the scene just after your friend called 999,' he says. 'It looked like he had blood on his clothes and between that and his history, we're very keen to find him. You don't have any ideas where he could be? An address or somewhere he hangs around?'

I shake my head. 'I don't know him,' I say. 'I didn't even know Jacob knew him until...'

He nods sympathetically. 'He was inside with Jacob for a while. He's not long been out again. Has a pretty nasty history,' he says, and taps his pen on his notebook. 'Don't worry. We'll find him sooner or later.'

He asks me to tell him what happened, right from the start, and he's patient while I talk and try to remember everything. He asks a few questions now and then, but mostly listens to me talk. It feels good to let it out.

***

I met Jacob six months ago. Well, actually I met him about thirty odd years ago. We were at school together right from infants until we left. Jacob was bullied, always the boy other kids picked on. I always liked him and tried to be his friend, even if it made me unpopular too. I remember one time he had a birthday party and his mum invited the whole class. Most didn't show up at all, but a few did come, but they were only there to laugh at him and find new ways to torture him after they'd been in his house and met his mum. I was the only one who stayed, and Jacob always liked me for that.

After school, I went to college, but, of course Jacob didn't. He was always different. I don't want to say slow, but he had difficulties. Maybe if they'd diagnosed things like that in those days, he'd have stood a better chance. But the world doesn't work like that and people who are weak, who are vulnerable – like Jacob – they end up being taken advantage of and end up at the bottom of the heap. I didn't know what happened to him after school. I went my way, he went his. But I thought about him a lot. I always liked him.

And then a few months back, I ran into him. We got talking and it was nice to catch up. After I left him on the bus, I wished I'd given him my number or something so we could talk again, but as luck would have it we saw each other again, a few times actually. It was like fate.

We started meeting up, going for a drink. I enjoyed his company. He told me his mum had just died. He was really broken up about it, and I think he needed someone to talk to. I didn't mind. I liked him. I'd liked his mum. And I knew what it was like trying to care for a parent. After a while, we started seeing each other a lot. I'd go round to his house, I'd cook for him, clean. He wasn't coping well, but when he was, I don't want to say normal, but I suppose that's the best word… When he was normal it was great. I was starting to fall in love with him. And I know people can't get their heads around that because of how he was, but it's true. I really loved him.

I had a flat with some friends, but I'd started staying at Jacob's most of the time. He'd get upset if I left. And the place was in such a mess, I thought I couldn't just leave him like that. He needed someone to take care of him. I guess his mum had done that until she died.

I didn't mind. I liked helping him. It was tiring, sure, especially with having a full-time job and taking care of my mum too. But I didn't mind.

And then, one day, Jacob asked me if I wanted to buy his house. He'd obviously inherited it from his mum, but he couldn't take care of the place. I don't think he wanted the responsibility. I'd mentioned before I'd like a house of my own, but there was no way I could afford it. So, he asked me to buy his.

I thought he was joking. I couldn't afford that place. I thought he was just being daft. But then, he'd written up this agreement. God knows where he got such an idea. And I don't know how legally binding it would be, do you? But anyway, he wanted me to start paying him, whatever I could each month. It was crazy. But to be honest, I liked the idea of living there. I knew it would never really be mine, and of course Jacob would still live there. I could hardly turf him out of his own home.

And I'm ashamed to say that at one point, I did wonder if he was trying to scam me somehow. Get money out of me and then throw me out when he was done with me. But Jacob wasn't like that. He was honest. He was too nice to do something like that. So, I agreed. I started paying him what I could and moved in.

It felt odd, to be honest. I knew I probably wouldn't ever own the house, that we'd need a solicitor to draw something up, but I didn't want to do that, in case anyone thought I was taking advantage of him. So in the end, I just lived there with him and decided it was sort of like paying rent. And Jacob got what he wanted, and we could be together. It wasn't so bad.

And then, he changed. He started forgetting things and blacking out. He even hurt me a few times. I thought about leaving. But I knew he didn't mean it. He didn't even know what he was doing.

I made him go to the doctor, and they were going to do tests, but Jacob refused. It was like he didn't want to get better. It was hard, but I stuck with him.

And, yes, then things got out of control. He lost it. He hurt me and ran off. I was scared and called the police, but I knew deep inside that it wasn't really him. Maybe I shouldn't have got the police involved, I don't know. Maybe that just made things worse.

He was always apologetic when he came back after an episode. And I believed him. Even when he said he was going to get help and never did. But I think it was too late this time. I think he came back to the house that day, after he'd attacked me, and saw the police and panicked. He didn't come home for a while. I was so worried, but I thought if I call the police again, they might arrest him for what he did to me. So, I just waited for him to come home.

And he did. Finally. But I guess he got involved with this Phil again. I came home from work. I saw Jacob in the house as I came up the street. It didn't occur to me that anything could be wrong, I was just relieved he was home.

I went rushing in, and Jacob tried to warn me, but it was too late. This guy, Phil, he hit me. He tied me up. I think Jacob must've blacked out again because he didn't do anything. He was so distant. I was screaming for help, but it just made Phil angrier. When he'd tied me up, he started trashing the place. He was looking for something, I think. Money, maybe. I don't know.

He was hurting Jacob, too, and I was begging him to stop. He knocked Jacob out. He was lying on the kitchen floor. I was desperate to help him, but I couldn't. I could hear Phil moving around. And then, finally, Jacob woke up. He untied me, and we tried to get away, but Phil got hold of me. He went crazy and attacked me, tried to strangle me.

Jacob ran at us. Phil threw me to the ground, and he had the knife, and the next thing, Jacob was on the floor too. There was so much blood, but I didn't know what'd happened. I didn't know he'd stabbed Jacob. He just stood there, and Jacob tried to grab him, but he pulled away. And then, he went for me again, and I think I remember seeing someone at the window. Cathy, I suppose. Phil let go of me, and I was sort of drifting in and out. He ran towards the back door, and then, the next thing I remember was waking up and seeing him stabbing her too.

He ran away, and I tried to get to her. I saw her phone. She'd called the police. I tried to stop the bleeding, but I couldn't. And then, I think I passed out again. All I remember is the paramedic standing over me.

God, poor Cathy. I don't know why she came over then. She looks after my mum. Oh, God, is Mum okay?

I don't know, I guess Phil must've broken the window when he was trying to get in. I don't know if he got there before Jacob or not. I don't know…

That's right, I'd changed the locks after the last incident. I was scared, I suppose. But I never intended to keep Jacob out. I just panicked. I was glad when he came home. Or I was until I saw Phil there too.

I don't know what I'll do now. Jacob's gone. Cathy's gone. Phil's still out there.

And what's going to happen to the house?

Chapter 57

The detective says he's spoken to Sasha and Kimberley. They were concerned about me and confirmed I'd found a boyfriend and had moved in with him. They didn't know much, though. I was a private sort of person. They passed on some mail that'd come to the old flat, including a letter from work. A formal warning about my attendance. The callous bastards.

But at least Doctor Turner confirmed things, probably because he felt guilty for letting it go so far. He should've been more proactive, should've done more to help Jacob and me.

Ethel from next door admitted she'd heard shouting and carrying on but was devastated she hadn't done anything to help. She'd thought it was the TV. Jacob had always had the TV on too loud. She'd told him Cathy had been to her house a few days earlier, asking about me and Jacob. She'd seemed concerned about something. It'll have been because Jacob had hit me, I said, and that seemed to satisfy him.

There was no one else to talk to, really. Cathy's husband, of course, but he knew nothing about why Cathy was there – she didn't talk much about work.

I was glad the temp had left, he couldn't mention our little transaction.

So really, it was just Mum left, and I wondered if they'd think her fit enough to talk to. I guessed they'd at least speak to other people at the home as this concerned Cathy now. And that made me nervous. What if Mum had been talking to someone else? And then, there was all this stuff about writing things down. I needed to see her and find out for myself.

**

I was released from hospital a couple of days after Jacob died. I knew I had to organise the funeral and make arrangements for so many things. It was hard being responsible for Jacob, and I would be glad when it was all over.

I didn't know what would happen with my job or, more importantly, with the house. No one seemed to be able to tell me one way or another. It was frustrating. I just wanted to move on with my life. 'I don't know where I'll go,' I say to the detective as he helps me get into a waiting taxi outside the hospital. It was Kev who came.

'You can get back in the house. We've finished in there,' the detective says. 'That's if you want to go back there, of course.'

'I do,' I say.

I know there's a chance I will have to leave my house, that I will have to find some other place, but for now, I smile at him and climb into the taxi, and before I close the door, I say, 'I just want to go home.'

***

Kev chats away to me as he drives, but I'm not paying attention. All I want is to go home and sleep and not think about things for a while. But I can't. I know I have to go and see Mum so I ask him to go back and drop me at the care home.

Kev looks puzzled, as if he wants to ask if I'm sure, but thinks better of it and just does as I ask.

We're at the home in a couple of minutes, and I realise I have no money, but Kev waves me off anyway. 'Just ring when you're done,' he says, and I can feel him watching me as I walk up to the building and he waves as I turn and look.

I walk into the home, down the corridor to Mum's room and can feel people staring at me. I know I must look terrible, but I wonder if they know. I suppose they must. They'll have heard about poor old Cathy by now.

I'm almost at Mum's room, trying to work out what I'll say to her when someone stops me. I turn and find Nora standing there, a funny look on her face. Behind her stands Dean, wearing the same strange expression. I wonder if they know, if Cathy talked or Mum did. I wonder if they believe it.

'Ms Cooke,' Nora says, and looks back at Dean before reaching out to me, a totally different woman to the one who'd been so rude before. 'I'm so sorry,' she says, and gives me a hug.

I pull back and nod. 'Thank you,' I say. 'And I'm sorry too. Were you close?'

Nora looks at Dean and then shuffles me towards the family room. I try to see into Mum's room, but the door is closed.

'Cathy was a lovely woman,' I say. 'I'm just sorry she got mixed up in it all. I don't even know why she was there. She–'

Nora closes the door to the small, stuffy room, and Dean stands there, his hands behind his back.

'What's going on?' I say.

'It's your mum, Polly,' Nora says.

'Has she had another stroke?'

Nora takes a deep breath. 'Your mum passed away. That's why Cathy came around. She insisted on telling you in person. She was very upset. She'd gotten close to your mum.'

I can feel my chest tighten, and the world blurs at the edges.

Mum's gone. That's what Cathy came to tell me.

Like you killed her.

I remember her words, hadn't paid attention at the time. *You killed him. Like you killed her.*

'I'm so sorry,' Nora says, and rubs my back as I lean forward, head between my knees.

Sometime later, minutes, maybe longer, I sit up and realise Dean has gone. No time to sit around with me, a grieving daughter and recent victim of terrible violence. But Nora is still here, still looking sympathetic.

'Her things,' I say, and Nora nods.

'We've packed them up. Collect them whenever you're ready.'

'I'll take them now,' I say, and ask to use the phone, summoning Kev back to help me take the stuff home.

In the back of the taxi, I rummage through a box and find some sheets of paper, words scrawled on them that look like the work of a small child, and they jump out at me. *Polly, fire, mad, Jacob, house, dangerous.* I screw them up into a ball and stuff them into my pocket.

Kev pulls up across the street from the house. He turns in his seat, grunting with the effort, and asks if I want him to help me inside. I shake my head and give my best Princess Di smile. 'No, thank you. You've done enough,' I say.

He looks like he wants to protest but instead nods and gives me his own attempt at a smile. I wonder if he thought there was something between us. But there is nothing, and he needs to know this. If I invite him into the house, he may never leave.

He's still looking at me, waiting, so I say, 'The place is a mess,' and look away as I gather my things.

***

I stand on the kerb, watching Kev's car disappear down the street, wondering if he'll come back, if he'll keep checking on me. I realise I made a mistake in calling him again, but I try to ignore that problem for now and focus on more immediate concerns.

I stare over to the house. I'll need to clean up, but I'm so tired I know I'll just go straight to bed and stay there for a long time, until someone comes and tells me I have to leave.

I take the ball of paper from my pocket, crushing it in my hand before tossing it into a bin, watching it vanish amongst the Greggs bags soaked in pasty grease and the half-drunk cans of Coke. I am making it go away.

I'm desperate for sleep, but as I cross the street, all I can do is think about Mum and how things turned out, and I know sleep is not going to come easily. But this wasn't what I wanted. This was never what I wanted.

I think about how much I'd started to hate the flat and the girls and how comfortable it was going to Mum's. I remember thinking that maybe I could go back home, that it wasn't unusual these days, that it wouldn't make me a loser. But we drove each other mad, and I knew we couldn't both stay.

I was only doing what I thought was best for her. She *had* been forgetting things, misplacing things. All I did was push things a little further. I didn't want her locked up, I just wanted her somewhere she'd be safe and happy and comfortable. She'd had her turn, and now, it was mine.

But no one would listen. No matter what I said, how many stories I told them, they just wouldn't listen. So, I had to push a little harder.

I knew she was taking a nap. She always did at that time of day. I went inside and put the sheets in the oven and then went to the shops. I knew she was safe, I'd planned to go back. How was I to know how quickly it would get out of control, that I'd get stuck at the shops? And it wasn't that bad, anyway, just a bit of smoke. I was hardly going to let the house burn down, was I?

And then, she had the stroke. And that wasn't my fault. I didn't do that. But it was me being punished. All I wanted was somewhere to call home, and they took that away from me too. It was all for nothing.

As I step onto the pavement, I realise I'm crying, and I realise that Mum is gone, and now, I have two funerals to organise and that life just isn't fair.

I rummage for my keys and my eyes go to the window of my house. And that's when I see him. Time slows down. I think I am mistaken. I'm desperate for sleep. I must be wrong.

But no.

There is someone in my house.

Chapter 58

I stand there, frozen, unsure what to do. My first thought is Jacob. That, of course, I'd be unlucky enough to get haunted. That even bloody death didn't get rid of him.

And then, I think maybe it's the police. Maybe they haven't finished with the house at all.

And then he turns. He's standing there in my house like he owns the place. I can see him clearly. I feel the heat inside me burn brighter. Not fear. Anger.

What's *he* doing in my house?

Phil stands in the living room, hands in pockets, hood pulled up. I grab for my phone as I meet his eye. He watches me standing there, useless, on the outside. He looks down at the phone in my hand. He looks back at me and wonders. Will I call the police?

But what if they catch him? What if he talks? They might not believe him, but they'll look more closely. Maybe I should just let him go.

But he's in my house. He knows he's taking a risk being there. There can be only one reason why he came back. He wants to hurt me.

I start to step forward, to go inside, to confront him, to get back what's mine.

But I've been here before. I've made this mistake before.

He moves forward, right up to the window, looking right at me. He smirks and raises his hand. His eyes never leave mine as he, slowly and quite deliberately, presses three numbers into his phone.

The anger turns to fear.

Phil watches a second more, and then, I turn and run.

Chapter 59

The bus pulls in at the stop, and I can see people staring at my red eyes and running nose. I've cried all the way here, knowing I've lost everything, but now, I'm done. Now, I have a plan.

I get off the bus and move my bag onto my shoulder. There's not much in it, but it rubs against my sore shoulder and ribs nonetheless.

It's raining again, and I'm soaked through already as I walk up the main road, past the takeaway and the newsagents, around the corner and off to the small road on the left.

I stand outside the house and notice it's much prettier than I'd thought last time. Perhaps it's the glow of Christmas lights from across the street that makes it look so nice. Or maybe I'd just misjudged it before.

I realise there are no Christmas lights up in this house, and I wonder if they'll bother at all this year. I think about the house I've just left and how I would have decorated it. How warm and festive I could have made it.

A car turns onto a drive next to me, and a couple get out and eye me up before going inside, carrying bags of groceries. I glance at their house, which also has no lights up and has an unwelcoming aura. There's a for sale sign outside, and I wonder how much these houses go for. Too much for me, at least.

I turn back to the house in front of me as the rain comes down harder. I can see someone moving inside, and I walk to the door and ring the bell. It takes a moment for the door to be answered and I wonder what I look like. A drowned rat probably.

When the door finally opens, a man stands there, a towel in his hand, and for a moment, I think it's for me to dry my hair with, but then, I realise it's a tea towel.

He looks at me with tired, red eyes, and I wonder if he's been crying just now or if he's been crying for days nonstop. He looks like he wants to say something, probably ask who I am, but something stops him. I imagine his throat is raw with grief. A little dog stands by his feet, barking and growling, and he tries to get it to stop.

He's better looking than I remembered. Taller, much slimmer than her. He'd probably be very attractive, if it weren't for the eyes.

'Yes?' he says eventually, and I realise I was right. His words come out gruff, definitely a sore throat.

'I'm sorry to bother you,' I say and step closer. 'My name's Polly. Polly Cooke. I knew your wife. I…' He looks like he's going to collapse, and the towel slips from his hands. I try to help him, but he pulls away.

'I just…I wanted to tell you how sorry I am about Cathy,' I say, and he lets out a spluttering cry. 'She was so kind. And the only reason she came that day was to tell me about my mum. My mum died, and Cathy wanted to tell me in person. I'm so sorry she…'

He leans against the door frame, tears in his eyes, rain pouring down my face.

'I just wanted to talk to someone,' I say. 'Can I come inside?'

He tries to say something but his words get stuck in his throat. But then, he stands up straight and almost smiles. He stands back, making room for me to get inside, the dog still barking from behind him.

'Polly,' he says. 'Of course. Come in.'

I step inside, into the warmth, and look around the place Cathy used to call home. Her husband closes the door behind me and stands there while I take my coat off.

'What a beautiful home,' I say.

Acknowledgements

Thanks to everyone at Bloodhound Books for their work on the book and for believing in it. To Stan for his input on the early drafts. And to Stephen, Mam, Dad, Donna, Jonathan, Maria, Chris and Diane for their continued support.

Any mistakes are down to Cotton and Tina who kept barking when I was trying to concentrate.

Made in the USA
Middletown, DE
08 April 2020

88139710R00139